THIS ARDENT FLAME

THIS ARDENT FLAME

BETH KANELL

FIVE STAR

A part of Gale, a Cengage Company

GALE
A Cengage Company

Five Star Publishing, a part of Gale, a Cengage Company

LIBRARY OF CONGRESS CATALOGING-IN-PUBLICATION DATA

Names: Kanell, Beth, author.
Title: This ardent flame / Beth Kanell.
Description: First Edition. | Waterville, Maine : Five Star, a part
    of Gale, a Cengage Company, 2021. | Series: Winds of
    freedom; book 2
Identifiers: LCCN 2020002211 | ISBN 9781432877378 (hardcover)
Subjects: GSAFD: Historical fiction.
Classification: LCC PS3611.A5492 T48 2021 | DDC 813/.6—dc23
LC record available at https://lccn.loc.gov/2020002211

First Edition. First Printing: June 2021
Find us on Facebook—https://www.facebook.com/FiveStarCengage
Visit our website—http://www.gale.cengage.com/fivestar
Contact Five Star Publishing at FiveStar@cengage.com

Printed in Mexico
Print Number: 01   Print Year: 2021

THIS ARDENT FLAME

CHAPTER 1

North Upton, Vermont, October 1852

A cold wind off the ridge followed me as I trudged down the worn path, the pack basket of late apples heavy against my back. Dark clouds scudded from the west. When the first small raindrops struck my cheek, I tried to tug my woolen shawl forward, to keep my dark hair dry. But the weight of the apples and their off-balance shift in the pack meant I needed to grip the shoulder straps with both hands, so I couldn't arrange the shawl any better.

"Drat. Drat, again." Had I spoken aloud? Well, nobody would hear my unladylike words. Cutting down through the field from my brother William's home, toward the center of the village, wasn't exactly ladylike, either. *Pfui.*

Since I'd been a little girl, I'd taken this track. Of course, back then, the house beyond the mill belonged to my father's older brother, Uncle Owen. Jerushah, my best friend, used to walk with me to visit Uncle Owen and Aunt Lina.

Jerushah. I shivered.

Larger raindrops pelted sideways in the wind, mixed with tiny ice pellets that stung. I regarded the half mile or so still to walk, then decided to take the shorter route through the patch of tall, wrinkle-leafed beech trees. No matter that the path was narrower, darker—it would take me home much sooner. And in the village, there'd be no wild animals to threaten me. Just in case some slow fox or larger beast lingered near the source of rich beechnuts, though, I started singing aloud for extra noise. My voice squeaked, alone, and off tune: "Blest be-ee the tie-ie that binds," I began as I ducked under the trees into deeper darkness, almost too dim to see at all.

A crash of breaking branches ahead of me made me jump and utter a small shriek. But the crisp clatter of hooves assured me I'd spooked someone's loose horse, so I caught my breath and was about to start the first line of the hymn again, when I heard a rattle of carriage wheels from the village road beyond the woods.

The stage! A letter, perhaps, from Solomon McBride—I blushed—or papers for me to set aside until Jerushah's brother Matthew could match them to others, at the scale works in St. Johnsbury where he now labored. I ran, despite the thump of the apple basket pounding my back and hips.

I reached the edge of the trees, slowed to a hasty walk, stepped toward the rough carriage road. And heard shouts.

"He's hurt," my father's voice called out. "Come help me carry him!"

Solomon? Solomon! Yet why should it be? I struggled again to straighten my shawl so as not to appear a hoyden, but a nearly eighteen-year-old young lady, and hurried ahead, with thin-soled shoes slipping on the wet soil and stones underfoot.

Anything could happen in these dangerous times. Especially if the man who courted you was—Well, my father and brother and I knew: Solomon was a spy.

But the vehicle slewed in the slick road was not the stage-coach, and the man being carried by my father and Mr. Clark into the inn could not be Solomon, for, as his cap tumbled to the ground, I saw a coarse mop of graying hair that matched his short beard. And such a drawn, pained face! As one of his dangling feet struck the stone hitching post, he cried out.

Echoing the man's pain, an agonized whimper came from the

wagon itself. I pushed closer, awkward with the apple basket on my back. My mother and Jerushah Clark's mother reached to assist a woman climbing down from the heavily loaded vehicle, more farm wagon than carriage for one's family. A small youth sat on the driving bench, crooning to the dark and sweating horse in front; behind, on a longer bench, perched a row of children, none of them older than seven, as best I could guess.

"Alice," my mother called over her shoulder, "bring those children inside."

"Surely," I answered, struggling to free my shoulders from the leather straps and place my burden on the ground with care, so as not to spill any fruit.

Mr. Wilson, arriving in haste from his store down the road, called up to the youth holding the reins: "Ease up. I'll hold your horse while the girl unloads the little ones, and then I'll lead your horse to the barn." He reached to take the uneasy animal by its bridle, and I dodged a large shoed hoof as I moved closer to reach up and beckon to the children.

I glanced at the youth with the reins and stifled a gasp of surprise: It was indeed a girl, her skirts tucked mostly under her and her hair covered with a rough cloth cap. I heard her whisper, "Me mam" and then seem to wake to her situation. She loosened her grip on the leathers, tied them deftly to a hook on the wagon's front boards, and twisted in her seat to talk to the small children behind her. "Step down with the lady, and mind your manners," she told them, heavily accented but clear enough. "She'll take you to Mam, inside, won't you, miss?"

"Of course." I stretched a hand to the first child, a small-boned boy with a pack of his own on his back. Without a word, five more followed him over the wagon board and down to the ground, huddling close to each other. Tears streamed down one little girl's face, but she didn't speak.

As small and thin as the children were, I wanted to wrap an

arm around each set of little shoulders. But instead I simply held out a hand to that first boy with the pack, and he gripped the next child, who grasped another hand, and, in a moment, I led the chain of what must be brothers and sisters into the chilly public parlor of the inn. Mr. Clark bustled at his stove, starting a fire, and the little ones stared around them.

The door that connected to the house opened with a clatter, and the mother pressed through it, wide and well skirted, calling her children to her. She seemed healthy enough, and she bobbed a half curtsey toward me. "Thank you, miss. I hope they were no trouble to you."

Her accent was even thicker than her daughter's. Oh! Were they Irish, then? Of course, that explained it. I offered a hand to the mother, saying, "My name is Alice Sanborn, and I live across the way. It's no trouble at all. May I fetch you something for yourself and the children?"

Behind me, Mr. Clark bustled back to his shelf of libations, then came out with a mug of cider that he handed to the oldest child. "Drink a bit and pass it around," he instructed. The child, a boy, obeyed at once, eyes wide. Mr. Clark continued, "I'll have tea ready for you, Missus"—He hesitated, waiting for a name.

"Mrs. McManus," the woman replied, straightening with some quiet pride. "Thank you kindly, sir, but it won't be necessary."

"It's only what I'd do for any traveler," Mr. Clark assured her. "There's no charge for this, Mrs. McManus. My wife will make your husband more comfortable, and I expect you'll be able to continue onward in an hour or so. She's a very capable nurse, and that leg just needs some proper care." He asked gently, "Are you headed far, ma'am?"

She shook her head, pulling off a shawl as she spoke. "Only a little farther, to St. Johnsbury." Her voice grew stronger. "My husband has work there, at the Gilman Mills, and we need to reach the town before evening."

I looked more closely at this Irish mother, and realized her bulk was more than most. She must be in a family way. No wonder my mother and Mrs. Clark had rushed to help her into the house. Traveling in her condition—dear heavens.

At that moment, my father stepped in with the youth who'd held the horse's reins. No wonder I'd thought she was a boy, with such short-cropped hair under the cap. She, too, gave a half curtsey, said "Miss," and went to stand beside her mother.

My father nodded to Mr. Clark, who said "Just a bad gash, nothing broken," and added more wood to the stove.

Thus assured, my father turned to me: "Stage just arrived, too. You'd best be seeing to the post, Alice. Hop to it, girl; he won't wait forever."

Out the door I raced, as the Irish children stared after me. My father meant: There could be a packet of papers from Solomon, or from the Gilman Mills. Our village of North Upton might be only a small dot on the map of Vermont, and a tiny cluster of people among New Englanders all—but we knew our duty, with work to be done today.

And there were my apples!

CHAPTER 2

I left the apples to wait for me outside the inn door, knowing I'd return shortly. This time, I did pull my shawl up properly over my hair, though I felt it catch on the hairpins at the top. Though my thick hair generally hung straight if I let it fall loose, damp weather made a mess of it, so I had meticulously fastened it into place in the morning.

Where the Irish family's wagon stood a few minutes earlier, the stagecoach now trembled, as the pair of horses still harnessed shoved each other at the water trough. Young Sam Walker, the driver, perched at the rear, tugging a small canvas sack out of a toppled stack of baggage.

"Miss Alice Sanborn," he called out merrily, and dropped the sack into my arms before bouncing down to the ground. "Take it straight to Mr. Wilson now, there's a girl, and I wager he'll pull out a letter or two for you. When's your beau coming back this way?" He lowered his voice. "I've only a couple of gray-haired folks in my stage this time. I could benefit from young Solomon's company for more lively conversation over the long stretches."

"I've no notion of his travel plans," I replied primly, "being as he's not my beau, just my correspondent."

"Ha!" Young Sam grinned. "Nobody but a beau writes as often as that man does to you, Alice. And I should know, I've courted once or twice myself. No, I'll not say more," he added, although I hadn't asked. "I'm off again right away to St. Johnsbury." He lunged for the harness of the nearer horse, scolding the massive beast and tugging its dripping face out of the trough.

A woman's voice called my name sharply from the inn. "Alice, I've hope of a letter myself in that sack. When you've taken it to Mr. Wilson, be sure to wait for him to pick out any items for me or Mr. Clark, if you'd be so very kind." Her last words were spoken bitterly, with acid.

My face blazed with heat, but I only answered, "Yes, ma'am," and nodded a quick farewell to Young Sam. Wilson's store, at the other end of the village, included the post boxes. Mr. Wilson would first sort out any deliveries for the Clarks and their inn, tuck them back in the sack, and let me carry them to their addressee. And, of course, anything for my own family could go with me also.

The rain fell steadily now. Behind me, splashes and a clatter of hooves confirmed Young Sam's departure. Ahead of me, a small cluster of men waited at the store, sheltered by the long overhang of roof at the front. I caught the scent of pipe smoke and a whiff of sheep manure, that classic pairing of working farmers lingering for an afternoon conversation. Two men from the other side of the village nodded to me, while Mr. Wilson himself held the door open. "Come right in, Alice, I know what you're after."

"Mrs. Clark wants her letters right away," I told him. I handed over the sack and said good afternoon to Mr. Hopkins, grandfather of twin boys I knew from the village school.

"Quite a commotion at the inn," the white-bearded man commented. "A passel of mackerel snappers, isn't that so? What are they doing here in North Upton?"

"Mackerel snappers?" I didn't understand. Mr. Hopkins grimaced but didn't add more, so I looked to the storekeeper.

Mr. Wilson handed me back the mostly emptied mail sack, with two letters for the Clarks in it, and one more, addressed to me, laid on top and franked with Solomon's bold signature across the corner. He frowned toward Mr. Hopkins. "That's no term to use in front of a young lady, Matthew. Irish, that's all he means."

"Papists," Mr. Hopkins grunted. "Fish on Fridays and can't say the Lord's Prayer the way it's meant to be." He asked again, "They have some business in North Upton?"

"No, just passing through to St. Johnsbury, but an injury to one of them. Mr. Clark says it's not so terrible as they thought, and," I added stiffly, "I'm sure they'll drive onward if there's still enough light."

"Plenty enough light to send them on their way out of here."

From the working of his mouth, I suspected Mr. Hopkins was about to spit, so I took my leave with thanks to Mr. Wilson and ducked back out into the chilly rain. The other two men came inside, already asking to see the just-arrived newspapers.

Solomon's letter slid cozily into a pocket I'd stitched to the inside of my short jacket, for later reading. Wetter with each quick step, I clutched the post bag under one arm and did my best to hold my skirts up an inch or two higher from the splashing puddles. Too late to think of my shoes and stockings, now soaked and very cold indeed.

What right did Mr. Hopkins have to speak so unkindly of the Irish? Mackerel snappers indeed; Papists, well, that term I understood, but the way he spat it out, it still sounded nasty.

Mrs. Clark opened the door as I reached the inn, and she grabbed in a most unladylike way for the mail sack. Then, over a muttered "Thank you, Alice," she jammed the door shut in haste.

No surprise that she didn't care to speak to me. Since her daughter Jerushah's death—the death of my dearest friend— she'd faulted me for the terrible illness and its dreadful conclusion. I faulted myself for it, too, in all honesty. But I'd promised myself to use the loss as incentive for work, instead: work toward freedom and justice for all.

Which perhaps would relate to something in Solomon's missive. I heaved my apples back to my shoulders and splashed across the road, then up the long muddy wagon track to home.

I left the apples just inside the door and called out to my mother, but heard no reply. No point going in with such wet feet—I wiped my shoes with a cloth, tugged them off along with my soggy stockings, and stepped cautiously ahead, not wanting to catch a sliver from the floorboards in my bare toes. Warmth from the woodstove and the scent of hot soup comforted me, but it seemed I was alone in the house. My father must be in the barn with the sheep—and my mother of course at the Clarks' inn, but she must have left our kitchen just a short while ago, or else the stove would have been cold.

Shoes stuffed with a twist of newspaper, stockings hung to dry, at last I could retreat to my own bedchamber, tuck the wet edges of my skirt out of the way while pulling on my other pair of stockings, and draw out the envelope that seemed to hold its own secret warmth against my chest. My heart. Perhaps I'd been too quick to deny that Solomon was my beau, considering how his letters lit such eagerness in me!

Thin pages rustled as I drew them out of the small envelope. For a moment I caught the scent of those strong hands, and of a distant locale. But it vanished at once, and I unfolded the pages. "To Miss Alice Sanborn, with respect and greetings from the wilderness of southern Illinois." Illinois! Frontier lands, raw and new and exciting. And—of course—the fierce political battleground where my own Uncle Martin owned a daily newspaper, doing his share to cleanse the stain of slave-holding out of the Territories to the west, in Iowa and wicked Missouri, with the Kansas Territory beyond them.

Quick scanning of the letter showed no mention of my uncle.

But oh! Solomon was coming east soon! For the election, he wrote. And to meet with Franklin Pierce himself, the New Hampshire man hoping to take the presidency of the nation.

In fact, the entire two-page letter, I realized, in cramped script on both sides of the pages, and crossing part of the final page again to include more, amounted to a description at length of why Pierce could not be allowed to win, and how Solomon meant to encourage the Vermont vote for Whig general Winfield Scott, "Old Fuss and Feathers," as his soldiers from the Mexican war called him affectionately.

My father would pore over every turn of phrase here, working out the politics and the moral stances of the candidates. But for me, I confess, it was the final line that meant the most, difficult though it was to read with the crossed lines of script: "Yours, most sincerely, Solomon McBride."

Mine? I wanted it to mean a great deal. Although the line before it, if I'd read it correctly, said, "Please convey my regards to your mother and father, and share this explanation with them." But still. I held the page to my cheek for just a moment, the word "Yours" brushing against my lips. Someday, perhaps. Why not?

A slammed door downstairs shook me out of the daydream, and I hurried to the kitchen, to find my mother in a tizzy. "Did you shape the biscuit dough, Alice? Your father's on his way from the barn. Oh, for heaven's sake, you've done nothing. Quickly now, or we'll keep him waiting too long, and you know he's sure to be tired."

We flew into action together, forming the dough (which I'd not noticed earlier) swiftly into round balls to tuck into a sharply heating oven, and a powerful aroma from the beef soup made my stomach aware of how late the day had become.

"You'll come with me to Mrs. Clark's tomorrow afternoon," my mother abruptly announced. "I want you to help carry some of the fabric, though you don't have to stay for long. We're making a Sunday skirt and cloak for Caroline—she's finally coming home at the end of the month, when her father goes to fetch her back."

I stared, a bowl in one hand, spoons in the other. "Who is Caroline?"

My mother spun on her heel and looked at me directly. "Don't ask more tonight. I'll tell you more when we're on our own tomorrow. But she is the other daughter of Mr. and Mrs. Clark, and she's been away for fifteen years. Hush now, not another word about this. Your father's coming in, right this moment."

A cold, damp wind swept the room as the outer door opened, then firmly closed, and my father's weary voice called out, "Found the last ewe down by the river. Just in time—It's dark and wild out there. Abigail, is that your mother's beef soup recipe I'm smelling? Heaven bless you, woman, I'm hungry as a bear."

My mother nudged me toward the pantry shelves, reminding me, "Fetch some jam, Alice. Don't stand there with your mouth open, you'll catch a fly in it."

What did this mean? How could the Clarks have another daughter? Their son Matthew, their daughter Jerushah (my chest clenched again in pain), the three younger children. There had never been another child there, so far as I knew or had heard. What secret had been kept? And why?

For a moment, I forgot about Solomon's letter. But only for a moment. I hurried back to the table and said, "Papa? I have a letter to share from Solomon, for after your supper."

My father's worn face brightened, and, behind him, my mother caught my eye and nodded her approval. Not so much for Solomon, I realized, but for cheering up my father on this late October evening.

Beth Kanell

Winter raced toward us, with every gust of wind. I shivered, even in the kitchen's warmth, and tugged at my damp skirts, hoping the woodstove's radiant heat would dry them while we ate.

CHAPTER 3

I woke on Wednesday morning from a confused dream of my oldest brothers, Charles and John. In the two and a half years since they'd left North Upton for California and the gold fields, home had changed so much: my brother William married and running the mill, my father's sheep flock three times the size it had been, and I—Well, truth be told, I wondered some days who I was, now that my two dearest friends were gone: Jerushah to her death from rheumatic fever, and Sarah, younger than the two of us, to a family far north in Coventry, Vermont, where her dark skin matched those around her. Letters came rarely from Sarah, but always with happy descriptions of her life at the home of the blacksmith and his family there. Letters from my brothers came to my mother nearly every month, often crossing hers to them, so that the answers to long-ago questions confused us often.

And no letters in the past six weeks. My mother insisted the mail could be slow, coming by ship, where storms could alter an arrival date by weeks or more. And across the Isthmus of Panama, too, and then another ship. But the absence of word preyed on my thoughts, it seemed, even when I slept. My dreams ranged from earthquake to fire to oceanic catastrophe, as well as mine collapse.

Shaking off the fears of the night, I threw the coverlet aside and at once wished I'd been slower. Surely there'd been a hard frost during the night. And the kitchen stove hadn't yet warmed my chamber. Shivers coursed down my arms, and I hurried to pull warmer garments over a linen shift. My stockings? Alas, the better pair still hung in the kitchen. At least they would be toasty warm.

"If you're going to the barn, you'd best be wearing William's cast-off boots," my mother advised over her shoulder. "And you should have worn them for apple picking yesterday. Your shoes won't last if you keep getting them wet."

"Yes, Mama." I endeavored to sound humble and apologetic, so she wouldn't continue. I earned a skeptical glance over her shoulder, then a half smile.

"Your father's ahead of you but not by much," she commented. "There's cornmeal pudding when you're done. Off you go." She thrust a slab of day-old bread with butter and maple sugar into my hand and resumed stirring.

Outside, the day gleamed gold and pale blue, as the laggard sun lit the leaves of the maples and turned the ground frost to a sparkling carpet. In three large pens, each fenced to its own entryway into the ground floor of the barn, masses of shaggy sheep crowded toward the structure, eager for morning grain. Thumping inside the barn suggested the horses in motion. I folded the last of my bread in half and popped it into my mouth all at once, to free my hands for the chores ahead. Horses to feed, plus one older cow and a bred heifer, not to mention the pen of laying hens and the bold cockerel that crowed as I pried open the heavy barn door.

But every moment spent with my father in the barn, where long answers couldn't take place among morning chores—just clipped comments on what needed doing next—was a moment's more delay in asking my mother about the mysterious "Caroline" and how the Clarks could have a daughter I'd never heard of.

By the time we finished, crossed the barnyard in bright

October sunshine, and scrubbed our hands raw in the pail of icy water my mother'd set on the step for us, my stomach twisted with hunger, and my curiosity ached for satisfaction. Cornmeal pudding with maple syrup and butter, dark, hot tea, and the last of yesterday's bread loaf satisfied the former. I stood to gather the bowls and washed them, listening for an opportunity to cut into the conversation about what portion of a pig to trade for, who'd smoke the bacon, and whether to take my father's boots to the cobbler today.

"Mama, about Caroline," I inserted tentatively. "You said . . ."

My parents exchanged glances. My father said, "It's a risky choice they're making." What did he mean?

My mother pressed her hands on the table edge, a sign she felt strongly, but her words came softly: "It's a mother's heart that's broken, Ephraim. She must bring the child home again."

"That's no child," my father warned. "That's a woman grown, and she hasn't grown up with her mother. There'll be trouble."

"But she knows her father," Mama replied. "You know he's gone to see her twice every year. Give it a chance, Ephraim."

"Give it a chance? It's none of my doing. It's the Lord God above that needs to bless this. Or the Lord may not."

Thumping his chair away from the table, my father carried his dark mood back toward the barn. As for me, I was more confused than ever. "Mama? Will you tell me, now? Who is she, and what is Papa so angry about?"

"Let's sweep while I explain."

At first it seemed my mother was providing the too-familiar but awkward explanation of how parents carried out the biblical command to "go forth and multiply." Then she added, "Sometimes, Alice, babies don't come quite right. From something while the mother carried the baby, perhaps the measles, or a bad fall. But sometimes they arrive with a trait, a way of being, that seems part of a family's particular burden. In Mrs. Clark's family, the Coffins, the trait that's present in quite a few of her relatives is being hard of hearing. From childhood. Being deaf."

"But Jerushah wasn't deaf! Nor Matthew, nor the little ones," I protested.

"No, but their first daughter, Caroline, came into the world that way. And it was a warning that other children of the marriage might have the same trait. Do you grasp what that means?"

Hushed, holding my broom but not moving it over the board floor, I asked, "Were the Clarks afraid? Afraid of more deaf children?"

My mother nodded. "Sore afraid," she confirmed. "And perhaps shamed. So that Mrs. Clark decided to place the child, once she reached school age, in a boarding school in Connecticut that takes deaf children and teaches them to read and write, and even teach. Caroline grew up to be a teacher after her schooling, and she's lived at the Asylum for the Deaf for fifteen years now."

Wait. "But the Clarks—they have more children! None of them are deaf. So maybe it wasn't one of those traits. Maybe it was from an illness, or a fall, after all!"

"Perhaps." My mother checked her bread dough, turned it, and covered the dough pail again. "The Reverend Alexander said perhaps it was prayer. Mercy from heaven. Who can say? But Alice, no matter the cause, Mrs. Clark needs Caroline to come home."

Now I saw the problem my father'd pointed toward. "Except it's not her home, is it? She only knows her father from short visits, you said, and she doesn't know another soul in the village. And how can she ever get to know anyone if she can't hear us, or talk to us. That is—is she dumb as well as deaf?"

A twist of her lips showed disapproval of my question. "Wait and see, Alice. Remember, such children may bring great blessings."

"Yes, Mama." Yet to myself, I repeated what my father had said: "That's a woman grown." Aloud, I asked, "Does everyone in the village know?"

"Just the older ones. The ones who knew the little child. After all, she left for schooling when you were barely walking—it's no wonder you don't recall her. And it's not your business to talk about this. Be thoughtful of Mrs. Clark's feelings. Now, if we're spending our afternoon with her, altering hemlines, we have a great deal to accomplish toward your father's noon dinner, and supper to follow. Why has your broom stopped sweeping?"

We laughed together, and I resumed my task, marveling: a new face for the village, someone who belonged but didn't—she'd be half a dozen years older than I was, but maybe she would be a friend anyway? If we could somehow talk to each other. I had so many questions, but at least as many tasks to complete, and I still needed to make another trip to the orchard—this season, the apples were my task alone for our household.

I wondered idly: Caroline, Matthew, Jerushah, the three little ones—that made six children, a small family really. Hardly bigger than our own: me, Charles, John, William. And two babies who'd died early, I knew. For the first time, it occurred to me to worry: Did my mother think she'd done something wrong to cause them not to live? Should our own family have been a larger one?

The Irish family passing through the day before came back to mind. Six, and the girl driving the horses made seven, and an eighth on the way. A young enough mother, and she'd bear three or four more, with time.

I put the thought aside and pulled on William's outgrown boots once again, to fetch split wood for the wood box and savor the outdoor air. When I opened the door to the yard, I balanced it against my hip, to swing an empty pail out the door with me for the smaller sticks. Then turned and almost bumped into a young woman—a girl—standing there saying "Good morning."

Curled ringlets cascaded around her pretty face, where rosy cheeks and bright eyes signaled that she'd walked from someplace. But who was she? I stammered the question aloud, then quickly apologized. "I beg your pardon! My name is Alice Sanborn. May I know yours? And how can I help you?"

She bounced on her toes as if I'd said something delightful and beamed a bright smile at me. "Almyra," she chirped. "Almyra Alexander. I've come to stay with my aunt, and she sent me to borrow two teaspoons for the church tea next Sunday. And you're the girl who can drive a carriage herself and who's been almost to Canada and back, aren't you? I feel we are sure to become the best of friends! Don't you feel the same?"

Now who was speechless? I fumbled, set down my pail, and finally said, "I think you should meet my mother and ask her about the spoons. Come in, please."

Already behind me I heard my mother's footsteps. Good, she would know what to say and do. The minister's niece, come to stay in North Upton? Heavens, the world was turning upside down.

But I would still need to fetch that wood for the stove.

CHAPTER 4

Thirteen years old. Almyra Alexander added "And a half," as she answered my mother's question. "Half a year can make a great difference in a young woman's life," she continued, with an angelic gaze both solemn and sincere. "In the past half year, I have seen a great deal of New England and New York, and I am most certain I shall return to Albany before next summer. For that, of course, is where a woman can make the most of her efforts against the evils of slavery."

She dabbed at her lips delicately with a handkerchief, as if anyone needed to dab like that after just a sip of tea. Too prissy, I though fleetingly—but already I could tell that Almyra's pretty manners reflected her strong determination to win over my mother, for she'd barely glanced at me since the three of us had settled at the kitchen table with a fresh pot of strong tea and thin slices of apple before us.

My mother attempted to regain the conversation. "But surely you must attend school," she pointed out.

"Oh yes," Almyra confirmed, her curls bobbing as she nodded. "My mother has been most emphatic about my studies. Which is precisely why I am staying with my aunt and uncle, now that the winter session starts here. My mother writes to me every Sunday, to inquire about what I've learned. I imagine," she at last glanced at me, a bright smile blazing, "that I shall join your daughter in the schoolroom in North Upton next Monday. It is most fortunate that your school is closed this week, so that I can attend on the next opening day."

Fortunate? Not quite. And "the next opening day" . . . Well, that was ridiculous. We'd only been out of classes for a week, while Mr. Gates—not the blacksmith, but his brother the carpenter—repaired damage from a heavy rainstorm and worn roof.

Other questions pressed, and I let this slide to ask instead, "You came all the way from Boston? To stay with the Reverend and Mrs. Alexander? Why?"

Again, Almyra's glance swept my way, before she faced my mother, as if the question arose from her, not me: "My father, the Reverend Charles Alexander," she emphasized pointedly, "preaches to one of Boston's largest congregations. And of course we are all most concerned to see our nation take a righteous stand at last. My father meets with the Boston Vigilance Committee, and when he heard that the Reverend Leonard Grimes—he is a mulatto, you know, and leads the Baptist Church in Boston—must travel to Albany to meet with Miss Anthony there, and Mr. Frederick Douglass, of course, well, my father could hardly let the Reverend Grimes travel so far on his own. What dangers he might face! And, of course, my mother wished me to meet Miss Anthony, and Miss Mott. They are Quakers, of course," her voice rose with a sort of joyful triumph, like a minister nearing the end of a good sermon, "but my mother says the Lord is making a new temple of His righteousness, led by women of several faiths, that we might abolish slavery, institute temperance across the land, and endow women with the rights of citizenry in this nation. From many, one—that's the nation's motto, and my mother says it will be shown to be the new standard of liberty. Don't you agree?"

Caught by Almyra's bold and wide-lipped smile of certainty, my mother dipped her head and replied, "Yes, indeed, how wise," as the cup of tea in her hand barely landed in place on the table.

I almost laughed aloud. My mother, hesitant and fumbling for words! I'd never seen the like. Nor had I ever seen the like of Almyra Alexander.

Still, the litany of great names spilled across the table called for more response. It was as if the year's news had stepped into our Vermont home and come to some sort of life.

"Have you really met all those people?" I couldn't quite believe it. "Even here, we know about Mr. Douglass. But Quakers?" I'd only seen a Quaker once, when Jerushah and Sarah and I were racing north last year. (Oh, Jerushah!) I remembered the man's wide-brimmed hat and strange form of speech. "And didn't you want to return to Boston afterward, with your father?"

"Oh, he didn't return to Boston," Almyra scolded. "How could you think that? Surely I would have accompanied him on his return. But he needed to go south to Philadelphia, which is a most important place to be for the national election, but I have no relatives there, and he'll stay in a boarding house no doubt, which can be quite uncomfortable for a lady. And when I said I wanted to see more of New England before returning home myself, my mother wrote to my aunt, and of course they wanted me to visit. I shall be here until the end of March, no doubt, and, when the inauguration is done, my Papa will collect me here for our return to Boston."

My head spun. Did thirteen-year-olds often travel like this, if they lived in the city of Boston? Were they all so worldly and so committed to causes? I blushed, suddenly caught up in thinking of Solomon, who'd grown up in that coastal city. He must think me so naive, so inexperienced. He would probably appreciate Almyra for her spunky spirit and wide acquaintance with figures of such importance.

A gust of wind rattled the windows and stovepipe, and rain

spattered loudly against the glass. My mother shook herself out of her momentary inaction and stood, signaling the end of the visit. "Alice," she said sharply, "there'll be no dinner unless you fetch potatoes from the attic. And the apples need sorting. Almyra, you'll excuse us, if you please. I daresay you'll join us Saturday afternoon, with your aunt? We're marking the last of October with a ladies' gathering to string apple rings to dry, and a few entertainments for you young ladies as well, I'm sure. Please convey my regards to your aunt."

In a trice, Almyra in cloak and decorative bonnet whisked out the door, calling a bubbly farewell and certainly not offering to help! With a basket on my arm and my mother's urgency behind me, I hurried up to the attic to gather potatoes from the boards where they were briefly drying before storage in the cellar bins—and to pull myself back together.

If this was what Boston guests were all like, I wasn't sure I wanted any more! But, to be honest, it wasn't the overwhelming torrent of news, information, and assumptions that bothered me so much, but a long, deep self-doubt. What could Solomon see in me?

Back in the ktichen, I deposited my basket of potatoes, stuffed my feet back into my brother's boots, and seized my pail again. The wood box wouldn't fill by itself.

If only I'd completed this task earlier! Now the heavy rain ran down my neck where my cloak didn't fasten tightly enough, and the battered straw hat I'd perched over my hair seemed to drink the water and then dribble it across my face. Or maybe that was the vigorous wind. I hurried to fill the pail with split and mostly dry maple from the shed, return its contents to the indoor wood box, then repeat twice.

"Once more," my mother suggested from her crouched position at the woodstove's firebox, adding to the fire so there'd be plenty of heat for her braised chicken and dumplings.

My thoughts went back to Caroline, the deaf daughter of the Clarks, who owned the inn across the main road from our small farm. Would she resemble Almyra? Confident, bustling, full of city ways? For a moment, it seemed a small mercy that she wasn't likely to be an ardent conversationalist. At least as far as I could guess. I knew nothing about the deaf. But I would learn!

Distracted, I piled more splits into my pail, my own hair now dripping down my face. Beyond the sheltered woodpile, near a pair of dripping apple trees, a movement caught my eye. I straightened up quickly. In reaction, a loud bang erupted, and two heavy-bodied birds flew toward the thicker trees up the hill. Ruffed grouse.

Another bang, this time from the barn door, announced my father. He waved, but hurried down toward the river instead of coming toward me. Uh-oh. Were there any sheep loose from the barn?

I toted in my pail and told my mother I'd check on what Papa was doing out in the rain. After all, I couldn't get much wetter.

Thank the heavens, Solomon wasn't likely to arrive in the village today. He would come on the stage when it next made its west to east transit, at least six days away. That would mean Monday, the first of November, just a day before the actual election. No, that would make nonsense out of his letter. Recalculating, I realized he must already be in Vermont, perhaps arriving in the state before his own letter reached me. Then, when would he visit North Upton? I tugged my straw hat down more securely, and hoped the visit wouldn't be sooner than my own next visit to the looking glass. A vision of Almyra Alexander's outrageous curls set my teeth on edge.

As I climbed over the stone wall into the field that ran along the river, I called out for my father to wait for me but didn't see him. I shouted again and this time heard him call back to me, so I followed the stone wall north, careful not to slip in the mud and sheep droppings. Alas, my skirt hem would be a disaster. I worked my hands inside my cloak to roll the waist, elevating the fabric a couple of inches. Who would notice my uncovered ankles out here in the field?

Now I heard something different over the chaos of rain and river. Something that wasn't my father. I dug my brother's boots into the slippery ground, trying to make haste.

CHAPTER 5

"Alice, stop where you are. Don't come any closer."

My father faced away from me, standing at the edge of the rocky bank along the river edge, gazing across it. He held one hand behind him, gesturing to me: halt.

Halfway across the river, half turned back toward him, a large, wet beast stood. Black fur, pointed face, nothing at all like the predators I knew—not a fox or anything like one, although it had four paws, all of them below the water just now. The smell of it reached me on a gust of air across the water: sour, with that deep unpleasantness of wet fur that often clung to the male sheep, the rams. Rounded shoulders, dark eyes. The beast gave a short moan, then clacked its teeth together loudly.

I kept my voice low, although I shook with fear for my father. "Should I fetch a pitchfork? What do you need?"

"No. Wait. It's leaving."

The black bear—I knew that must be what it was, from children's stories, though I'd never seen one before—clacked its teeth again. A threat? Then it turned its strangely human gaze away from us and toward the far side of the river. All at once it seemed to decide, and a heavy paw rose out of the water, then descended again, further across the current of autumn run-off.

As if the first step had released the animal from its stance, it proceeded methodically, and surprisingly quickly, across the rest of the channel and up onto the bank. A moment later, it was gone, disappeared into the thick woods. Even the sound of its passage vanished almost at once.

"Papa? If there's one, are there more? Would it try to break into the sheep barn?"

"I don't know." My father turned from the noisy waters and met my gaze, solemn and thoughtful. "I haven't seen one here since I was a boy. It could be they're breeding back. We'll add another bar to the lower barn door, and I'll talk with the other men, find out whether anyone else has seen this, or others."

"Would it try to eat you? Is that what it meant, clacking its jaws like that? Why didn't you do something?"

"Ease back a bit, my girl. Bears are a sight more likely to eat a lamb or maybe a small ewe—your grandfather told me those tooth sounds only mean you've come too close and made the animal uneasy. The way a horse might stamp its forefoot."

We walked side by side up the slope to the barn's wide wagon door. Thoughtfully, my father moved the heavy boards one way and the other. "It needs a better latch," he decided. "But first I want to talk with the others. Go help your mother, Alice. What were you about? Did she send you to fetch me?"

"No, not at all. I was fetching the split wood for the stove, and I need one more pail full now, to top up the wood box."

Together we eyed the shed and the entry into the mudroom. "Time to move a stack inside," my father decided. "When I get back from the store, and after I work on the barn latch."

In confirmation of the shifting weather and its demand for more wood, a flutter of snowflakes descended, holding separate and pointed for an instant on my woolen sleeves. A sharp gust of north wind tossed more of them in my face.

"I'll tell Mama you've gone," I said. "Should I ask her first whether she needs something?"

"Not now. If she needs an item, you can fetch it for her later." He started down our cart trail toward the village road, his pace accelerating, and I realized I'd best hustle and bustle if I wanted to stay warm enough in my task.

I seized my pail and examined my very muddy skirt. Mama would scold. Worse yet, there'd be no walk to the village store for me until it dried out. Who'd want to appear to others as an immodest hoyden, with soaked skirts and layers of wool petticoats clinging to her legs? Ugh.

Inside, one task ended and the next began; I sorted apples in the time until Papa returned for his noon dinner with Mama and me, then helped carry fabric for Mama, to the Clark home. Then I went back to apples, setting aside any badly bruised or spoiling ones for the horses, and arranging the others in baskets for the apple party ahead. Which left me free to daydream and ponder Solomon's letter and what might take place when I saw him next.

Solomon Duncan McBride. Though I'd seen him first more than two years ago, and raced north toward Canada that cold and bitter March of 1850 with his help, to protect our dark-skinned friend Sarah, since then my time in his company added up to less than twenty-four hours. Dark haired, with deep-brown eyes and small, neat hands and feet, he came from Boston and traveled to New England and New York and even to far-off Pennsylvania, carrying messages and urging political action toward a change of government, a natural liberty for all American people, no matter their skin color or origin. He'd confided in me that his political work was for William Seward, senator from New York and the best orator, countering Daniel Webster's bitter failure. Why, Seward had even declared there was a higher law than the Constitution! One that guaranteed the brotherhood of all mankind.

I rolled the phrase across my tongue quietly. These noble ideas were confirmed in our Vermont village by our minister and his invited guests, all preaching Seward's declaration (as well as the Gospel), enjoining us to stand up for the enslaved as well as the poor and imprisoned. For slavery is the ultimate poverty and prison, is it not?

Truly, Solomon's stance and labor for these most vital ideals appealed to me powerfully. His warm personal presence appealed also. But, I told myself, it was the ideals and actions that mattered most, first, and best. How could any young woman my age love a man who did not stand for such?

Heavens! I'd daydreamed the word "love," a word I had no right to consider. And yet—how could I not think that Solomon McBride would make a fine romantic beau and, someday, husband? I closed my eyes to better picture his smile, his tender eyes, gazing into mine. The warmth of his hands on my shoulders. His quiet, firm grip of my hand.

At any rate, Solomon and Mr. Seward must be sorely disappointed. Solomon hadn't said as much in his letters, which of course I always provided to my parents after reading them. But I knew the Whig Party meant Mr. Seward to be nominated the past summer, at the Whig national convention. Southerners hated Mr. Seward passionately, for his opposition to the cruel institution of slavery that made possible their cotton plantations and enormous wealth. As a result, his name did not carry through the national balloting in June. Instead, after thirty-five rounds of voting, the name of New Hampshire lawyer Franklin Pierce entered the competition. And Pierce won the nomination by the necessary two-thirds of votes in the forty-ninth ballot.

I recalled Solomon's letter from the end of June: "Not only is Pierce a doughface, softened by treacherous sympathies with the South; he is vain, a heavy drinker, a man who'd sell out his morals as quickly as he would his family. His wife, a shy and sickly woman, is said to have fainted dead away upon word of the nomination."

But there was another aspect to Solomon's travels and politicking, a far more risky one: In secrecy, he carried papers of apprenticeship signed by Joseph Gilman himself, owner of the massive manufacturing mills in nearby St. Johnsbury. And those papers, with the blank space ready to insert a name, became documents that could guarantee a degree of safety for a Negro man struggling for freedom. If such a man reached the state of Pennsylvania, just north of the dangerous Southern-leaning state of Maryland, and he held such a set of apprenticeship papers for our Vermont firm, he could travel in almost certain safety. Which, in turn, might allow him to assist the escape of other enslaved men and their families.

I smiled to myself. Linking Matthew Clark, Jerushah's older brother and now a junior foreman at the Gilman Mills, to Solomon via transfer of such papers: that was my small task over the past two years.

Until the end of June, four months ago. Indeed, it had been four long months since Matthew had passed any papers to me, and Solomon must know that, for he'd never asked about more and had not visited North Upton since midsummer.

How could I have ignored this situation? Had something gone wrong with the plans and their effects? Could it even be somehow my fault?

Now that I saw the gap of time, I knew I should speak with Matthew and find out.

Easier said than done, though. With the bitterness that Matthew's mother held toward me, I usually stayed away from the inn, watching only for Matthew's visits to our sheep barn, where he'd leave a valise of documents that I'd shelter until Solomon visited again.

It seemed clear I should talk with Matthew soon, for Solomon's visit could be at any day. But how?

Two dozen baskets heaped with firm apples sat around me, occupying the entire floor space of the cool and dim front room, our parlor. And two pails of discards stood next to the door to the kitchen. By the quiet gray of the room, I judged it must be almost five o'clock. My father would be in the barn. A clatter at the door and the banging of stove lids told me my mother had just come home.

I lifted the pails and stepped into the kitchen. "Mama," I told her, "I'll just take these out to the horses." She nodded, testing the heat at the rear of the stovetop, and I added, "Too many crushed apples though for just our horses, and Papa doesn't like the sheep to have them. So I may take one pail across to the Clark stable, past the inn."

My mother shot a sharp glance at me but said only, "Don't linger, Alice. I only have two hands. You're needed here to set the table and bring up more butter from the cellar."

"Yes, Mama. I'll be right back."

I flung on my outer garments and sped toward the sheep barn. Leaving one pail just inside the barn doors—Papa must be outside in the sheep pens, out of my line of vision—I raced with my second pail, crossing the village road at a diagonal to avoid the front windows where Mrs. Clark might watch, and bolting into the small stock barn where the inn housed the horses of guests, as well as its own.

Three horses munched steadily in their stalls. I hastened down the aisle between them and, to my relief, found Matthew oiling leather tack at the back of the barn.

I set my pail in front of him, said quickly "for your horses," and added, "Matthew, I need to talk with you. Can you meet me in the tunnel after supper? About seven o'clock?"

Calm as always, Matthew nodded and added, "Seven thirty's the soonest. But I'll be there."

"Thank you!" I turned and forced myself to walk slowly past the horses, so as not to disturb them, then ran back to our sheep barn to turn out the apples there, to our horses "Old" Sam and Ely.

As I latched the barn door behind me to return to the house, my father called out to me, walking toward the barn from the river.

"That bear again?" I hated the notion.

"No, there are no fresh tracks." He patted my shoulder, and we walked together.

Looking down, I realized a thin layer of fresh snow now clung to the cold ground. "Is that how you knew to look for the bear this morning?"

"Of course," my father replied.

All the complicated questions of life, like the presence of a bear in a place that had no bears, or the freedom of an enslaved Negro child like Sarah had been, could be answered with a simple choice: the right one. That was how my father's affirmative struck me at that moment. I hoped I, too, could say "of course" to the next important question that came my way.

For now, I needed to see that supper went smoothly, so I could enter the tunnel as planned. I reminded myself: bring a candle then, and wear William's boots.

CHAPTER 6

Wind rattled outside the dark windows. My mother drew the curtain shut over the pane of glass near the kitchen table, to hold a bit more heat in the room. From her baking and soup, a fragrance of home surrounded us, with the warmth and hiss of the fire in the iron firebox.

"Definitely a bear," my father repeated. He'd told the tale of our beastly visitor to my mother and Aunt Julia, who sat over their tea with woolen stockings growing from their clicking needles and exclaimed at all the right points of the story.

Aunt Julia asked again, "Are you certain, Ephraim, that your sheep are safe if there's a bear in North Upton? Mother used to tell us about bears and always mentioned how hungry they were."

"First of all, it's just one bear," my father said patiently. "None of the others who were at Wilson's store today have seen any. It may not even stay. And one bear alone will look for easy sustenance: corn fields not well cleared, dead stock left unburied, even scraps tossed out after a meal. And apple trees and such."

I blanched. All those visits I'd made to the orchard on the ridge this past week, and I could have met this grown bear at any time.

My father muttered something else, which I couldn't hear, but apparently my mother grasped the matter. She snapped, "Filthy animals. Don't even think of it."

"Only if they're not well tended. The ones that the McLarens have in Barnet are fine creatures, clean and well trained. I've had it in mind for a while."

My mother wouldn't argue further in front of Aunt Julia, but I could hear in the snap and clatter of her knitting needles that she had more to opine.

"What kind of animal?" I asked cautiously.

"Scottish collie," came the short reply. "Sheep drovers use them to keep the herd moving. They'll make plenty of noise for a bear, even scare away a wolf, if there are any left of those to come around. It's a working animal, and," my father repeated firmly, "I've had it in mind."

Aunt Julia intervened, inquiring instead about my brother William's wife, Helen, and whether she was carrying another child yet. This discussion sent my father to the barn to check on his sheep and his door latches, and I excused myself to read in the parlor. I lit a candle there, and a second one, just a stub but enough for the task I had in mind. Boots came from where I'd set them aside earlier, behind an armchair. I tugged my skirt down lower to hide my feet and re-entered the kitchen.

"Mama, I think I left a cup down in the cellar. I'm going to look for it."

A short nod agreed that I might step out of the kitchen and descend the steep wooden staircase toward the butter cooler, the cream shelves, the bins of carrots, the empty ones waiting for the potatoes—and the old, almost hidden door that led to the ancient tunnel linking our farmhouse to the inn across the road. Jerushah and I had used it two years ago, to exchange messages; it was a grim and damp place, often with water lingering at the lowest point, and of course "dark as sin," as my father would say. Jerushah, Matthew, and I had all passed through it when we needed to quietly get word to each other. Since Jerushah's death, I hadn't entered it. After all, the catastrophic cellar tumble that led to her death took place when she'd been looking for a message from me, one that I should have taken to her in some safer way. I had no desire to enter that passageway ever again.

But for Solomon's sake (or so it seemed), I could do this. Armed with my candle stub, I slowly pried the door open, wedged it with a half brick to prevent it sealing again, and began the trek underground.

Fortunately, Matthew met me close to my end of the tunnel. In the flickering of his own candle, he looked intense, perhaps angry, unlike his usual calm.

I whispered an apology and said, "Solomon's coming to town before the election. Are there papers for him? You haven't left any in the barn, have you?"

Matthew stared at me, then replied: "Here I thought you were well up on the news, Alice. Don't your parents talk about the politics and such, and read the newspaper, at your home now?"

"Of course they do! And I do also, if I have time!"

"Then what are you thinking? John Gilman's running for governor of the state. How could he possibly have time or even enough privacy to provide more papers now? Plus the new fugitive law makes it all so much more risky for the men. Think, Alice. Honestly, you're the clever one, not like that little Almyra Alexander who's bouncing all around the village, aren't you? Try to act like it."

Embarrassed and angry, I protested. "If I were helping fugitives to freedom, I wouldn't let an election stop me from keeping up my share of labor."

"Girls!" Matthew groaned. "Go back to your kitchen chores, Alice. If Solomon and I need you to move more papers, one of us will say so. Right now, it's more important to change the laws. That's the fight that matters. Abolition must take place, or the nation's damned."

And with that startling statement, he spun around and hurried back into the darkness of the descending tunnel.

How unfair! I stamped my feet in irritation as I headed back into the house cellar, remembering at the last minute to latch the tunnel door behind me and pick up an empty cream-settling tin to carry up with me.

"No cup there, but a pan that needs cleaning," I said quietly as I returned to the kitchen. I made a show of scouring it out and setting it aside to dry before taking a seat at the table with my mother and her younger sister.

Least said, soonest mended. But still, could I find out an answer to one niggling question while my father was out in the barn? I picked up a sock to darn, began stitching, and waited for a pause in the conversation.

"Mama, did you ever want to have more children? Someone commented at the store that our family is a small one, and I wondered."

Silence, without even the clicking of knitting needles. I looked up and saw Aunt Julia and my mother with pursed lips. I held still, dreading that both of them would scold me at once.

To my surprise, my mother began a reply. "There are many things that cause a marriage to have fewer children," she said quietly.

"Like Mrs. Clark and her daughter Caroline?"

"Yes. Or like a man sustaining certain kinds of injuries. And that, I think, is sufficient answer to your question. Tell your Aunt Julia about Mrs. Alexander's niece who came to visit! She's been as curious as a cat."

"Do tell!" crooned Aunt Julia. "Is she really as pretty a young thing as your mother tells me? And what kind of dress did she wear? With a hoopskirt? And the latest Boston fashion for her shirtwaist, I'm sure of it. Come, Alice, details if you please!"

Half an hour later, my very weary father returned to the house, and Aunt Julia's husband collected her a few minutes later. I rinsed out the teacups and made my way to my chamber, my thoughts churning around the election, Solomon's return to North Upton, and the increasing nuisance of having a pretty girl from Boston entering every conversation.

Just as I drifted off to sleep, I wondered: If the election next week and the changes in the laws were so pressing, would they help Sarah's parents and brothers and sisters leave the South any sooner? I must write to her, first thing in the morning. After, of course, walking the village to see whether Solomon had arrived.

CHAPTER 7

Friday morning began auspiciously: My brother William, already scented from the barn, stood in the kitchen with my mother. They broke off their conversation, and my mother said, "William just offered to help fetch the last load of apples. Eat quickly, Alice, and you can ride with him to the orchard and then bring the apples down in his wagon. I don't want you up there alone, with a bear someplace nearby."

My brother grinned as I hurried to dish up my oat porridge and splash it with maple syrup and a spoonful of butter. "Ever seen a bear in person, Alice?"

"Yesterday! I saw the one that Papa followed, while it crossed the river. William, have you seen it, too?"

"Not yet! And I don't much want to. If we have a choice on which animals come back again, it's elk or caribou I'd want. Or even deer." He smacked his lips. "I remember venison roasts from when I was small."

My mother nodded. "Good eating. I hear you can still find them in the woods up north from time to time. But not up here among the villages and roads. Stop talking, Alice, and finish your porridge. There's a lot to do, and I want you back here by mid-morning. Mrs. Alexander should bring Almyra, and Mrs. Hopkins brings Eleanor, and there's Helen of course." Her counting continued and added to fifteen women, grown and younger, planning to be at our house to string apples on Saturday afternoon. Oh! No wonder everyone was hurrying.

43

"The barn chores," I mumbled around a mouthful.

"Done," William assured me. "Or close enough. I came an hour ago. A bit of milk's setting in the pans, and Papa's already off to Upton Center for new barn latches."

William's wagon and horse waited in the yard. A mound of golden hay and a dozen pails of corn made an ample load. "Winter feed for Harvey," he confirmed, clucking to his horse as we rolled forward. "You can help me unload it all, at my shed, and we'll have a fine empty wagon for your apple pickings."

"William, have you heard from Solomon? Have you seen him? He said he'd come for the election."

"Of course. But don't count on seeing him in Upton 'til after the balloting, little sister. He's sure to be rousing the votes in St. Johnsbury, where there are more to gather. You've read about Winfield Scott? What a president that man might be! We could stop slavery from expanding into the Territories and move to end it in the states as well."

Not until after the balloting? How unfair. And, yet, I knew Solomon must take every step he could, to press our nation toward a new direction. "If women could only vote, we'd help Mr. Scott to be elected president," I pronounced.

William laughed. "Women don't want to vote, Alice. Women have men to do such hard things for them, as you should know. Getting old enough to be thinking that way yourself, aren't you?"

My arguments with William on behalf of suffrage for women caused only more laughter. Perhaps I needed Almyra Alexander to talk with him about the wonders women could perform, if we had more say in the affairs of state!

Having the wagon at the orchard made everything easier, since I could stand on the side boards and reach higher in each tree than I'd been able to extend on my own. And, of course,

William harvested at a good pace himself. The sun warmed us more as it grew closer to midday, and bits of tree bark clung to my damp clothing and made their way under my bonnet, into my hair. But sack after sack, we finished the best picking quickly, happy with each other and our efforts as William urged Harvey back to the village and the family farm. William himself lived with his wife Helen in a small house next to the mill, where he cut lumber.

"No milling today, William?"

"Not until Papa's back from Upton Center," he explained. "He offered to fetch what I need to repair the main belt, if I'd take you apple picking." He bumped my shoulder in fun. "Couldn't resist a morning doing something different."

"And Helen? She's coming tomorrow, isn't she?"

A cloud of worry drifted back between us. "I hope so," William said quietly, without adding more.

Helen's sorrow over the loss of their first baby weighed heavy on them. William grieved, too, I knew, but it was harder for a woman. Especially a woman not yet expecting again. I closed my eyes for a moment, to wish Helen a new start.

The wagon swung wide into the track to our barn, and the horse slowed. Ely, my father's younger horse, nickered from the paddock. Papa must have returned.

Where to put the rest of the apples, that was a conundrum. The parlor, filled with baskets of apples I'd already sorted, could not take much more. The barn, of course, stood too far from the house for the gathering. At last, we cleared one side of the mudroom, the entryway between the door and the kitchen proper, and wedged the sacks of apples along it. My bed-chamber of course then became the temporary receptable for a heap of winter cloaks and spare boots and such.

Then my mother took charge of my every minute for the rest of the day and evening, polishing silver teaspoons, slicing bread, baking two pies, a quick supper of hot pork gravy on biscuits, and an evening of stitching the skirt hems she and Mrs. Clark had pinned up.

"When will Caroline come?" Candles made a poor light for stitching, so I sat close to the oil lamp at my mother's side.

"Mr. Clark leaves in the morning," Mama replied. "Of course, he'll stay over for the Sabbath and return on Monday."

The timing baffled me. "He can't possibly find a stage that's as quick as that, Mama. All the way to Hartford, Connecticut, and back? It must take at least two days each way, maybe more."

"He'll take the train," my mother said briefly. She cut off further questions by asking to see my stitches, then insisting that I take out the last row and set them fresh with a tighter, smaller measure. "This isn't some growing girl we're dressing," she reminded me. "She's a young lady, and she may even teach some pupils. Her clothing must be as well finished as she'd find in Connecticut."

The train! Why hadn't I thought of that? After two years of railroad cars reaching nearby St. Johnsbury . . . Well, but I'd never been on a train myself. Of course, I'd seen the passenger cars lined up at the station once or twice, and even the massive locomotive. But not in motion. For a moment, an unexpected longing filled me: How I would love to take a journey on the railroad, see Boston or Albany someday. Places that Solomon saw as he took Mr. Seward's messages and raised up fervor across New England and New York.

I looked critically at my own skirt, still needing a good brushing from the day's activities. It certainly looked humble, compared to what Almyra wore. Aloud, I wondered: "Do you think we might be able to pick out a length of goods so I could make a fresh Sunday shirtwaist, Mama? For a winter's evening work?"

"I should think so. If your stitches improve, Alice. See

whether you can complete that hem neatly."

She left her seat to check the woodstove and bank the firebox down for the evening. The scent of rising yeast filled the room as she checked the batter set aside for the morning.

With a hundred tiny stitches to form, I tried to concentrate. But my thoughts drifted instead to counting the hours ahead: tomorrow, stringing sliced apples with our neighbors; Sunday, the Sabbath, of course; Monday, Caroline Clark's return— would it be soon enough in the day for me to meet her? Probably not. Tuesday then, since she would be just across the road. Even Mrs. Clark must allow me to pay a call of welcome to her daughter, I hoped. And Tuesday was also the balloting, in Upton Center. So, Tuesday evening—no, more likely Wednesday morning: Solomon McBride. At last.

Ouch! A hidden pin caught my hand. Careful not to bleed on Caroline's newly hemmed skirt, I paid closer attention. My mother turned up the lamp wick a bit and said, "Just another twenty minutes and then to bed."

I nodded without looking up, for fear she'd guess the reason for my blushes.

CHAPTER 8

At noon on Saturday, I cleared a space at the kitchen table for my father to enjoy his dinner. Piping hot chicken pie and a slab of the graham bread with a mug of strong, dark tea kept him mostly silent, while Mama and I continued our supper preparations: pans of biscuits for the ladies, and a rich chicken gravy to spoon over them.

"No pudding?" my father inquired.

"Apples," my mother replied succinctly. A pudding at suppertime would be quite a treat, and entertaining guests at supper might be a reason to serve such a sweet—but this gathering was for work, not for frivolity. Besides, anyone who wanted to follow their supper with a morsel of juicy apple might easily do so, for we would all be slicing and stringing.

After a timid knock, the door past the mudroom opened a few inches, and my cousin Timothy Palmer's round face peered inside. "Uncle Ephraim? Mr. Wilson sent me to tell you. The papers have arrived."

"Close the door, Timothy, you're chilling my stove," my mother called out.

My cousin, nearing fourteen years old and sturdy across the shoulders, sometimes helped my father in the barn now. I nodded to him as he entered, but the filthy state of his boots moved me toward him: "Hold there, Timothy, or we'll be sweeping after you."

He gave me a confused glance but stopped before entering

48

the kitchen itself. "I only came to fetch Uncle Ephraim."

My father already had his long woolen jacket half on and said, "Abigail, I may be gone for an hour or more."

At my mother's inquiring look, he added, "Daniel Webster. He died on the Sabbath, and today will be the printing on his life and on the funeral services. And more."

I couldn't help my annoyance showing: Daniel Webster, the great silver-tongued orator of New England, owed a debt of conscience to us all. A mere two years earlier, in the nation's senate, he'd tipped the balance into passing the terrible Compromise of 1850, including the dreaded Fugitive Slave Act. Replacing him in office with Charles Sumner soon followed, but the terrible new legislation put my friend Sarah Johnson and her family—all but Sarah were still trapped in the South's enslavement—into greater danger than ever. I felt no regret for the death of Daniel Webster!

Nor did my father, I knew. Still, he must read and discuss the newspaper's report with the other men of North Upton. Just before the door closed behind him and my cousin, I remembered to ask: "Papa, did Mr. Clark leave this morning, as planned, to fetch back Caroline?"

"Of course he did," my father replied. "If you weren't such a lay-a-bed these days, you'd have heard his carriage leave before dawn." He smiled, taking the sting out of his comment, and shut the door firmly.

Now the remaining preparations for our gathering must be swift. I set aside my father's plate and fetched the knives from the drawer, along with a whetstone, to begin sharpening each. My mother and I circled each other in a steady progression of tasks, hers mostly at the stove, mine from cupboard and sideboard to table, and fetching the other two chairs from the front room, as well as barrels for more seating. Even so, some would have to stand up while coring and slicing and, my favorite task, setting the slices onto long strings to hang in the attic to dry. We would need enough for forty pies at least, over the long winter, and the other ladies likewise. My heavy-laden returns from the hillside orchard would show their measure this day!

As the day's light dimmed, we moved pots and kettles among the hotter and cooler places on the woodstove, and, when the first knock came at the door, my mother had just poured water over tea leaves in the brown crockery teapot. She called out a welcome, as Mrs. Hopkins and Eleanor and the younger Hopkins girl, Anna, pressed past the coat hooks to make room for Mrs. Wilson, her sister, Miss Chance, and the minister's wife, Mrs. Alexander—accompanied, of course, by Almyra, in a satin-lined cloak trimmed with fur at the wrists and collar. Then I lost count, as I scurried to place cloaks in the parlor and match each two persons with a basket of apples between them, a sharpened knife, and some lengths of twine. Thank goodness most of the women brought their own blades, so we had enough to go around, just barely.

Cups of tea circulated, and a plate of gingersnaps, as the clicking of knives on wooden boards and cheerful gossip rose up in a merry chorus.

I scanned the group: Helen had not arrived, but Mrs. Clark sat at the far end of the table, next to Mrs. Alexander, their voices lower than some.

Almyra pressed around several people and re-settled herself next to me. "I'm likely to jump up and down to refill the teapots," I warned her.

"No matter," she laughed. She eyed Mrs. Clark, then asked me in a low voice, "So, this Caroline who's coming home to the Clarks on Monday—what is she like? My aunt said she's a teacher and has no hearing at all, is that correct?"

"That's what my mother says," I returned as quietly as I could. "But I've no idea what she's like, since I must have known her when I was tiny but have no recollection of it." My thoughts lingered on Jerusha, who'd never told me about this older sister of hers. How strange, that our small village had such secrets. Or at least, such silences.

"Will she teach in the village school, then?" Almyra asked.

"Oh, I'm sure she won't! How could she? Besides, we have a schoolteacher already, you know. Miss Wilson."

"But she's leaving in the spring," Almyra said. "She's marrying Jasper Blake in Upton Center, you know."

I didn't know. I felt my cheeks heat up with annoyance. Why should Almyra know this ahead of me? This was my town, not hers!

She watched me, amusement sparkling. "It's not your fault you're late to hear," she pointed out. "The minister's wife knows before almost anyone else, for her husband takes part in the marriage. Have a care, Alice, you're slicing through the core!"

"Jasper Blake is a terrible storekeeper," I spat with irritation. "I can't imagine why anyone would want to marry him and starve from lack of payment."

"Oh, you never know. Sometimes a clever wife can improve a man's business, while she attends to his other needs as well," Almyra whispered. "She strikes me as a very eager young wife to be, you know."

Now my cheeks flamed. How could she say such a thing! Ladies did not speak of such topics, not ever—or, at most, only to hear their mother's advice for marriage.

Entirely unbidden, I thought of Solomon McBride. Did men speak of the eagerness of young women, when they talked among themselves? How horrible! Still, I pictured myself leaning close to Solomon, assuring him I'd care for him in every single way, allowing him to feel the warmth of my affection and—Dear merciful heaven, I sounded like a heroine in some absurd serial story from a low-class newspaper. I dropped an apple on purpose, to take a moment under the table to compose my face and steady my hands.

A sharp breeze gusted through the room as the door opened and quickly closed again, presenting my brother's wife, Helen, at last. Murmurs and calls of greeting circled the table, and we pressed closer to each other as Helen slid into a seat next to my mother, and Anna Hopkins fetched a crate from the mudroom on which to settle herself next to Almyra. To my enormous relief, the two began to chat about a new pattern for woolen stockings, and I bent to my basket of fruit with fresh attention.

It took just over an hour for the first round of baskets to empty, and with "many hands to make light work," bowls of biscuits and gravy soon reached each guest. My mother stood at the stove, watching over us all and offering second helpings to those who cleaned their dishes swiftly. I refilled the two teapots—Helen had brought hers, thank goodness—and then summoned Anna to assist in fetching another round of baskets of apples for the group.

Now some sliced more slowly, and others fumbled with placing the slices onto the twine. Only a few of the women, mostly the older ones, completed their work with sufficient speed to begin a third basket full. But it must all be done, if we were to feel comfortable with winter's provisions.

I noticed Almyra leave her work and seek out Anna and Eleanor. The three of them approached my mother, who gestured to the big iron tureen on the shelf. Almyra fetched it, set it on the floor, and directed the others in carrying water from the hand pump to the tureen. What were they doing? I looked to my mother, who shook her head indulgently. Mrs. Alexander rose and trekked around the others, to supervise the process.

"Young ladies, I must caution you to attempt this only in fun," she lectured. "Our Lord warns us to avoid fortune tellers and gypsies and such, so you must see this only as a game, not a hint of the future."

My mother nodded her agreement. My grandmother Palmer at the far end of the room snorted in a rather unladylike manner and kept stringing her apple slices.

"Come on, Alice," Almyra called to me. "Fetch us half a dozen good-sized apples with the stems still on them, and we'll have us a proper apple bobbing!"

Oh! Now that I understood, I was surprised at the indulgence Mrs. Alexander and Grammy Palmer were showing for such foolery. But I gathered the right sort of apples and moved close to the small group of giggling girls.

Almyra set them into the tureen of water and announced the rules: "Hold your hands behind your back, and be sure your braids are pinned back," she told the younger girls. My own braids, of course, were pinned tight to my head, befitting my age. This sort of game was for youngsters, not for me.

But Almyra called out to Eleanor, and then also to me: "We need more girls, to make it challenging. Remember, the first one to catch an apple with her teeth will be the first to marry!"

A chaos of splashing, laughter, and exclamations followed, as the youngsters pressed against each other, wrangling for position and snapping at the bobbing fruits in the water. Eleanor and I, by unspoken agreement, stepped back from the game and showed our mature selves in so doing.

Of course, it was Almyra who captured the first apple. Exclaiming happily, she stood dripping with the apple snug in her sharp, white teeth. After a laugh of triumph, she plucked the apple from her mouth, first taking a neat, circular bit of the flesh. She waved the bitten apple in the air and announced, "I'm going to be married first, I do declare! To a Boston man, no doubt!"

A wave of smiles and laughter circled the room; everyone already knew Almyra would return to Boston in the spring and supposed her meaning accordingly.

But as I caught the mischief in her glance toward my own self, a chill ran along my backbone: Was Almyra Alexander hinting she'd be pursuing Solomon McBride when he returned to North Upton? My own Solomon?

I sped back to a seat at the table and plunged my knife into the next autumn-scented apple, shaking with a fury I'd never before known.

CHAPTER 9

Matthew Clark, in his Sunday best, walked past our pew in the North Upton church. His mother held her head high and proudly as she stepped with him along the aisle. Her tall, broad-shouldered son gestured for her to precede him onto the polished wooden bench in front of my mother and me, and then he clumsily dropped his psalter in the center aisle. The book made an embarrassing thump as it struck the floor. In picking it up, he also fumbled with two thin sheets of paper that slid out from the pages. As he stood again, he placed one back in his psalter, then glanced at the other and said to me, "Oh, this one must have dropped from your own psalter, Alice. Here you are."

Of course I hadn't dropped anything, but I managed to hold my face uninterested and said, "Oh, thank you, Matthew," as I tucked the folded item into the back of my book. A few minutes later, as we rustled the pages before us, I slid the missive up my sleeve and made sure the cuff held tightly buttoned to keep it secure.

Solomon! There could be no other reason for Matthew to pass a message to me, and it must be urgent, or he'd never have done so in such a public place. Hymn after hymn and through the Rev. Alexander's sermon on the moral obligation to partake in the election according to Christian values, the time dragged. But at least the presence of Almyra Alexander in her elegant Boston-style shirtwaist and half-hooped skirts no longer burned.

Let her think she could catch Solomon—I knew better.

This attitude seemed un-Christian at the least. I made an effort to focus again on the hundred-and-seventh psalm with its clear anti-slavery message, as the minister pointed out: "He brought them out of darkness and the shadow of death, and brake their bands in sunder." I particularly loved "They that go down to the sea in ships, that do business in great waters," because again I thought of Solomon and his seafaring relatives. Such a difference from farming in northern Vermont!

Anticipation lifted my heart. Outside the plain church windows, sunshine beat on the nearly bare hills, corn fields emptied, distant trees glowing in a rich red-brown. Oh, such a long final hour of worship . . . Amen, Amen.

"Mama, I'll go increase the fire in the stove," I offered, "and stir everything, so don't hurry."

My mother raised a questioning eyebrow as she continued to accept warm greetings from Mrs. Wilson and some others, speaking of how enjoyable the apple gathering the evening before had been. I gestured discreetly toward my stomach, and she nodded, assuming I needed to hasten home for some urgent need. No matter. It wasn't exactly an untruth.

Ahead of me my father strode, anxious to see that the sheep did well, before settling to his noon dinner. When I'd left the church folks far behind and turned into the track toward our house, I stepped aside and paused at last to retrieve the note from my sleeve and, with trembling hands, unfold its careful creases.

Solomon's penmanship, most surely. But so brief! "No time for N. Upton. Departing by 10 a.m. train, the day after the election. Messages can reach me in care of Miss Farrow until then. Yours in haste and with regret, S."

No! So close, and no visit? In an agitated state, I completed the route to the house, setting the note this time securely in my pocket behind the waist of my skirt, and hastened into the kitchen, adjusting the air to the woodstove, adding another split of maple, and ensuring both the pots on top and the iron dish inside the oven sat correctly for the heat.

William and Helen arrived before my mother; my grandmother and both my parents entered the kitchen all at once, and soon we sat at our meal, taking turns to comment on the Sabbath lesson and morsels of news. Helen marveled that Caroline could return to the village: just another day and she'd arrive.

"Did you help at the birth?" I asked my mother.

She shook her head. "I'm not much older than Anna Clark and didn't have skill to offer. Her mother, Mrs. Simpson, came from Rutland and stayed with the family for the last month of Anna's confinement, and then with the birth. I always wondered, though."

"What did you wonder?" Helen asked.

"Whether it could have been—Of course, Mrs. Simpson has passed, and I don't care to speak ill of the dead. But still. I heard there were Irish girls who boarded at the Simpson house. I read that a lot of the Irish in Rutland had come down with fever and spots, with Mrs. Simpson hurrying out of town hoping not to have the illness herself, and Mrs. Simpson never mentioned it to Anna until afterward. It's said the disease was a German one, with risks for women."

This conversation clearly unsettled the men, and they excused themselves to sit in the parlor, while Helen and I cleared away the dishes and pushed my mother to say more. Grammy Palmer cut in: "The good Lord protects his own. If Emma Simpson was a God-fearing woman, then there was nothing to fear in her home. It's possible, Abigail, that this deaf child was sent to young Anna for a trial of her faith."

From her cross expression, my grandmother clearly felt the

infant daughter should have stayed in North Upton, deaf or not.

I pressed for more detail: "How old was she when her parents sent her away? She wasn't an infant then, was she?"

"Seven years old," my mother confirmed. "She came home for summer the first year, but with Matthew and Jerushah to care for, Anna couldn't manage the extra burden, and the child seemed happier staying at the school, they said."

My grandmother snorted loudly. "When I was a young woman, we managed what God provided, without fuss or questions."

The aggravation in her tone reminded me of the fierce scolding she'd once given me when I was very small myself, one of the few times I'd known her anger. What was it for, back then? A broken teacup? Perhaps.

My mother interceded. "I believe we have more stitching to complete, for Caroline's Vermont skirts. Mother, will you join us?"

"I'll not be sewing on the Lord's day," Grammy Palmer replied crisply. "In my day, that wasn't done. I'll read aloud to the three of you if you must complete your commitment, however."

So, Helen, my mother, and I took up needle and thread and listened to a not very inspired reading from a ladies' improvement column.

If only she could read to us the columns on the election, I thought. My father made time to read several papers from around the state each week, but how could I do so? Of course, when winter set in, we'd have time for other reading among us, and I hoped to enjoy the novel that everyone talked about now, *Uncle Tom's Cabin*, by a lady from Hartford, Connecticut, Mrs. Stowe. But since Jerushah's death, the cozy sessions of reading together in the Clark home were gone, and I'd be perusing the book on my own, with its moral descriptions of the perils of both slavery and escape.

Which of course took me back to thinking of Solomon, whose every action must pursue the end of enslavement, through political success first of Mr. Seward, and now of Mr. Scott, in our presidential election. I must read Mrs. Stowe's book soon or have him think me ignorant.

At that moment, a plan came to mind, and I realized I'd need to put it into action by morning, if I wanted a chance to see Solomon before he once again left Vermont.

The scuffing of boots and louder voices heralded my father and William, out of the parlor and crossing the kitchen.

"The post," my father said. "I'll be back shortly."

My mother nodded. Of course my father wouldn't linger at the store on the Sabbath. Indeed, none of the men in North Upton would, though I'd heard that in larger towns, men drank and played cards even on this day of the week, when they met to collect their letters and appraise the news of the day.

William gathered up Helen for the ride back to their house by the mill, and Grammy Palmer took advantage of the opportunity to join them in their wagon. I wished I had a reason to go out into the afternoon sunlight on this late-autumn day.

But instead I lifted a woolen petticoat and began its long, tedious hem. Best to accept the trials of the moment, in exchange for the possibility of the morrow.

I said to my mother, "Perhaps we might go to meet the train tomorrow, to welcome Caroline before her ride from St. Johnsbury to North Upton. We could match that thread you wanted for your new bodice, and visit Mrs. French to see the latest hats."

This last notion betrayed my scheming to my mother, who knew quite well I had no interest in millinery fashion. She laughed though and replied, "Perhaps we might indeed, Alice.

Winter will be here any day, and I've an itch to go to town myself. Let me talk with your father after supper. We might even look at some fabric. After all, now that we have a Boston girl in our village, we'll have to catch up with the times, or be sadly flat by comparison."

Her sympathetic twinkle assured me she'd guessed some of my feelings. I felt a twinge of guilt, knowing I should tell her about trying to cross paths with Solomon in town. Well, least said, soonest mended. If I only saw him "by accident," I'd have no reason to regret the effort!

The squeak and bang of the outer door told us my father'd returned, and he set two letters on the table. "I'll be going to West Barnet on Tuesday afternoon," he announced cheerfully. "There's a sheep dog ready for me." He looked more serious for a moment and added, "Alice, Mr. McLaren says one of the district schools there has an opening for next summer. So, you'd best come along and meet him, to make sure you'll be considered for the post."

CHAPTER 10

"Today and tomorrow, I have obligations to meet, so with regret, I will not return to study with you until Wednesday in the forenoon. I thank you for pardoning this unexpected absence."

I signed my note to Miss Margaret Wilson, then looked again to make sure my sentences were properly punctuated. It wouldn't be Miss Wilson certifying me for teaching after this term, but the local superintendent. Still, he would surely ask her opinion, as well as examining my teacher preparation documents. Although I hoped for a future that involved Solomon McBride, I must be practical in the meantime. At least, that was Mama's instruction to me: "Once you've managed a schoolroom," she'd advised me last summer, "you'll be able to manage anything else."

The sun crept over the east hill of the village, bright in a pocket of blue sky for the moment. Mare's tails of thin cloud predicted changing weather by afternoon, but Mama and I would be fine in our wagon with Old Sam pulling us; he knew his way to St. Johnsbury, but he knew the way home, even better.

From her position now at the woodstove, Mama managed a frying pan and a kettle, as well as biscuits in the oven. She warned me, "Your father will be in for breakfast in another quarter hour. If you want to carry your letter to the school, you'd best do it now."

My short jacket wouldn't do, this early in the day—now it

61

was the first of November, and felt like it, frosty with a biting brisk wind from the northwest. I flung on my cloak, fastened it quickly, and skidded out the door, barely staying upright on a thin skim of ice over the step.

The schoolhouse stood at the far end of the village. I walked to the main road rapidly, almost trotting, and veered to the left, past a half dozen houses, the woodsmoke fragrant in the sharp breeze. Hurrying helped me warm up and would get me home sooner.

A small fire hissed and spat in the schoolroom stove. Miss Wilson must have already come in to start the classroom warming up. I placed my note at the center of her desk and bolted back out the double door—and nearly tripped over Almyra Alexander.

"My aunt said eight o'clock, and it's only seven thirty," she proclaimed in some frustration. "Do the older classes start earlier? I saw you coming through the village!"

"Eight o'clock for everyone," I reassured her. "Go home and stay warm a little longer, while you can. I'm headed to town."

"Then who will study with me?" Her wide eyes and rising agitation assured me: for Almyra, the focus of each moment was herself.

Pretend you're the teacher, I told myself. Manage this. I smiled coolly and said, "Miss Wilson will see you to your books, Almyra. You wouldn't be studying with me anyway, as I'm past the lessons and am preparing to teach."

"To teach?" She squeaked in excitement. "Are you old enough to teach, Alice?"

"Of course. I'm nearly eighteen, with a year of preparation already."

"Oh! I thought you were only sixteen!"

Aggravating though this was, I could ignore it, if I were a teacher. I summoned another calm smile and said, "You were mistaken, I'm afraid. Pardon me, I need to return home. You should also, Almyra. I wish you well on your first day of studies here. Good day!"

The twitch of a curtain at the minister's house assured me that someone, probably Mrs. Alexander, kept an eye on Almyra. As I sped home, I heard occasional voices and doors, as others in the village pursued their morning efforts.

My father, already half through his biscuit and bacon, nodded and continued to chew. My mother must have already eaten; she was examining the contents of her traveling bag and reminding my father about his noon dinner.

"You're sure you don't want me to drive you ladies to town? I could let Timothy work alone for a few hours."

"No, Ephraim, we'll be fine. Old Sam knows me, and the way is simple."

"Old Sam? Abigail, I told you last night, he's not walking well. I was going to hitch Ely for you. Maybe I really should come along."

"Not at all. Ely will be fine, and even Alice has driven him."

This was true, but not exactly something I wanted to discuss. I hadn't really driven Ely much, just when Solomon needed a break, as we'd driven a long hard road carrying Jerushah home, two years earlier. Still, clearly we "ladies" would have more freedom if allowed to drive to town on our own, so I nodded to my father and said, "I'm sure we'll be fine, Papa. And you said you need to go to Barnet tomorrow for the sheep dog, after you cast your ballot, so you need to be in the barn today, don't you?"

Which settled things, indeed. Twenty minutes later, with the school bell ringing behind us, my mother and I guided Ely and the wagon down the river road, headed for the big town of St. Johnsbury, the arrival of Caroline Clark, some window shopping for hats and some spending on ribbons and thread, and, I was sure, a completely accidental crossing of paths with a certain political young man I looked forward to surprising: Solomon.

After the first half mile, the sun warmed deliciously, and the river sang softly beside the old road to town. My mother began to sing old songs—"Down in the Valley, Hear the Wind Blow," and other sweet tunes. I sang along, feeling less rebellious and a bit regretful about what seemed like it might be a deception. Finally I said, "I suppose Solomon might be in town, seeing as the election is tomorrow."

"I suppose he might." My mother smiled without taking her eyes off the road. "It certainly wouldn't surprise either of us, would it?"

"Not at all." I heaved a sigh of relief. "He's probably too busy to come calling, though." There, I had revealed the contents of my little note, without getting Solomon or myself into trouble. I couldn't help adding, "You like him, don't you, Mama?"

"Yes, of course. He's a hard-working man showing loyalty and perseverance. If all men were like him, we'd see the end of slavery quickly."

"In the North," I agreed. "And maybe the West. But not the South."

"No, not the South. Your father says . . ."—she hesitated, then continued—"Your father says the longer and deeper this difference over slavery continues, the more likely it is to split the nation. I suppose Solomon and Mr. Steward must be aware of that risk."

"Yes, I'm sure. Mama?"

"Alice?"

"Did Papa court you for a long time?"

"Oh, that was years ago," my mother said dismissively. "There wasn't time for such things. He knew I favored him, and he just up and asked my father for my hand, a month or so after I finished school."

"Oh." That seemed discouraging. I'd known Solomon for almost two years, and he didn't seem any closer to talking to my father. Was I imagining that he favored me? A Boston man, traveling all over the East, he must meet young women everywhere. My chest seized up, and my throat felt choked.

Perhaps my mother followed my thoughts, for she said gently, "When a man has committed to a cause, he may not look to court or marry, Alice. You have more choices than just Solomon. Take the teaching position and sample a little more of the world. You'll see things differently."

I didn't want to see things differently. I wanted Solomon to come courting. I thought of the warmth of his hands, and the mingled scent of saddle leather and soap and hard-worked muscles that clung to him.

But I was thinking about this the way Almyra thought, wasn't I? Solomon had a mission, and it wasn't focused on me. Eager to change the subject, I took a risk and asked my mother the other question I'd mulled over: "Mama, the other day, did you mean that Papa was injured somehow, so that you didn't have a larger family?"

"Easy, Ely. Whoah, now. Whoah." She eased the wagon toward the side of the road, letting a rider pass in the other direction. The man tipped his hat to us. "That's Judge Paddock," she told me as she encouraged Ely back to a slow trot. "You remember, Miss Farrow lives at his house."

Miss Farrow: the dark-skinned woman with a past life of enslavement, the one who'd brought my friend Sarah from Pennsylvania, after Thaddeus Stevens offered to help her family purchase their freedom, one family member at a time.

"I never met Judge Paddock, just Miss Farrow," I replied. "Is he a good man?"

"He is," Mama confirmed. "I expect he's on his way to talk

with our men when they collect their mail today, to encourage them to cast their ballots for Mr. Scott." She paused and said, "Your father owned a horse once that didn't pull well, and it caught him against the barn wall in a way that did damage. You're not to mention that I told you. Now, what do you think of Mr. Scott as a candidate for president?"

"Me? What do I think? Why, Mama, we women cast no ballots. Why should I think about Mr. Scott?" Besides, the Mexican War hero was more than sixty years old, and, from what I'd heard Papa saying, the man's views were plain and clear: dug in against the Southern slaveholders, as a matter of both Constitution and the higher law of God. I said this aloud.

"That's right. Just because a woman can't vote, Alice, doesn't mean she can't influence the course of moral choices. You must always study these matters, so you can support the wise choices of others, my dear."

Did she mean, support Solomon? I cheered up again, and, when my mother began to talk about her planned purchases in town, I paid close attention and offered to take on some of the tasks myself.

"Not this time," she demurred, patting my arm for a moment. "Let's do this together. My girl's becoming such a fine young woman that I'm counting our time together as a pleasure today."

Oh! Now if I did see Solomon, it would be with my mother at my side. Well, considering how confused I felt about his not coming to court me, perhaps that would be for the best.

Ely's trot became more labored and slowed to a walk as he drew the wagon up the long hill that led to the Plain, where the shops lined the main street. I expected we'd go directly to the livery stable there, but, instead, my mother clucked to Ely and turned him down a steep slope toward the river side of town. "I believe the train arrives at eleven," she explained, while we both braced ourselves with our feet against the front of the wagon, our backs on the bench, to be able to pull on the brake and hold back the buggy from picking up speed. "Easy, Ely, slow down now."

The train! Thinking of Solomon drove the notion of Caroline Clark's arrival from my thoughts, but now I wondered eagerly: Would she look like her younger sister, Jerushah? Would I know her when I saw her?

My mother, being more pragmatic, reminded me: "Mr. Clark and Caroline will have to walk from the station to the stable, for their horses and carriage. We'll settle at the midpoint of their route and prepare to greet them." She nudged her traveling bag toward me. "There's a packet of cookies and a new handkerchief, lavender scented, in there. Pull them out, and we'll give them to Caroline when we meet her. I've heard that the deaf may compensate by having other acute senses, so we shall befriend her with aroma and sweetness." She laughed as she saw my excitement. "Be a lady, now, Alice!"

Then she focused entirely on guiding Ely, whose ears perked up at the long, shrieking whistle of the oncoming train.

We pulled up to the station, and I slipped down from my seat to hitch Ely to one of the posts, then climbed back to sit beside Mama, hands over my ears. The ground shook beneath us, and every horse along the rail stamped and rolled its eyes.

Oh! Nobody had told me how enormous the locomotive would be, or how powerful, tugging its train of passenger cars into St. Johnsbury. Whistles blew, men shouted, some in thick accents that surely must be Irish, and, with a squeal of metal and wood and more, the monstrous locomotive eased to a stop, smoke lingering around its massive stack.

Jerushah! No, I rebuked my pained heart firmly: not Jerushah. Caroline Clark was stepping down from a car, one hand resting on her father's shoulder, the other grazing the edge of the doorway as she maneuvered a full skirt with undoubtedly a hoopskirt underneath it. And so beautiful!

Tears dripped down my cheeks, as I realized: this is what Jerushah never had the chance to be.

My mother handed me a handkerchief, one of her own; the scent of rosewater in the cloth pulled me back to myself, and I sniffed hard, wiped my face, and delved within for a smile with which to say, "Mr. Clark, and Caroline, it's good to see you here."

CHAPTER 11

Mr. Clark beamed with pride as he held his daughter's hand in the crook of his arm. "Why, Mrs. Sanborn, how kind of you to stop! I know you'll remember my little Caroline, though she's a lady now. And here's Alice." For a moment his smile vanished. I didn't blame him; to think of Jerushah's death hurt all of us who'd loved her. But he resumed after a breath. "Alice, this is my daughter Caroline. Caroline . . . ah, wait just a moment."

Releasing his daughter's arm, he delved into a satchel dangling from his other arm and drew out a piece of card stock. On it were the letters of the alphabet, each with a drawing of a hand in a different position.

Caroline had already given a half curtsey to my mother, and dipped a small nod toward me, with a sweet quiet smile. Now she turned to look at her father's face, made a small gesture toward me, and tapped the card that he held. Letter by letter, he pointed: *A, L, I, C, E.* He spoke them aloud as he spelled, and then said, "Alice. Alice Sanborn."

The tall, well-dressed young woman tapped the card again and turned to look at me. She held up a hand and, one at a time, made five gestures, then tapped it again and looked at me questioningly.

Oh! She had spelled my name with her hand! I was entranced and pressed closer. My turn: I reached over and tapped the letters *C, A, R, O, L, I, N, E,* and the smiling, silent woman produced a quick sequence of hand movements that clearly matched the gestures for those letters.

I turned eagerly to my mother. "We can talk with each other! We can spell words and messages this way!"

My mother patted my hand and let Mr. Clark reply: "Alice, it's much better than that. You can also say a word with just a single movement, like this." He demonstrated a tender touch to a rounded cheek and said aloud, "Girl," then tugged at an imaginary cap brim and spoke "Boy!"

With so much to ask and say, and no time to do so, I vibrated with excitement. I wanted to learn this new language of signs and gestures. Even more, I wanted a new friend.

What insight this young woman in front of me must have, for she saw, I believe, the mix of sorrow and hope in my face at that moment. She drew a line down her own cheek as if a tear crept down it, reached for her father's hand, and held it in position in front of her to point to the letter *J*.

A half dozen tradesmen carrying bundles pressed past us, knocking the card from Mr. Clark's hand. He stooped to collect it, and I took the moment to hand Caroline the packet of cookies and the pretty lavender-scented handkerchief. My mother pulled me gently toward her and said to Mr. Clark, "We'll see you in the village, I'm sure. Perhaps Mrs. Clark would care to bring Caroline to call on me on Tuesday, while Alice and her father are out of town. Now, Alice and I have errands, and some shopping. Your horse will be ready for you?"

"Of course," Mr. Clark assured us, and, with his daughter's hand back on his arm, he headed along the wooden boardwalk toward the stables beyond the station.

My mother, in turn, drew me to our wagon, and, after an encouraging scratch of Ely's ears, we boarded and rode back to the Plain to commence our small commerce.

Walking alongside the shops, we exchanged greetings with quite a few people who knew my mother, and we peered through the windows at the bounteous goods in the Gilman company store. At a grocer's, we purchased tins of baking soda and cream of tartar, and small packets of cinnamon sticks, nutmegs, cloves, and a larger one of hard black peppercorns. There was no need to visit the baker, of course, since my mother made our breads and pies. But she chose half a dozen fine candles that she said would give better light for winter reading than the ones we made from sheep tallow.

In each shop and outside between them, I flicked my gaze around, hoping to catch a glimpse of Solomon. My mother finally commented, "Are the flies bothering you, Alice? You're as twitchy as a new-broke mare!"

Then she laughed and said, "I doubt you'll see that young man at a grocer's. But I do have need of some goods from Dr. Jewett, and the waiting room of his surgery is almost sure to hold a bustling group of gentlemen talking about the election. Come along, and we'll see whether I'm correct."

What a delight for my mother to name my longing and facilitate a possible connection with Solomon! She seemed for the moment like an older sister, teasing a little and fully aware of what I longed for. Strange though the sensation was, I confess I felt both charmed and hopeful.

We lifted our skirts to the tops of our shoes, no easy task while also carrying our bundled treasures. But to let them drag while crossing the street would soil them sadly with the horses' leavings. The knack was to raise the fabric just barely enough, and not reveal any glimpse of ankle! Or at least, to make it appear that any such glimpse was purely accidental. Anticipation speeded up my breathing, and I felt new heat in my cheeks. Arm in arm, we navigated across the mud and muck, to the long brick home of the doctor with its white-painted extension for his medical office and dispensary. Two horses stood hitched to a granite post in front, evidence of at least a few people within.

The warmth of a group of men in vehement discussion, and the sharp scent of them, caught us immediately as we stepped inside. Along the wall we faced at first, shelves and drawers overflowed with bottles and tins of remedies. But along the other three walls of the room, wherever windows did not interrupt, books and pamphlets stood in rows, lay in stacks, and overflowed from corners. Six men sat at an oak table, some with chairs tipped back, and two of them puffing smoke from powerful tobacco in their pipes. A stoneware jug with its cork set aside indicated the hour had advanced well past noon.

Dr. Jewett, thin as a rail with a slender moustache and white hair, sprang up to greet us. "Mrs. Sanborn! Do I have a packet for you? I don't recall a letter. Are you well? How is your husband?"

As my mother sorted out answers to all of this and provided a short list of "simples" that she required, I stood blushing, drawn to the amused and warm gaze of the man I'd been hoping for so long to see: the dark-haired Solomon himself, a long lock of hair dangling across his forehead, and a mug of cider in his hand.

He rose in gentlemanly fashion and politely greeted my mother, then introduced the men at the table, some of them leaders of the town whose names I knew from the inner pages of the newspaper. One, named McLeod, looked more like a farmer. To my mother's gracious nod, each of the men bobbed a half bow from the waist. We'd interrupted, I could tell.

But courteously, Solomon allowed us into the discussion by saying, "You fellows must admit that the clear vision of a God-fearing woman is a powerful force toward truth and justice. Here's just the sort I mean: Mrs. Sanborn here hosts a table of men who stand for both the Union and the end of slavery, and

I'd wager her daughter's been raised with the same views. Perhaps," he teased, "we should allow the fairer sex to take up the ballot, if it will speed correction of the nation's pathway!"

All the men chuckled. Aside from a handful of outspoken women of cities like Albany and New York, nobody really believed women were fit to take part in an election. How could they be, sheltered as they were?

Recalling Almyra's outrageous statement of the week before, I spoke up: "There are those who say the nation could benefit from outspoken women who stand for their faith, so that we might abolish slavery, institute temperance, and endow women with the rights of citizenry." I hazarded, "Would that not be of use to your plans?"

The men laughed loudly at the mention of temperance, and one refilled his glass and another's. Dr. Jewett, weighing a powder onto a sheet of paper, spoke without looking away from his care. "The Bible endorses wine," he pointed out, as the merriment continued. "It's folly to attach temperance to abolition, for the one is a matter of moderation for the wise man, and the other an absolute moral necessity."

"Which is why Franklin Pierce can't be allowed to win the presidency," said a wide-girthed man of middle age whose name I didn't know. "That fool of a doughface will let the South walk all over him. And there's no chance at all for repeal of the Compromise of 1850, with its outrageous fugitive slave provision, if Pierce takes office."

I looked at Solomon, whose face now showed grim resolve. I asked, "He won't take office, will he? Franklin Pierce? Isn't Vermont dead set against him in the election?"

"Vermont, indeed," Solomon confirmed. "But as a son of New Hampshire, he'll carry the Granite State, and as a compromise candidate for the nation, I fear he'll draw the vote in many other locations as well."

"Ay, true enough," growled a deep Scottish voice from another man, Mr. McLeod. "Let's place our ballots for Old Fuss and Feathers tomorrow, our General Scott, and then put our shoulders back to the wheel. I've heard Gilman's open to a second term later, in office as governor of Vermont. And he's growing stronger in his views."

Dr. Jewett examined the list, then handed a final packet to my mother and inquired, "What do you hear from our brother-in-arms, Martin, out in Illinois, Mrs. Sanborn? Is there hope for a stronger approach to banning slavery from the Territories?"

"As to that," my mother said pleasantly, "I'm sure it's Ephraim you'll want to speak with, for such expansive news. Alice, I believe our errands are complete. Shall we take a luncheon at the tea shop, before heading home?"

Solomon crossed the room at once. "Allow me to escort you there," he proposed. "As I've no opportunity this week to pay a call in North Upton in person, you shall recount the news of friends in your village, and I'll consider the time well spent."

My mother agreed and permitted Solomon to carry her traveling valise, now filled with brown paper sacks and packets. He held the door for her, and I followed, and, when he caught my eye and flashed a wicked grin at me, I nearly tripped on my own skirts, heading from the porch to the short steps toward the road. I swear he smothered a laugh, as he took my arm for a moment to steady me, then released it and walked appropriately next to my mother across the road and over to Mrs. French's flower-adorned porch with its welcoming doorway into the tearoom.

I stepped modestly behind the two of them, concentrating on my skirt and also the fine cut of Solomon's coat, and smiling at a wicked girlish thought: If Almyra could only see this Boston beau of mine in person. Silly little thirteen-and-a-half-year-old flirt that she obviously was!

CHAPTER 12

We settled comfortably around a neat table in Mrs. French's tea room. That is, Mama and I were comfortable; Solomon clearly had not visited the place before. After all, the very name *tea room* declared its occupants to be female. Men, of course, dined at the restaurant by the railroad, or at one of the taverns in town.

But Mrs. French greeted us warmly and assured Solomon: "Mr. McBride, you're far from the first kind-hearted gentleman to escort the ladies of his acquaintance into my parlor. That said, here's a pot of good black tea to start with, and you'll all partake of the oyster stew, I'm sure, with some of our good Cross crackers."

Perhaps the presence of a gentleman encouraged our hostess to add a little more to the bowls of stew and to the dish of crackers, with a side dish of fresh butter. My mother sniffed approvingly at the deep-yellow spread and opened the conversation, as the lady of the table should do: "What is your position in tomorrow's elections, Mr. McBride? Clearly Vermont will vote for General Scott, but I gather he is unlikely to take a majority of the states."

"Very unlikely indeed," Solomon confirmed. "Of course, he won't be able to speak as president until after the Electoral College casts its ballots next March, but it seems we must face the presidency of Franklin Pierce."

My mother remained calm. "I doubt he'll be able to slow the

turn of this nation toward ending slavery," she predicted. "A nation is like a very large boat: once it has begun to make the turn, it must complete the arc of motion."

Solomon looked impressed. "Well stated, ma'am, and, if I may, I'll carry those words with me to others."

"To Senator Seward?" I asked, to show I recognized this large canvas under way. "Why can't we elect him as president instead, when he's the better candidate?"

I won a small smile for my question, then a long explanation about the two-party system, Democrats and Whigs, the national conventions, the many rounds of balloting. All of which boiled down to, Daniel Webster had steered New England, was now gone, and one must recognize the enormous Southern hatred for Senator Seward and his staunch abolitionist position. And thus, alas, compromise on General Scott, a war hero and barely able to scrape enough Southern votes for the position.

By that point, our empty plates were gone from our table, and only my mother was still sipping tea.

"If I may, ma'am, I'd like to make a request."

My mother stiffened slightly, her shoulders squared. If Solomon wanted to call on me, he was asking the wrong person at the wrong moment.

But instead he continued, "I know St. Johnsbury is the railroad town, and word circulates that, in time, it will supplant Upton as shire town here, the new county seat. But there is a great deal of culture and education among the ladies of Upton, and especially North Upton. Might you be willing to assess for me their positions on the election and the changing winds of our movements of Abolition and Temperance? I would value your letters and thoughtful summaries, and it would be of great help to Mr. Seward as well."

How could my mother decline? As we rose from our table, I realized the political point of the meal. So I pressed forward for myself by saying, "I could do the same among the younger women, of course."

"Of course," Solomon agreed, smiling. "I would appreciate that, Alice. Perhaps your mother could enclose your letters with her own."

Foxed! Foiled! Boxed into a corner. I glared at Solomon, whose eyes sparkled with mischief, quickly hooded before my mother could see. Well! It would serve him right if someone else came courting me, now that I surely had my first teaching position just ahead.

With great dignity, I donned my short jacket and bonnet and announced, "I believe it's time to collect Ely and begin the journey home. The light is so short at this time of year, isn't it, Mother?"

I turned toward the door and began my exit, suspicious that smiles were being exchanged behind me, but too cross to turn and look.

On the road home, conversation lagged. My mother regretted that we hadn't visited the millinery shop. I regretted more than that, but kept my lips closed over the words. A conspiracy of Solomon and my mother did not suit my thoughts for the day.

Annoyed and irritated, when we reached home, I helped to carry bundles into the kitchen, then offered to lead Ely into the barn and brush him down. My mother, so cheerful that I still felt laughed at, agreed and began to prepare supper.

There are few things as satisfying and distracting to an upset mind as the ritual of brushing down a horse after a long day of travel. In a home with brothers closer in age to me than William, Charles, and John, I might never have discovered this pleasure. But my father had invited me into the sheep barn as a small child when I showed interest, and when his flock grew past a hundred, he relinquished some of the simpler tasks to me, with the agreement that we would not discuss them in front of my mother.

So, as the light failed and the barn turned dim and almost quiet, the sheep settling in their pens, Old Sam drowsing and Ely methodically consuming a handful of oats and then an armful of long hay, I drew the curry comb through and then the bristled brush again and again, stroking the dry, loose hairs free, letting the road dirt fall, inhaling the reassuring scent of horse and sheep and fodder. And trying not to think of Solomon.

This procedure benefited me a great deal, until the moment when, after hanging the brush in its place and turning toward the door, I slipped my chilled hands into the inner pockets of my cloak—and felt the rustle of paper, where I knew there shouldn't be any.

Bolting out of the dim barn, I stood in the last gleam of western light to make out the words. There was no greeting, just a message: "Will send word soon about Sarah's brother *F*."

Oh! The possibility that Sarah's brother might emerge from the South's cruel hold lit my heart with joy and excitement. Though I knew my uncle Martin must be correct in tackling the monster of slavery head on, it still mattered so much to see each individual person escape the shackles. Perhaps Sarah would come to North Upton to fetch her brother Franklin, if Solomon could transport the boy to us, and then I would get to see my dear friend again! I thought of her sweet gaze, from dark eyes above smooth, brown cheeks and her rare, delightful smiles. Wonderful!

But Solomon must mean this news to stay just between the two of us, for he hadn't said anything in front of my mother. I took a deep breath to calm my chest and ease the exhilaration from my own lips and eyes. One more thought assisted in this process: Solomon had not used my name or signed his, and the note bore no mark of affection of any sort. Only in case the scrap of paper fell into the wrong hands? Or because he didn't have emotions to express to me?

It occurred to me, as I paused to latch the barn door, that the role of a young woman, to be modest and await a clear message of interest from a young man, did not suit me well. In fact, it rubbed me wrong, like brushes moved against the hairs.

So I entered the kitchen with pursed lips and an air of annoyance, which my mother ignored, only asking me to set the table and slice some bread.

A gust of cold air through the room announced my father peering into the room. "Abigail, can you hold for another few minutes? I want to check the sheep and lock the barn."

He darted back outside and returned shortly, hanging a damp coat to dry near the stove and setting down a cloth sack of yellow-skinned apples. "Went up on the ridge, looking for bear tracks earlier," he explained, "and there's still that pair of old trees where the Hutchinson place stood. No tracks, but it seemed a shame to waste the best apples."

We settled quietly to our meal, and then my mother and father exchanged details of their day. When he heard about tea with Solomon, my father's eyes sparkled. "So, Seward must have a plan to move forward. Still, I'll cast my vote for Winfield Scott tomorrow in Upton Center, as we head to West Barnet. Alice, while I tend to the sheep in the morning, you can outfit the wagon with an old blanket and some burlap sacks for the collie, and we'll bring a small cake of maple sugar for the McLaren farm, to sweeten the payment. I'm taking them one of our young rams to exchange." He added, "The school superintendent and Mr. McLaren will meet us at the district school first, at eleven o'clock, so we'll need to start out by seven. Then we'll go to the farm."

I dreamed again that night of my distant brothers Charles and John and woke early, aching and concerned. Still no letters from them. I knew my mother wrote to them twice each week, so something must be awry in the post. They couldn't possibly both be hurt, could they?

There wasn't time to worry. I splashed my face with icy water, braided my hair, and fastened it, neatly coiled, atop my head. With my better skirt and the new "waist" my mother'd made from cutting up one of her own, and a lace collar, I felt both adult and elegant. Over a quick bowl of oatmeal with butter, my mother gave me last-minute suggestions, then added her own stickpin to my collar as an extra touch.

Clouds hung heavy. My father tossed the carriage blanket into the wagon to cover us in case of a snow flurry and heaved the young ram, bleating madly, into the back. Wrapped in burlap sacks and bound, it couldn't injure itself by getting to its feet or jumping out. But the journey certainly began in a noisy fashion!

The road to Upton Center wound along the river, five miles of well-traveled and solid footing for Ely, who didn't seem to mind pulling the wagon for the second day in a row. At the town hall, my father hitched Ely to a post and advised me to climb down and walk around a bit, before the longer ride to West Barnet. I exchanged smiles and short greetings with several other women passing by, but of course the only people entering to cast their ballots were men.

It took longer than I expected, but at last we were on our way again, around the village green and onto the winding road along Joe's Brook. We passed through a covered bridge, Ely's hooves thumping and echoing in the passage, and then my father eased the horse up into a trot, watching carefully for other conveyances headed toward town. Twice we pulled off to the side of the road to allow farm wagons laden with hay to pass by, but those men only casting ballots seemed, like my father, to have made their journey early in the morning.

At Ely's trotting pace, the wagon bumped and shook too

much for conversation. But I enjoyed riding with my father and not being subject to my mother's pressing and inquiring and such. Only the rather dim light of the day worried us both, with the unpredictable November snowfall it presaged.

The tiny flakes began in thin bursts, uncertain and whirling on currents of wind. I pulled my shawl more snugly around my head and across the lower part of my face, and my father buttoned his coat collar to the chin. Just another mile or so to go.

There! The Joe's Brook School, a reassuring brown and gray twist of smoke rising from its chimney, stood squarely on a plot of land on the opposite side of the road from the river. No lights glowed in the windows—I supposed the teacher wasn't expected to light a lamp until the December darkness, which would often linger 'til noon. But a glow of lamplight would have cheered the little structure. Inside, unpainted rough walls could also benefit from civilizing, I thought.

A class of four children of wildly varied ages and sizes occupied the schoolroom. One, standing, recited the day's lesson on rivers of Europe. The teacher, a few years older than I, sat upright behind her desk, a finger following a list on the page before her. "And now the rivers that flow into the Black Sea, Isaac?" she prompted, in a rather stern voice.

Two men standing at the back of the room nodded toward her, then came to the classroom door to greet us. "Let's sit in the cloakroom," the taller one proposed. He gestured to a small table already surrounded by four chairs. "Miss Sanborn, this is Mr. Elijah McLeod, and I'm James McLaren. And you, I'm sure, are Miss Sanborn's father, Mr. Ephraim Sanborn, is that correct?"

"Indeed," my father agreed, doffing his hat and pulling out two chairs. Now I knew I must have grown up on the ride from North Upton to West Barnet, since my father held the chair for me to settle my skirt before seating himself.

In a jolt of recognition, I realized Elijah McLeod had been in Dr. Jewett's office the day before, and I smiled—which made it easier to nod and smile also to Mr. McLaren. "How do you do," I replied. "What a fine location for a school. Is this the usual count of pupils, or are some missing today?"

The two Scotsmen exchanged glances, and Mr. McLaren replied, "There are three more boys who should be here, but they are older and less reliable in attending. And one primary student, a girl, home with an earache."

I gave a sympathetic nod and decided to be direct: "Are the older boys difficult to manage in the classroom?"

Mr. McLeod laughed, surprised. "Aren't they always, at that age? Miss Hall does well enough with them, on the whole, when they come. Could you control the older students, Miss Sanborn?"

There, he'd given just as direct a response. "Yes," I said firmly. "Predictable consequences for misbehavior, ample planning of material to keep them busy, and meeting their parents ahead of time should suffice to rein them in and have them learning."

"Are you an eldest child yourself, Miss Sanborn?"

"Youngest child," I countered. "With a very firm mother to learn from, and experience in the classroom myself as an assistant while studying these past two years. Here are my letters of recommendation and my qualifications." I laid out three pages, and the two men bent close, reading the details. My father tipped me a small wink, then regained a solemn expression and gazed at the pages with the others.

The taller man, Mr. McLaren, looked up. "You would also ensure a moral study of the books of the Bible?"

"Not as such," I replied, detecting the catch in the question. "Of course, the students must arrive at school able to make moral decisions, but it is the task of the parents and their own religious body to teach such things. We would, of course, open each day with words from the Book of Psalms, and the songs the children sing would include an occasional hymn. But our Constitution forbids the government to favor any particular religion, so a well-run academic classroom leaves such matters to others. There is enough to teach in mathematics, reading and writing, geography, and the like. Don't you agree?"

Out of the corner of my eye, I saw my father's small nod of approval. And the two men pushed back their chairs, each smiling within his short "winter beard."

After a few more niceties, the men proposed to take my nomination for next summer's term to their school board, and we all rose. Mr. McLeod rode off first; Mr. McLaren proposed to lead us to his farm down the next side road, where he said his wife would be pleased to have us join them for the noon meal before we set off again for home.

Once the young ram was unloaded and gratefully back on his legs in a paddock alongside a snug barn, a bit smaller than ours and more newly built, and Ely under a shed roof with a blanket and some oats, I followed the men toward the house. As we reached it, a sharp barking startled me, and I pulled back. Just in time to save my skirt! Two dogs leaped outside and immediately sat next to Mr. McLaren, looking to him for direction. One was clearly younger than the other, not quite fully grown.

"Watch the new sheep," he told them with a short gesture. To my astonishment, both trotted to the paddock where our ram paced, and lay down where the barn roof hung over, creating some shelter from the increasing snowfall. The ram, after backing away frantically, seemed to sense their calm and edged toward them.

"Come in out of the cold," a woman's voice urged. "Coffee's ready, and a fine rich stew if I say so myself as shouldn't." She beamed at us, a wide generous smile making her plain face a pleasure to behold.

My father and Mr. McLaren moved aside for me to enter first, another sign of my new arrival at being an adult, even if only for the moment. I kept in mind that Mr. McLaren wanted to see a strong, firm, educated person to teach the school. Best to behave that way! And for all of the noon dinner, indeed, I did.

Afterward, as we hitched Ely to the wagon and brushed off the inch of snow on its boards, Mr. McLaren brought the younger collie to us. Speaking as one might to a fellow farmer, he introduced the eight-month-old dog, whose name was Chester, to the two of us. At some length, he explained to the animal that it must take care of us, and he suggested that I climb up and allow the dog to sit next to me. "If you'll place a hand in his fur and talk with him quietly, he'll understand his task and ride with you politely," Mr. McLaren assured me.

This was only the second time I'd touched a dog, and I worried that the animal might snap at me with its sharp teeth. But the warmth of the thick, white and black fur felt good, and I began stroking and speaking to Chester. As I did so, my father slowly climbed to his own seat, reached down to shake hands with Mr. McLaren, and eased Ely into a steady walk toward the road.

For a moment the animal turned his head to look back, and gave a soft moan as if worried. But then his gaze returned to my face, and he pressed closer to my skirt, so I could feel the warmth of him all the way through my woolen petticoats. Was he grieving for his master? I bent a bit closer and kept talking—some long-winded tale of our farm and our sheep, and telling him many of their names from when our flock had been smaller and I'd known each one—until the farm buildings were hidden by a bend in the road, and my father urged Ely to a steady trot.

I tugged the carriage rug across all three of us and kept assuring the collie that he would like his new home, and his flock of sheep, and more. His melting eyes never left my face, all the way home to North Upton.

So it wasn't until we pulled into the village, snow light on our garments but not enough to impede travel, that my thoughts skipped to my mother and her anticipated guest of the day: Caroline Clark.

Would Caroline still be in our kitchen? Would she see what I felt so strongly—that in this day of applying for my first teaching position, I, too, had left my girlhood behind me and become a young woman, a teacher—just like her? I wondered.

CHAPTER 13

"That animal will make a mess. And get hair into my bread dough. And soil the floor."

My mother's voice rose as she berated my father, who'd fed the collie, taken it for a walk before supper and another afterward, and now was making a pad of a horse-blanket remnant atop a folded burlap bag, at the foot of the steps to my bedchamber. The dog sat next to me, intent on the argument, turning from one person to the other. I felt his body tremble, and I reached into the warm fur again to pat him. How terrible to lose your "person" and your home all at once, and sit in a strange place with someone's anger aimed clearly at you.

"Chester," I whispered. "It's all right, Chester."

"And," my mother added in a triumphant sweep of logic, "whoever called a dog Chester? It should have a good Bible-fearing name, like Ely or Samson."

I'd forgotten that Old Sam's original name was Samson. Wasn't there anyone named Chester in the Bible? Even in the "begats" section?

My father yielded a short distance: "Then call him Jesse. It's close enough, and I'm sure he'll understand. Right, Jesse?"

The dog stood and trotted across the room, looking into my father's face for a command. He probably expected a sheep to take care of.

"Papa . . ." I began hesitantly.

"No need for you to comment, young lady," my father said

firmly. He rubbed the dog's ears in a friendly way and pointed toward me. The dog followed his gesture. "Jesse, take care of Alice."

At once the animal returned to my side. My name? Did he know my name?

I said, "But I need to go to bed, Papa."

"Go," he agreed. "I think the dog will make sure you get there, then come back to the foot of the stairs. He knows where his bed should be."

And my father was right. "Jesse" followed me to my bedchamber. I hung my skirt where it could dry, draped the waist over the top of a chair, and slid into my sheets and blankets atop the featherbed. "Good night, Jesse," I tried. He kept watching.

From the kitchen I could hear thumps and clangs as my mother evidently put protections into place for her stores of food and the rising bread dough. A few minutes later, as I was starting to wonder how long the dog would stare at me, my father called softly, "Jesse. Take care of Alice. Here, boy."

The dog gave me one more appraising look, then headed down the stairs, the scratch of his toenails letting me know his progress. From the sounds, I gathered he'd settled on his blanket pad, as expected, and a few minutes later my parents' voices faded off, as they, too, went to bed. Morning would be here soon enough.

Thank goodness, when it arrived, no disturbance of bread dough or dishes or floor seemed to have taken place. I heard my father quietly invite Jesse outside and guessed the dog would be fed in the barn, like the other farm animals.

At last, I could ask my mother about Caroline Clark's visit the day before.

"There's not much to tell," she admitted. "She left one of

those alphabet cards with me, and I learned a few more of those words she does with her hands: mother, and father, and bread." She performed them so I could copy and learn. "And Mrs. Clark seems very happy to have her daughter home."

Some reserve lingered in that statement. I pressed: "And Caroline, will she be happy here?"

My mother looked disturbed. "I don't know. She's accustomed to being an adult, a teacher even. And Mrs. Clark may not know how to fit that into her home. Jerushah wasn't quite grown up when they lost her, you know. It takes time and effort to see your child as an adult, even when you've gone together through each day along the way."

I nodded. Having just experienced a day of being an adult, away from my mother and working to gain a teaching position of my own, this made sense.

An idea struck me. "Could we start a sewing group or some such thing, to bring the women and girls together, so Caroline could have more people get to know her?"

"Perhaps. But I've been thinking it should be a reading group instead, Alice. You and I, we have a task for young Solomon McBride. If we gather around that novel of Miss Stowe's, *Uncle Tom's Cabin,* and read it together, the conversations should give us room to assess and report as we've agreed to do. Moreover," and my mother's face now glowed with fervor, "we can nurture the moral standing of Abolition and Temperance among the women and girls of the village in this way."

Abolition and Temperance? Almyra Alexander's influence, I immediately guessed. Our new visitor's outspoken ways were lighting an ardent passion in my mother. From, I admitted, some very ready embers and tinder.

"When would we meet? And where?"

"We'll need either the schoolhouse or that big front room that Mrs. Clark has," she proposed, so quickly that I was sure this wasn't an entirely new idea. "I will speak with her later today. And I think regularity is important. Say, Saturday afternoons. If we offer cookies and tea, it will gain us a good group right away."

And so it was done, just that quickly: when it turned out Mrs. Clark wasn't willing to provide her front room, my mother organized the North Upton Ladies Auxiliary, declaring that its second goal, beyond literary enrichment, would be to organize committees to take care of or plan for the church's routine needs. Mrs. Alexander leapt into this with enthusiasm, offering to bring refreshments for the first gathering.

"And," my mother said to me the next day, "we need to write to Solomon today about the group."

"But we don't have anything to tell him about people's views yet," I protested.

"Of course not. But we could benefit from one or two more copies of Miss Stowe's book right away. And who better to purchase them and send them north?"

News of the election, with the obvious success of Franklin Pierce as president, had subdued all of us, but this notion at least perked me up, with something to be accomplished.

We sent a letter the next morning, written neatly and briefly by my mother, and with my signature next to hers at the end. The address was care of Senator Seward; I wondered how long it would take to reach Solomon.

Saturday morning's mail included two items for my parents, and I pressed close to watch my mother open them. The first, in Solomon's rounded script, bore his franking signature on the outside and was addressed to my father, but she did not hesitate to unseal it. Inside, it said only, "Delivery reached Philadelphia. Please advise Warren in West Upton to expect arrival next week."

"What does it mean?" I asked. "Is it about the books?"

"Not at all. And not for you to know about. This is your father's business." Stiff though the words were, my mother didn't scold—she just set the note aside.

The second one came with unfamiliar handwriting. I held my breath. Bad news about my brothers, conveyed by some stranger? Oh no!

Unfolding it in a way that kept me from seeing inside, my mother stared a moment, then looked again at the franking on the other side. She pointed out to me what the name was: Seward!

The contents, directly from the senator, said Solomon's business had taken him some distance away, so the great senator himself had opened my mother's request, and two copies of *Uncle Tom's Cabin* would arrive via one of the Gilman salesmen on his way back north the next week. And it closed with, "Yours most appreciatively, William H. Seward, Sen."

Without warning and without even a knock, the door burst open with a gust of cold air and a cheerful "Hello!" in an unmistakable Boston accent. Almyra! I jumped toward the door as my mother swept the notes from the table into her apron pocket.

The thirteen-year-old didn't seem to notice. "My aunt has sent me to borrow four more silver teaspoons," she said, bouncing with enthusiasm. "Is it true? Do you really have four of them?"

I couldn't resist. "We have six," I announced, knowing how unusual it was. "I'll wrap them and bring them with me."

"Oh, but she wants them now, to make the table perfect! She's set it all up in the schoolhouse, even though I think it would have been lovely in the church sanctuary. Isn't that a marvelous word, *sanctuary*? And I'm to bring them straight away."

I read my mother's rather shocked look easily and said, "I'll bring them myself, Almyra. We can walk together. I'm sure my mother will be glad for some peace to prepare herself, and she'll follow us in a few more minutes."

With the precious four teaspoons wrapped and placed securely into a lined basket to carry, and my own self bundled into a cloak to deflect the sharp wind under a bright, clear sky, I walked alongside Almyra, listening to her constant babble about the others at school, and the letters she had from her father in Philadelphia. "And then he took Miss Anthony and Mrs. Stanton to meet Mr. Stevens—he is a representative to Congress, you know—and they all went to dinner at the restaurant by the railroad station, which is open all day and almost all night, because there are so many trains, did you know that?"

"No, I didn't know that," I inserted quickly, "but did you say Mr. Stevens? Mr. Thaddeus Stevens?"

"I don't know; my papa just wrote 'Mr. Stevens of the House of Representatives,' " Almyra replied, pausing to bounce on her toes and focus for a moment. "Does it matter?"

"Then it must be Thaddeus Stevens, who is a member of the House for Pennsylvania. He grew up in Barnet and went to the academy in Peacham, you know. Upton Center counts him as one of ours, for his mother lived here when he was born!"

"What a funny name, Thaddeus. Is that in the Bible?"

I was glad to know the answer: "No, it was a general's name first, someone who came from Europe to help us fight the Revolution. Thaddeus Stevens is a patriot, and an ardent abolitionist, of course."

"Of course," Almyra echoed. "Any man or woman of honor truly must be so. Alice, do you know Mr. Stevens?"

"Not yet," I answered. Which baffled Almyra, and revealed to me how much I was counting on seeing Solomon in person again soon, and becoming part of his life, working for the freedom of all Americans and an end to the grievous sin of slavery. And this meeting today would give me reason to write to him, and to add my contribution to his work. I clenched the basket handle more tightly and resumed walking toward the schoolhouse.

"So, when exactly is your father coming back from Philadelphia? The election's over now."

"Yes, but the Electoral College hasn't yet taken place, and he must see to that, so I doubt he'll arrive in North Upton again until the end of March. Isn't that wonderful, Alice, that we shall spend an entire winter getting acquainted! You know, Miss Wilson says you were the best student in the school. Aren't you going to study any more, now that you are becoming a teacher yourself?"

"Of course I will keep studying! Any good teacher never stops. But this week I've needed to take care of other things." I bit my tongue to avoid saying "You wouldn't understand," that phrase of my older brothers that always annoyed me so much.

"Oh, good!" Almrya bounced again, her skirts swinging in such enthusiasm that her ankles showed clearly. At her age, she probably had no idea what that suggested, but it was time she learned to behave.

We'd arrived at the schoolhouse, and I followed, still half listening to the babble of news and wondering and postulated explanations.

Inside, several women who'd arrived early were talking with Mrs. Alexander. She summoned us, took the basket and its contents from me with a word of thanks, and courteously introduced her niece and me to the others. Of course, I already knew most of them, but there were two, sisters from West Upton, who were new to me.

"This is Margaret Johnson, Alice, and this is her sister, Catherine Warren," the minister's wife told me. "They both live in West Upton and are members of the Congregational Church in Upton Center. You know, of course, that group has already passed a resolution condemning slavery. So they are here to advise us, should we need their assistance."

"Oh! That is so gracious of them," I replied. And I hope I hid my surprise. Things seemed out of hand if forwarding a church resolution had come to mind already. I thought this would be simply a reading group! Mrs. Alexander seemed very similar to her niece, I decided.

Almyra tugged at my sleeve. "Come see the arrangements," she pleaded. "I made them myself." In glass vases, evergreen branches and sprigs of berries took pride of place along the center of a long table garbed in ivory lace and set with tiny china plates and matching cups and saucers. This simply could not be all Mrs. Alexander's—and when my Grammy Palmer entered, I saw here assess the decor in the same way. I escaped Almyra for a moment and sidled over to hear my grandmother's opinion. "Borrowed from the Gilman family that lives in Upton Center," she hissed to me. "I've seen the set before." Ah.

My mother arrived then, with her copy of *Uncle Tom's Cabin* in hand. I saw several others carrying theirs, too. Good. The copies from Mr. Seward would ease the sharing, but not be essential for our beginning.

A few minutes later Mrs. Alexander called the meeting to order and quickly dealt with an election of officers—she of course would be president, and Miss Wilson secretary (with a hint of dismay on Miss Wilson's part, but what could she say?). My mother was declared the group librarian, which apparently had some prestige, since this would be halfway a book-centered alliance and halfway for the church.

The part of me that hosted my father's calm good sense whispered "Too many cooks and too many directions," but, like Miss Wilson, I felt little choice: If reports for Solomon were to reflect the opinions of the ladies of our village, I must endure. Besides, I could already see that this group would take action, and action was needed. One thought of Sarah and her family and their struggle for freedom made me determined to see this through.

My mother announced that the group would read aloud (and hear) both chapters one and two of the book, a large helping for a first time. But I soon understood her decision, for the first chapter ended very dolefully, but the second suggested action could be taken.

Also, reading two full chapters left little time for politics, which I felt was wise for the time being. Instead, the women and girls around me set aside the shock of the book in just a moment and dove happily into the indulgence of tea and cookies and gossip.

For Solomon's sake, I counted: fifteen married women, one single (Miss Wilson), and four teenagers, plus a few small children on their mothers' laps.

Determined to make the most of this, I set aside my tea and began to walk around the table, as if looking for someone, meanwhile listening to the various conversations. Several regarded the book and the issues. Most did not.

As I came to the far end of the table, I realized my mother and Mrs. Warren, whom I'd met earlier, were deep in conversation. My mother caught my eye and beckoned me over.

"Mrs. Warren's husband raises Morgan horses," she told me. "And they have a marvelous connection with a pair of livery stables that our Mr. Stevens has patronized in the past. I've told her we'd love to come and visit her next week, perhaps Tuesday?"

I nodded obediently, while thinking quickly. My mother had no interest in horses, none at all. What hid beneath her words?

All at once I recalled the cryptic note Solomon had mailed to my father: "Please advise Warren in West Upton to expect arrival next week." Could my parents both be assisting Solomon in something secret? With a lurch of hope, my heart jumped to the nearest conclusion: Sarah's brother must be coming North.

"Oh, Alice, come quickly; your brother's wife, Helen, just gave me the most marvelous report on the Temperance bill in the legislature! You didn't tell me she was so knowledgeable!" Almyra bubbled and bounced, then tugged at my arm.

Helen? Sure enough, she sat, pale but composed, on a padded bench at the side of the room, a cup of tea balanced on her lap. But knowledgeable? About a Temperance bill? I followed Almyra, wondering what other surprises and secrets circulated in the room.

Beyond the tall windows of the schoolhouse, I noted the belated arrival of the stagecoach, pulling up at the Clarks' inn. Hmm. Mrs. Clark was not in the room, and neither was Caroline.

I thought suddenly of the Irish family who'd come off the stage not so long ago. Who rode it now—and would any of them step off and stay in North Upton?

CHAPTER 14

Tuesday dawned fair, if cold. My second wool petticoat added bulk under my skirt, but much-needed protection from the sharp air. Although I offered to help my father with water and feed for the sheep, he declined. "Timothy will be here after breakfast," he said. "Hold your skirt clean for the visit you're making with your mother today."

I expected we'd drive the wagon, with Old Sam, but my mother had planned otherwise. "It's too far to West Upton for Old Sam. And your father says Ely is reliable enough now to draw the buggy, since the roads have so little snow as yet. You'd best go watch him hitch the horse, Alice, in case there's no help at the Warren farm. I know you have a good head for that."

A rare compliment from my mother! I bustled outside after we'd set the kitchen in order, and, under Papa's guidance, I set the harness in place and made sure Ely would be comfortable. "It's not that different from the wagon hitch," I told my father.

"But you can't make any mistakes," he cautioned, "or the buggy won't stay upright on the curves. Take it all off, and do it again, so I know your hands are practiced, as well as your eyes." Jesse the collie watched me also, prepared to "herd" me if necessary, but otherwise staying close to Papa's heels.

At last we set off to pay our call. Settled side by side on the buggy's bench, with a heavy carriage rug across our laps and second-best bonnets and cloaks, I felt we must look quite elegant: two ladies out for a drive. Once again, the notion that

I'd shed my girlhood and become an adult occupied my thoughts. But I kept them to myself, instead watching my mother's careful driving, expecting she'd permit me to take the reins when we reached the straight section of the road. Indeed, she did, and I quickly learned that she who holds the reins experiences more of the chill winds than otherwise!

Ely's steady trot carried us at a good pace. As we neared Upton Center, my mother again took the reins, slowing the horse to a walk, well to the side. We passed some wagons and one carriage, as well as two horses hitched at the store. This reminded me of the stagecoach arrival on Saturday, and its return tomorrow. So, when we left the village behind us, riding behind Ely's brisk trot again on the long hill toward West Danville, I asked, "Mama, did anyone arrive on the stage on Saturday, while we had our ladies' meeting?"

My mother shook her head. "Only the mail. And Matthew Clark followed it back to St. Johnsbury. You may know that he came out to visit with his sister Caroline for the day."

"I didn't know that." Cautiously I added, not wanting to seem like a gossip but very curious, "Mrs. Clark and Caroline didn't join us Saturday."

"And that's exactly why. With Matthew home to visit, they declined to come to the meeting. Mrs. Clark is reading my copy of the book this week, and most likely you'll see the two of them next Saturday."

"Is there any teaching position for Caroline nearby?"

"I wouldn't think so. There are so few children born deaf, there's little need for her skills here. I did hear of a family in Guildhall with three deaf children, and I know Mrs. Clark has written to see whether they might wish to hire her daughter. But I doubt much will come of it. Few families can afford a private tutor in that way."

Three children deaf in one family! "A family disorder? Or an illness?"

"I don't know." Mama drew the reins back to slow Ely as we crested the hill, then gave him room to trot again on the flat stretch when we could see clear road in front of us. Ahead to the right, the wide waters of Joe's Pond glimmered in the bright sunlight. Our route lay along the lakeshore for some distance. "Bear in mind, Alice, many people believe the deaf are also unable to learn. You can see for yourself how untrue that is. But it's the cost of difference, that it's seen as crippling."

"Isn't it crippling, though, Mama? Caroline can't do so many of the things we all expect to do in our lives."

"But she already has an education and experience in a career," my mother pointed out. "Which sets her ahead of present company, my girl."

Oh! I laughed uncertainly. "I'll gain experience this summer, Mama. And you know I've assisted Miss Wilson already."

"You've missed the point. She's capable and using her skills. Not crippled in any important way. Think, Alice. Haven't you seen this in someone else already?"

I puzzled over what my mother was asking. "Do you mean Sarah? That her dark skin makes her different, and disadvantaged?"

"Precisely. And where does Sarah shine as being well educated, skilled, and accepted by the people around her?"

That was easy to answer: "Among people like her, with the Hayes family in Coventry, and with Miss Farrow, and—But Mama, how does this thinking fit with the politics of Abolition in the nation?"

"My point's made, Alice, in exactly that. Abolition of slavery is a moral principle; any Christian must see its absolute necessity. God's creation as man or woman or child should never be taken as property or abused. And, God willing, we'll see our land freed of the dark sin of slavery soon. But how we shall conduct ourselves with more difference among us, that is a question for the mothers and teachers to consider already, so that we can lead with our actions. And"—my mother shot a sideways glance at me, then refocused on driving Ely—"your young friend Almyra, though she could learn more moderate speech, is correct in naming temperance as a matching necessity, a condition under which we can lead and teach."

After this long speech, we both fell silent. I felt uneasy, as if my mother had compared me to Almyra and found me less than I should be. Disturbed, I wondered whether Solomon might feel the same way. If only he would write to me again!

"Mama, why do you think there's been no letter from Charles or John? Are you concerned that they're injured or ill?"

"Not at all," she said crisply. "If that were the case, someone would let us know. I'm sure we'll hear from them soon."

We slowed for the turn onto a narrower road, leaving the lake behind us. A wide brook lay to the left of this road. "How much farther, Mama?"

"A mile or less. A farmhouse and several barns, but I think we'll see the horses sooner."

Sure enough, not far along, fenced pastures opened to either side of us. Most Novembers, they'd be snow covered by now, but instead today they showed green grasses. It might be mostly frozen forage, but a group of horses browsed at the end of the pasture closest to the outbuildings. Their brown coats gleamed in a way that Ely's did not; I wondered, were they oiled in some way?

"Stop bouncing on the bench, you're making it harder for Ely."

"Yes, Mama."

Two men came out of a long barn shaped differently from ours. Because it held horses instead of sheep? Perhaps. The men looked in our direction, and one turned toward the kitchen door of the house; the other stood waiting for us.

"Mama!" I gasped. "They are black men!"

My mother teased, as she slowed the buggy further and angled it onto the wide drive: "Did you think they only lived up in Coventry, where you delivered your friend Sarah? Don't you remember Charles Hayes coming this way and stopping to see you, after Jerushah's passing? You didn't think he came to Upton only to visit you, did you, Alice?"

Actually that's exactly what I'd thought. Miss Farrow even said she'd asked Charles to come see me then, and the memory of his quiet and prayerful presence still calmed me. But, of course, anyone traveling so far might have other visits to make. Still, in West Upton? I had no idea!

"Close your mouth, or you'll catch flies," my mother added, still amused. She drew Ely to a halt and smiled at the young man reaching for the bridle. "How do you do? I'm Mrs. Sanborn, and this is my daughter, Alice."

The man raised his cap politely. "Please to meet you, ma'am. Ethan Smith's my name. Mrs. Warren said you'd be coming today. If you'll let me stable your horse for you, you can go right on in. And Miss," he nodded toward me.

Soon we sat at a highly polished table, taking tea and fruit cake, exchanging polite news. Mrs. Warren in her own home dressed more simply than at the Saturday ladies' gathering, but the fresh fabric of her skirt and the froth of lace for her collar spoke of financial comfort on her farm.

The second black man, an older one who'd introduced himself as Henry Harris and then gone back to the barns, reappeared. "Mrs. Warren, pardon me," he said quietly. "Did Mr. Warren leave a list of the sheep he wanted moved?"

"He just said the older group, Henry. Is that enough guidance?"

"Yes, thank you. Ladies," he added, with a tip of his work cap, as he left again.

I blew out a sigh of relief. Something familiar. "So you do raise sheep, not just horses here?"

"A few," Mrs. Warren confirmed. "Nothing like your father's flock in number, I'm sure. But we don't depend on them the way we do the horses." She announced with a modest glance downward, "We have purchasers come from all down the East Coast for our Justin Morgan horses, you know."

Curiosity, my besetting drawback, pushed me to ask: "Is that how Mr. Harris and Mr. Smith came to work here? Did they hide with the people who traveled north to see your horses?"

Mrs. Warren tapped the table to emphasize her words. "No man has ever had to hide to find a job with horses in Vermont, Alice. There are substantial livery stables in Hartford, near White River Junction, and more in Woodstock. St. Johnsbury may be a bit slow to develop the same, but, now that the railroad has daily trains, I'm sure the need will be felt and met. At least half the workmen at the livery stables are black-skinned, you know. It's a trade that's never been isolated to one group of men or another. Although," she added with a twinkle, "you'll find women to be mighty rare in the livery stables. I daresay it's the skirts that aren't a good fit with either the animals or the tasks."

My mother took advantage of the topic to introduce a related one. "Now, Mrs. Warren, about the Johnson lad."

"Yes, Mrs. Sanborn, of course. We expect him by the end of the week and will be glad to keep him for a fortnight or so, as he recovers from the long journey. Then I presume you'd like to provide for him to travel north. I understand you're in correspondence with his sister, up in Coventry?"

"Yes, my daughter's been to visit Sarah, and I've sent her a letter about her brother. I believe she'll try to find suitable transport of her own to North Upton, to meet her brother hereabouts."

All this was news to me. I looked back and forth between my mother and our hostess, unsure whether to feel exhilarated at learning what was taking place, or offended that nobody had told me sooner. Perhaps both.

In the name of manners, however, I opted for asking my own questions, as if I had not been entirely taken by surprise. "Won't Sarah's brother Franklin want to ride north right away, himself? Why should he delay?"

Mrs. Warren looked a question at my mother, who shook her head. "I haven't told Alice," she admitted. She reached out for my hand, held it firmly, and said, "Alice, you know the South doesn't let go of whole men readily. Your father raised a substantial sum, but it wasn't enough to purchase the freedom of any of Sarah's family, until the accident happened."

"Accident?" I heard my voice rise, but I couldn't help it. "Accident? To whom? Mama, what happened?"

The men from the barns had just re-entered the house and stood in the doorway, listening, as my mother finally told me: "To Franklin, Alice. He's lost a leg. He'll not be riding again for a very long time, if ever."

CHAPTER 15

Suspicious. That summed up how I felt about whether my parents kept further secrets from me. Discovering they knew so much—but hadn't told me!—about the condition of Sarah's brother and when and how he would arrive made up half my frustration. The other half, of course, came from letters flying around New England that clearly excluded me, even though they concerned my life.

The one advantage of the moment was, of course, permission to send a letter immediately to Sarah, disclosing that I now knew her brother would come soon and offering to share my bedchamber with her, as soon as she could travel to North Upton. I signed my name at the finish, then took the page to my mother to show her, before taking it to be posted.

"All things considered," I said stiffly, "I believe adults write and post their own letters without review by others."

"Quite right," my mother agreed, "and pay for their postage, as well as for their own room and board. And when you are doing all of those, you, too, will post your letters without review." She softened a bit and added, "You write in a lovely hand, Alice. Sarah will be grateful to hear from you. And, of course, you may read my own letter to Charles and John. I believe there is room for you to add some words, should you choose."

Saturday morning I looked for a reply from Sarah, even while knowing the timing made it unlikely. I wondered also when we would hear from Mr. and Mrs. Warren. Surely Sarah's brother must arrive there at any moment. Were it not for the scheduled Ladies Auxiliary meeting, I'd have asked permission to ride to West Upton myself.

Chapters three and four of *Uncle Tom's Cabin* did not break any hearts as we read them aloud that afternoon. Almyra sat beside me, and whispered, "I've read all of it. The next chapter is purely anguish, Alice. Purely terrifying anguish. Wait 'til you hear it."

I shrugged. How could it be worse than the situation of enslavement itself, the terrible pride and error of those who treated people as property? But I didn't want to discuss it with Almyra. Instead I whispered back, "Have you heard from your father?"

An admonitory look from Miss Wilson hushed us until the reading concluded and tea was served. The cookies on hand seemed oddly tasteless for ginger snaps, until I began to sniffle and realized it was not the cookies but my senses: dulled by the start of a head cold. Nor was I the only one to dab with handkerchief or to cough in a ladylike manner into the cloth; at least half a dozen others in the room seemed to be likewise afflicted.

When we finally reached home, I visited the barn to see my father and his now-inseparable companion, Jesse the collie. "Pulling the rams out of the flock?"

"Not yet," my father said with a grunt as he and Jesse maneuvered a ewe into position to examine her hindquarters. "Another ten days, I think. There are still a few ewes that haven't taken yet." He gestured to the dog. "This one's good, Jesse, put her in the other group." Amazingly, the collie did exactly that, then returned to cut the next ewe toward my father.

I asked, "Any word yet from the Warren farm?"

"Not yet. But Matthew rode over there this morning. He should have word for us tonight."

My father and the Clarks still managed to get along, even though Mrs. Clark clearly hadn't forgiven me even a shred of responsibility for Jerushah's death. Would Caroline's presence change that? I realize I still hadn't visited with the young woman I had wanted so much to meet and befriend. I should do so, soon.

But I felt so tired. I left the barn and trudged up the stairs to bed, not rising again until midday on Sunday in a silent house. Vaguely I recalled my mother's hand on my forehead in early morning, and something about not getting up.

When I fumbled my way out of the blankets, my head spun. I wasn't fit to reach the "necessary," the outhouse. Gratefully, I realized my mother had set the chamber pot near my bed, and I used it, then crawled back into my warm nest and slept until supper.

The scent of chicken gravy reached through the haze of my sleep. At first, I thought it meshed with Charles and John coming home, some feast in my dreams. But, as I woke more fully, I felt my stomach growl mightily in hunger. A day without eating! I reached for my skirt, which I realized had been brushed clean for me, and slowly dressed.

My mother must have heard, for she arrived to escort me down the stairs, an arm around my waist. "Slowly, slowly," she urged.

Indeed, supper must have already passed, for the plates sat in the dry sink, ready to be cleaned. But she spooned piping hot gravy onto a split and buttered biscuit, and I slowly ate my way back to myself.

My father came from the parlor, a newspaper under his arm. "The state legislature has taken up a bill like Maine's, to forbid the sale of liquor," he announced. "I venture it will take another week to discuss, and, even so, it's hard to guess whether it will pass."

"It will," my mother said with determination.

I only commented, "I'm too tired to think about it." Then I remembered to ask: "Sarah's brother?"

"Safely arrived at the Warren farm," my father confirmed. "Matthew saw him yesterday. Worn from travel and still not strong, Matthew says, but just give him some time."

"Sarah?"

"At the end of this week," my mother answered. "But if you wish to share your bed with her, you'd best get well quickly, for she won't thank you for a cough or cold."

"Good night," I replied, thankful to have reason to go back to sleep.

On Tuesday morning, finally sitting at the table with my parents for an ordinary breakfast, I asked whether I could ride to West Upton to meet Sarah's brother.

My mother said firmly, "Not yet. If you keep improving, I'll allow you to go with Sarah on Saturday morning to fetch him, though. Now, you're well enough to mind the baking, I believe. I'll put the loaves into the oven, and then I need to go to the attic and check the apples to be sure nothing's molding. Ephraim, is the post in town yet?"

"I'll see. Don't look for me to be quick, Abigail. There's sure to be discussion of the liquor bill, and I want to be sure Gilman's cousin knows we'll stand behind him for a dry state at last. Oh, I'll leave Jesse in the barn, but there shouldn't be any alarm."

Feet propped up in front of the cookstove, a fresh cup of tea at my side, I tackled the only task for which I had the energy so far: reading the past two issues of the newspaper. I examined the articles on the liquor bill with care, and related letters. It seemed our county stood divided on the matter. Another piece told of negotiations in Washington around the Kansas Territory.

I wondered idly whether my uncle Martin had traveled that far west, or remained deliberately in Illinois, where newspapers could probably sell more easily. I should ask my mother whether she'd heard from him in the past week. My earlier suspicions came back to me: Could Uncle Martin have written news, and my parents not told me about that, as well?

I drowsed in my chair, until someone calling in the barnyard woke me.

"Abigail! Abigail!" my father bellowed as he banged the door behind him. "Alice, where's your mother?"

"In the attic, Papa. What's wrong? What's happened?"

"Abigail!" he shouted up the stairs. "Letter from Charlie and John. They're on their way home!"

The three of us, much cheered, read and re-read the letter that had just arrived, postmarked from Los Angeles, a Spanish-named city that my father assured me was in the southern part of the Gold Rush state—clear evidence my brothers were already en route when they posted their letter. They said nothing about whether they had gold or how much. ("Of course they want to keep it quiet, for their safety," my father crowed.) Two friends, named Walter and Isaiah, were traveling with them. They described a mixed group on the ship they were about to board, from railroad men to families headed back East, and expressed shock at seeing shackled African men taken on board, being shipped to Southern plantation owners. And they hoped to be home in two months. The letter's date: the 13th of August.

Nobody wanted to say aloud how frightened that made us. Almost a month longer than my brothers had forecast, and they had not arrived home. I stared at my father, who abruptly declared he needed to be in the barn. A clang of stove lids showed my mother heating more water for tea and moving two iron kettles of meat and gravy aggressively across to a hotter location over the firebox.

I'd had enough of recovery. I needed to be outside, where I could beat my worries down to size. I found my cloak and boots and made my escape.

Clearly, I'd gone to bed on Saturday in one season and emerged from the house today on Tuesday in something entirely different: real winter had arrived.

Wind buffeted me as I wobbled a moment in my boots. Snow lay six inches deep on the ground, with only a faint depression where our track out to the road should be. The last of my father's boot tracks lingered near the house but otherwise had vanished. Blasting from the northwest, an icy mix of snowflakes and wet, icy pellets blew into my face and shocked me to fresh alertness.

This was no time to hike the ridge or even climb to the closest apple orchard. I tramped down the track anyway and took the turn toward the store, where a single indoor light shone, but no carriages or horses stood out front. Even the village houses huddled without anyone out their doors; threads of woodsmoke vanished just above the chimneys, and, although it could not even be noon yet, a dimness like dusk hovered around it all. I wondered whether this was what fear looked like—or was the dark day an omen of something terrible that had overtaken Charles and John?

The marvel of knowing that the people around me had purchased, somehow, the freedom of Sarah's brother Franklin dwindled next to the horror of his missing leg, from some accident I didn't yet grasp. Solomon's refusal to court me suddenly seemed clearly an indifference or worse. And I doubted that the monster of slavery that stalked the land could ever be tamed, any more than the wickedness of fallen humanity.

Drawing my shawl and cloak as closely around me as I could, I persisted in pounding my way down the road, to the far end of the village, and stared out into the heart of the storm. A bear?

One of the few wolves that still stalked through from year to year? A catamount? None of that frightened me like the possible deaths of my brothers on a ship bound for the Isthmus of Panama, or in the jungles of Panama itself. Or, I realized, perhaps at the hands of robbers who'd realized the gold in John and Charlie's pockets. Jerushah's death from the previous year reared up inside me, fierce and fanged, tearing at my heart.

In the noise of the storm, a small pocket of something else formed: a voice in my memory, of Miss Farrow, the wise and formerly enslaved woman in St. Johnsbury who had reached out to me on the day of that terrible funeral. "When it strips us of the people we love, we blame ourselves, and we blame our God," she'd said. God? I hadn't thought of God in days, barely even saying my prayers at night. What must God think of me—not even taking steps to fight for Abolition this season, not standing up for what was right? But how could I? If something had happened to my brothers, I knew I'd never stand for anything or anyone again.

Another memory of that sorrow returned to me—the words of Charles Hayes, who had come to sit with me and lay his prayer upon me: "I surely am sorry about Miss Jerushah. I imagine you'll miss her, all your life. That's a good thing, you know. It's a sign of how much you cared about each other, isn't it?"

Now I repeated in a whisper the last part of what Charles Hayes had said, as he prayed that day. He'd said to God, "Fit us to labor for Your freedom and Your justice."

Something took hold of my shoulder. I whirled, crying out in part fear, part hope: "Charles Hayes?!"

But it was, strangely and improbably, Caroline Clark. She touched my chest with her gloved hand, then pointed at her own. Then gestured toward the village.

I didn't have any will to resist. I placed my hand in hers, and we began to walk together. A moment later, a four-legged creature bounded up to us, circled us, and herded us further forward.

Jesse.

"The Lord is my Shepherd," I whispered into the wind. And walked back to my house, with Caroline and Jesse at my side.

CHAPTER 16

To my surprise, Caroline Clark, despite reconnecting with her mother and three much younger siblings, and, of course, Matthew and her father, felt lonely. At least, I believe that's what she told me as we sat at the kitchen table and finger-talked and gestured and sometimes just looked at each other. In the background, my mother continued preparing the next meal; my father, after much praise for Jesse, had taken him back out to the barn to work more with the sheep in their pens, after a walk across the road to let the Clarks know their eldest daughter had come across to visit.

So, being lonely for her friends in Connecticut and her "real life" of teaching there, Caroline spent a great deal of time sitting at the window, writing letters by what light entered, and dreaming of the people she missed. Which is how she'd seen me tearing my way through an outer storm. And an inner one.

How could I tell this calm young woman, half a dozen years older than I but so much more experienced in many ways, what storm beset me? Did she know how Jerushah had died—the long ride through winter weather as we took Sarah north toward the Canada border, the weeks of illness at the Hayes home in the very northernmost part of Vermont, the perils of returning to North Upton, with Solomon driving and Jerushah still frail and failing, and then her plunge into rheumatic fever and her deathly collapse in the cellar of the inn?

We wept together at the table. My mother quietly set a pot of tea beside us but did not interrupt. I removed from my pocket, where I'd kept it for so long, the last letter that I wrote to Jerushah, the one she never saw, and unfolded it for Caroline:

Dearest Jerushah,

I hope indeed that Providence will never require me to abandon my friends, and I do not mean to abandon you. Let us seek permission from your mother to exchange letters in a more normal fashion, perhaps through Matthew's hands. If you share with her our correspondence, it may be that she will allow her heart to soften so much sooner, and we will spend hours in each other's company again.

Do not fear that I will leave behind our friendship, in spite of the labors I find in front of me. The more that I think about the situation of the coloreds of our land, the more I understand that we must convince the Slave Power as a whole to give up its pursuit of human bondage. Only evil can come of such a terrible institution.

I hope that you are feeling stronger with each day, and that the summer sunshine is brightening your home, as it is mine. Tell me about your grandmother and her visit with you, and what you are stitching—for I know you so well that I cannot believe you are idle, even if your health is not yet recovered.

Let us think of Sarah today and celebrate what God has wrought, that Sarah has already attained the freedom with which her life should ever have been endowed, and that her father and family are soon to follow her into this happy state of affairs.

Fondly, and with deep affection, I remain Your Friend,
Alice

And then we wept a little more. Caroline told me, in small phrases that I grasped, in between others that remained mysterious, about a friend of hers named Nellie, at the school in Hartford, and something about Nellie having to go home and take care of her mother. She gave me a taste, also, of the joy she felt in teaching. It seemed there were many more small children, even in Vermont, who enrolled at the school because they could not hear, and their parents could not teach them well. In Caroline's glowing eyes and sweet smile, I saw the affection she felt for them, and pride in her work.

When my mother realized our struggle over how to explain "time" to each other, she brought from the parlor my father's *Old Farmer's Almanac* so we could demonstrate dates of before, and after. Would Caroline stay in North Upton? No: She showed me that she'd take the train back to Hartford on the second of January. Did her mother know that? Either Caroline wasn't sure of the answer, or she didn't want to say it outright to me. But I suspected, from her circling around, that Mrs. Clark didn't want to admit it. Yet the date stood out, and it seemed Mr. Clark accepted it.

Supper interrupted, just as we'd begun to worry together about my brothers and their delayed return from the gold fields of California, and whether they were safe. My mother squeezed each of our shoulders and conveyed that she believed God would bring them home to North Upton. Her faith seemed unreasonable to me, considering all the dangers out in the world. But I felt better for having bared my heart to Caroline, and I didn't need to argue about it with my mother.

"Now, girls, the day's over. Caroline, Mr. Sanborn will walk you to the inn," my mother announced, with enough gestures that Caroline followed her words easily. "And Alice, you need more rest."

I watched through the tilted upstairs window until snow and darkness closed around the pinprick glow of my father's lantern, Caroline at his side. My mother arrived in my chamber with a hot brick to place inside the covers and shooed me into them, puffing out my candle. "Sleep well, Alice, and don't rise too early in the morning. Your father and I will manage the chores. You need to be well for Sarah's arrival."

Happily, by Friday morning barely a sniffle or sneeze lingered. I kept up with barn and house tasks, dashing outside at even the smallest hint of a horse in the village, and finally at mid-afternoon the stage pulled up, Young Sam the driver ringing his bells and a great commotion in front of the inn. With my father at my side, I hurried down the track to the road.

"Sarah!"

My friend, already on the ground, released Mrs. Clark from a warm embrace and turned toward me, beaming. "Alice! I'm here!"

"So I see," I laughed as I rushed up to enfold her. "Dear merciful heaven, how tall you are!"

The little dark-faced waif of two years back stood in wide skirts and neat boots, with a hat that cupped her face charmingly. Behind me I heard the voices of other people from the village, and Almyra rushed up to exchange hand clasps and names. I could tell from her envious glance at Sarah's attire that the needlework and millinery of the Hayes household stood up under "Boston" scrutiny quite well. So there! Pride and a rather wicked sense of triumph cheered me greatly.

I could afford to be generous. "Almyra, would you like to come to the house with Sarah and me, for some hot cocoa?"

"Yes, of course I would! Thank you! Mr. Young, you'll let my aunt know I've gone visiting, won't you?"

Mr. Young? Oh! Young Sam, who clearly admired Almyra deeply. He blushed and stammered and assured her he'd carry her message to the minister's house down the road before leaving the village. She tossed him a flirtatious glance. And he was even older than Solomon! Did Almyra charm every unmarried man who crossed her path? Now, now, that was an unkind thought. When I realized Sarah's smile spoke to the same observation, I giggled and looped an arm around each girl's shoulders, and, with my father carrying Sarah's satchel ahead of us, we slid and skipped our way to the house.

A feast of girl talk, as well as sweet biscuits and our cocoa, warmed the kitchen merrily. Sarah described the four Hayes brothers and their parents for Almyra, who marveled at the adventures the family shared up north. She presented a tatted lace collar to my mother, a pouch of tobacco to my father, and caught my eye as she set back into the valise a small packet that I knew must be for me—for later, after Almyra's visit.

Then, of course, we began to talk about the election, and the politics of the nation. Sarah asserted that the newly elected president—of course it was not final until after the electoral college vote later in the winter, but no doubt they'd follow the popular vote—could not stand in any way for Abolition. "And your friend Solomon says the Whig party is collapsing from its weakness around ending slavery," Sarah added.

"You've seen Solomon since the election?"

"Oh no, Alice, but he did send a short letter after he met my brother Franklin. Isn't it amazing? I haven't seen him for so many years, and, finally, tomorrow, I will!"

Now Almyra wanted to know more, and Sarah described her parents and her brothers and sisters stranded in the South. She told me their "master" had moved them to southern Maryland, not far from the nation's capital, and continued to keep his prices for their purchase terribly high. "So it is hard to thank Providence for the loss of Franklin's leg, and I'm sure it's been terrible sore and hard for him, but at least Mr. Thaddeus Stevens fought for a better price. Alice, your father's help means so much. I know he gathered more than a hundred dollars of the funds himself."

We all shivered as Sarah named the prices again that the slave owner sought: a thousand dollars for her father, Mr. Johnson, and the price had been three thousand for the rest of the family as a group, but Franklin's five-hundred-dollar purchase counted against that. How could anyone raise such funds? My father's farm, now prospering with its very large flock of sheep, cleared a profit in a year of about fifty dollars.

Almyra, of course, didn't hesitate to ask what I'd never dared: "Does that man hurt your family, Sarah? Is it like in Mrs. Stowe's novel, where the overseer uses a whip and flays the men in the field? Does the owner's wife intercede for your mother at all?"

"Oh, no," Sarah replied, "he's not a terrible master. Of course, he doesn't allow any black workers to leave the farm. And my mother worries that if there's a bad year for the crops, he might sell my brothers, because they're good workers and could get a much better price than the master's asking for the family's freedom. But this was a good year, which is all we can ask."

I noticed she'd avoided answering about the owner's wife. But I was horrified at the conversation and tried to stop this direction of talk: "What do you hear from Miss Farrow?" The former slave who lived in St. Johnsbury wrote often to Sarah, I knew.

"She's well, and she told me Mr. Gilman is spending more time with Dr. Jewett lately. Which must, truly, be a Godsend, I believe."

"I don't understand who those people are and why it's a Godsend," Almyra interjected.

"Mr. Gilman owns the Gilman Mills in St. Johnsbury," I explained. "He's a very important man, and he was just elected governor of the state. Solomon says his opinion can sway what takes place in Washington. And, though he's an abolitionist, he's the kind who wants to ship former slaves to Africa, to send them home, as he sees it. But Dr. Jewett understands clearly that slavery itself must end, in the name of all that's right and holy."

Sarah continued from this: "So, if Mr. Gilman, soon to be Governor Gilman, is spending more time with Dr. Jewett, we have more hope that he'll take a stand for immediate Abolition."

Almyra nodded with enthusiasm. "I see! And which women here are leading the movement for immediate Abolition?"

Sarah and I stared. I found my voice before hers and replied, "Women don't do that here, Almyra. We encourage the men. And we remind them that they must do their duty in forging better laws and standing for what's right. We are the power that enables them to work for God's will."

"Old fashioned nonsense," Almyra pronounced. "Women are not children. Abigail Adams herself, wife of the second president, told her husband to pay us particular care and attention in crafting the nation's independence. Remember?"

I wasn't sure I'd ever heard that said, even in school lessons, and I struggled to recall the strengths of President Adams. I wished Sarah would speak up to counter this astonishing statement.

Instead, my mother, opening the stove door to add a split of maple, quietly confirmed Almyra's pronouncement. "It's not simple, though, to lead when the men are the ones who own the property and business and who make the public stands, more often than not. Almyra, you should recite the rest of what Mrs. Adams wrote to her husband in that particular letter."

I stared. "You know about letters from Mrs. Adams to her husband?"

"Her grandson Charles Francis Adams published some, a

few years ago," my mother said. "Come, Almyra, say the words with me: 'If particular care and attention is not paid to the ladies, we are determined to foment a rebellion, and will not hold ourselves bound by any laws in which we have no voice or representation.' "

My friends praised this statement, while I sat dumbfounded. I suppose I should have expected my mother to know such things—she led much opinion in our church—but it sounded . . . Well, it sounded rebellious. And my mother was not a rebellious wife.

Once again, I wondered whether Solomon McBride wanted a wife who knew such things, the kind who could summon the words of a president's wife to buttress her opinions. No wonder he had not come to call! I must write to him this evening and assure him that I knew more, day by day.

The light in the kitchen had faded gradually, and I realized we now sat by lantern glow, as well as several candles. Almyra seemed to realize the time at the same moment. "I must return to my aunt's home," she said with regret. "Will I see you in the morning, Sarah, and Alice?"

My mother's glance warned me to be discreet. Freedom shouldn't be put at risk in casual conversation: None of us knew how much Almyra might say to others, and the horror of the year's new laws lingered as a warning. So I said only, "Sarah and I have an errand to run tomorrow, Almyra. We'll meet you at church on the Sabbath, though."

Sarah and I offered to take a lantern and walk Almyra home, then return, and my mother agreed that some fresh air seemed timely. "But don't dawdle, girls. Mr. Sanborn will be in for supper soon, and I want you here on time."

We hurried into our cloaks and talked of light topics as we passed through the village, escorted Almyra to the minister's home, and turned back in the dark, cold onset of night to make our return. As we reached the inn on our way back, I saw Caroline gazing from a window and waved a greeting, hoping she could see who was outside. Should I have invited her earlier?

Life seemed so complicated. What suited my friendship with Sarah wasn't a good fit for when Almyra came to call, and neither of them could be quickly introduced into the connection that Caroline and I were forging.

And that was only the "distaff" side of my life! How did women engage in friendships and also sustain their roles as wives and mothers? Or even—How did they know for sure when a young man was courting them?

At that moment, Sarah resumed her description of what she'd learned to cook and sew over the past year, and I was glad to be distracted from my thoughts.

CHAPTER 17

The snow swirled outside the kitchen window.

"It might be easing a bit," I told Sarah. "I can see the barn better now."

She stood up from the table, where she'd been reading a Bible passage, mostly to herself but sometimes aloud at the surprising parts. It was the story of Joseph and the way he could interpret dreams. We both knew the scripture, word for word, and Sarah loved the parts about sheep and goats. Shepherds! And each time Sarah said "sheep" aloud, Jesse the collie, lying at my father's feet, seemed to expect her to produce some for him to herd.

I was too frustrated to laugh. "Papa, Old Sam could manage this snow. The Warrens must be wondering why we're not there."

From behind a sheet of newsprint, my father said, "The Warrens know why we're not there. It's snowing in West Upton, too, Alice. I told you before: When the roads have been rolled, we'll go. That may be this afternoon, or it may have to wait until tomorrow."

"But tomorrow's the Sabbath," I protested. "You won't go so far on God's day of rest."

My father set the page down and exchanged a long look with my mother. She seemed to signal him, and he sighed. "If it's God's own work to be done, we can do it after church. I'm going to the barn."

Sarah looked puzzled. She said, "I don't understand."

"I do," I said with a groan. "Even with the sleigh, Papa won't hitch up Old Sam to go until the roller comes through. It's too much work to pull anything in deep snow."

"No, I understand that. It's the sheep in Egypt I don't understand. Isn't it all sand and desert there? How can sheep thrive, when Pharoah welcomes Joseph's family?"

"Look in the atlas," my mother recommended. She kept knitting as she talked, turning the heel on a sock. "A good question should lead to discovery."

As if I hadn't heard that before. Still, I fetched the atlas for Sarah, and soon her excitement overflowed: "Two kinds of sheep in ancient Egypt, and listen, it was the desert dwellers who depended on sheep the most, for milk, and meat and wool. How did they do that?"

"Think. And read some more. Find out how people live in the desert in the first place," Mama suggested.

I sighed and sat down next to Sarah. "I might as well learn more about Egypt's sheep myself. I expect I'll be teaching school next summer. You never know what a student will want to learn."

By midday we understood more about desert life, and the frequent green belts along the Nile, its tributaries, and so many other rivers. It couldn't be less like a Vermont snow season. But because Sarah and I studied it together, we kept seeing how it compared to the way fugitives were coming out of the South, finding their way North despite dangers and the terrible power of the Fugitive Slave Act, which transformed ordinary, kind people into frightened informers.

Sarah said, "The Hayes family doesn't often bring home the newspaper. Alice, have you seen news of fugitives coming to Vermont?"

I nodded. "Along Lake Champlain, because it's a route to Canada," I confirmed. "And the minister talks about churches in Burlington where parishioners quarrel all the time about who owes which duties to whom, and how they should help."

My mother, taking a pan of cornbread out of her oven, commented, "I believe there's more agreement about Temperance than about Abolition, in Burlington and Montpelier. Every week the news from the state legislature wrestles with how to stop drunkenness. Less so for how to change the laws in Washington."

A bang of the door brought my father into the kitchen, and Sarah and I scrambled to set out spoons and plates for the noon dinner.

"Roller just worked the village road," my father announced. "We'll depart after our meal."

That added a great deal of cheer to the room, and, in next to no time, clean plates and covered dishes and a banked fire sent us all four out to the sleigh, with hot bricks for our feet, and merry anticipation. Only a few flakes tumbled from the half-cleared sky.

"You're sure you want me to come along, Ephraim?"

"I do, Abigail. It's a fine showing, a family out for a Saturday drive of the fine Vermont roads. And you're the person who's talked with Mrs. Warren at length. Moreover, if young Franklin needs some relief on the journey, you'll know best how to make him comfortable."

With my father to drive, Ely drew the sleigh swiftly, gliding over the rolled roads. My mother admitted that we skimmed with great speed behind the younger horse. "I would not have dared to drive Old Sam so quickly," she confessed and smiled at my father. In his fond glance at her, I could see a flicker of the young couple from so many years ago.

Indeed, no further snow fell, and we arrived at the Warren farm in not much more than an hour. As we pulled up the drive, Sarah gripped my arm. She whispered, "What if he's forgotten me? What if he is different now? What if . . ."

I patted her hand and then her cheek. "He could never forget you. You're his little sister. And I'm convinced that he needs you. Go be the blessing in his life."

Her eyes lit with delight. "Oh, Alice! Oh!" She leapt from the sleigh, barely resting a hand on my father's arm to climb out, then froze, staring at the farmhouse door. A young man, about the age of my brother William, had opened it. Maneuvering a pair of wooden crutches that made him stoop somewhat, he came out onto the swept porch and gazed at us one by one, at last settling on my friend.

"Sarah?"

"Oh, Franklin!" As if a spell had released, she pelted up the shoveled pathway, skirt and petticoats swinging, arms outstretched. When she reached him, she pulled up short, unsure whether or where to touch him as he balanced on the wooden sticks. At last she leaned forward with great care and placed her cheek against his.

And then everyone moved again: my mother to lift down a pie she'd brought to give the Warrens, my father to turn the sleigh around and then release Ely from the shafts, and one of the men from the barn—was it Mr. Harris?—to walk our horse out back for water and grain. Mr. and Mrs. Warren welcomed us and urged us to come in for tea; my father agreed but cautioned, "We'll need to depart in half an hour, I'm sorry to say, for the darkness settles early, and the cold temperatures with it."

How different it was to sit in the parlor with Mr. Warren and my father, as well as the women, and Sarah, Franklin, and me. Everyone perched politely on the stiff, formal chairs, and my parents shared an elegant loveseat corded in gold braid. The men discussed the news of the week, especially the commentaries on Daniel Webster, who seemed to have escaped his tarred-black reputation as a traitor to New England by dying. I guessed from my mother's tight lips that she might be thinking the same thing I was: Here we sat, with two young people whose family suffered the actual lash of the Slave Power, and Mr. Webster had betrayed the moral requirement to respect them, by allowing slavery to extend into the western Territories. How could he now be a good man in death?

But Sarah seemed deaf to the conversation. She held her brother's hand tightly and gazed only at him—a shy, sad look for just the briefest moment at the empty pinned-up leg of his trousers, and, otherwise, the entire joy of her heart glowing in her eyes as she smiled tenderly at Franklin.

Would I ever look at my brother William in that way? Perhaps, if I thought he'd been lost to us. Which reminded me of the uncertainty we all felt about Charles and John, and I wanted to speak up, in order to be somehow reassured that these oldest of my brothers weren't lost at sea. Still, the careful formality of the parlor kept me hushed. My bodice pinched across the waist, my collar felt overly snug, and my feet, damp now, remained chilled from the journey.

I forced my attention back to Sarah instead. Soon, thank goodness, the half hour ended, and my father stood to thank our hosts again. He turned to Franklin: "Do you have a valise for us to place in the sleigh, young man?"

Franklin eased to stand with his two crutches. "It's at the door," he said softly.

Sarah said, "I'll fetch it," and my father nodded, then quietly moved to Franklin's side to guard his balance if needed. Mr. Warren did likewise, and his wife, smiling at my mother, held the door for us all.

Outside, the low sun threatened to sink behind the western hills in a very short time, and the air snapped at us, already colder than when we'd arrived. Mr. Harris brought our horse, and my father hitched him between the shafts. In a flurry of helpful hands and "pardon me" and "there we go," Franklin and Sarah slid under a pair of woolen blankets and a thick bearskin. My mother began to direct me to Franklin's other side, then changed her mind and sent me around the sleigh to squeeze under the covers next to Sarah instead, sandwiching her slight frame. And, with my father's hand under hers, my mother took her position on the front bench, with a farewell wave to our hosts.

Ely, clearly well fed and eager to pull again, took us down the road at a lively clip. I asked, raising my voice to carry to my father, "Will we reach home before dark?"

"Ely intends us to," my father chuckled. "Soon enough, Alice. Abigail, why don't you start a song for the ladies in the back row? It will cheer us along our way."

We sang "Green Grow the Rushes, O!" and "Widdecombe Fair," and when we tried "I Am a Poor Wayfaring Stranger," even Franklin knew some of the words. The part with "I'm going home to see my sister" made my eyes burn, and I choked up on the last verse, with "brother" in it. My mother moved us onward to hymns after that, including the new one we'd just begun singing in church, "My Faith Looks Up to Thee." I asked for "Old Hundredth," which my mother liked to call the Doxology, and we'd just started it when my father called out to Ely, to slow him.

Trying to lean around my mother without unbalancing the sleigh, I saw something capsized at the side of the road, with a small horse struggling and slipping. Next to him stood a man in a long coat, flourishing a whip and shouting. "Gee there, you blamed animal. Gee up. Haul it, you lame old creature. Or I'll send you off for stew meat!"

The slap and slash of the whip cracked loudly, and the horse whinnied in pain, lunging against the harness, one foot banging against a runner of a half overturned sleigh. The animal cried out again, and I did, too, without thinking. "Papa! Do something!"

My mother half turned and glared at me. "Hush, Alice! Silence!" She hissed, "You'll make things worse if you call out. Bite your tongue, child."

I turned to see why she wasn't scolding Sarah and Franklin and realized they had vanished under the covers. Sarah peeked from underneath, one hand across her mouth, the other grasping her brother's shoulder. How could I not realize the slash of a whip would terrify them? I bit my gloved hand to silence myself and cautiously reached the other hand downward, to brush against Sarah's cheek.

She dodged my touch and slid further into the darkness, curling around her brother, who in turn had his eyes tightly clamped shut, his body shaking with cold or something worse.

I realized that if Sarah and Franklin were hiding, I wasn't helping them, by showing so clearly where they were. In the gray twilight, I pulled upright and sat like a lady, only leaving one hand below the covers to say "I know you are there."

My mother held the reins with just enough pressure to let Ely know she was there. My father, nimble and quick, stood on the hard-rolled snow of the center of the road, talking to the stranger. "I'll ease your sleigh upright, so the horse can draw it forward," he offered.

The stranger, his long, black coat panels flapping like crows' wings, stamped angrily on the road and cursed his horse for clumsiness. But he accepted my father's offer and held back from slashing again and whipping his animal, while my father eased the wooden platform back onto its rails, letting a heap of blankets and packages tumble as he did so.

Flash! Slap! The whip flailed in the air, causing the horse to lunge again and my father to leap sideways.

"Hold back, man! I can't get your horse steady if you do

that. If it's your belongings you're concerned about, still, hold back. We'll gather it all together."

My mother bit her lip angrily, and Ely took a nervous step backward, making our sleigh shake a bit. Instantly she took control of herself, crooning quietly to Ely and easing the reins a moment, then gathering them again. The horse must not try to back up with the sleigh; he'd only hurt himself.

In the moment I'd been distracted, my father had maneuvered the stranger's sleigh into position and gripped the bridle of the other horse. To my dismay, I saw a red, bleeding wheal on the animal's flank, and what looked like another, partly healed. I could tell my father had seen them, too, by the grim expression on his face.

He steadied the horse, helped the animal to draw the sleigh back onto the rolled road, and turned to look at the man stomping toward him. I thought he'd speak for the horse, but instead he thrust out a hand and said, "Ephraim Sanborn at your service, sir. May I ask where you're headed? Perhaps I can be of some help."

"Pshaw," the man spat. "I don't need any help, if you'll just replace the items you've dumped out of my sleigh. I'm headed for Littleton, and I'm in a hurry."

My father pulled his hand back and began lifting bundles. In a deep voice, which to my ear was deliberately slowed, he said, "Might be a bit late to make it to Littleton before dark, sir. You'll find a good hotel in Upton Center, just a few miles ahead of you."

"Damned horse," the stranger cursed again. "Stupid and slow and clumsy. Any livery stables in this Upton Center of yours, where I might find a better animal?"

My father gave a slow nod and added the last blanket, shaking off snow as he lifted it. "Might be something available."

"I'm off, then." The man jumped into his sleigh and slapped

127

the reins, and the horse leapt in pain and fear, jerking the sleigh forward.

I cried out through my glove, afraid the sleigh would capsize again and the horse be further beaten. But somehow it kept the road, and it headed away in front of us, rapidly.

"Fool," my father said as he climbed back to sit next to my mother. "And now we'll need to stop at the stables on our way, Abigail."

"Yes, Ephraim," my mother agreed as she passed him the reins. My father talked softly to Ely for a moment, then eased him forward.

I patted the bench next to me, but Sarah whispered from below, "We'll just stay here for now, Alice. You understand."

And I did. So I leaned forward to talk quietly with my mother. "Mama, can we do something about that terrible man?"

She patted my arm over her shoulder and said only, "Your father has a plan. Sit back, Alice. Don't make it harder for Ely."

We reached Upton Center just as the sun dipped beyond the mountains. A faint pink and gold glow suffused the sky, but I knew it wouldn't last long. Night was falling.

My father slowed Ely and eased our sleigh up against the side of the general store, just around the corner onto the North Upton road. He ducked his head to look around, then headed for the inn. My mother seemed to understand what he had in mind, though I hadn't heard them discuss it. Once again, she held the reins calmly. She suggested, "Alice, you may want to slide down under the blankets now with Sarah and her brother. It will help the three of you stay warmer. It's going to be a cold half hour ahead."

A mere five minutes later, my father jumped back to his seat and clucked to Ely to start the last stretch toward home. My mother said only, "You found Judge McMillan?"

"I did," my father replied, then focused on driving the sleigh.

I wanted to ask more but could recognize a closed moment when I saw one. With a sigh, I angled down from the bench and curled against Sarah, trying not to bump into her brother, who kept his eyes closed. Together, Sarah and I softly sang one psalm after another and had just started my favorite, the Twenty-Third, when the slowing of the sleigh signaled our arrival in North Upton. Minutes later we turned up our own track to the barn and soon were inside the house, where my mother swiftly brought the stove fire to flames again, and the scent of warm chicken stew and a pudding assured me we were safe.

Sarah led Franklin into our much smaller parlor, to show where she'd made up a bed for him. I stood in the doorway, uncertain of how to help or what to say.

At last Sarah turned to me and said, "That's how some of them always sounded. Especially in Virginia, even more than Maryland. Mean, and with a whip. What's your father going to do?"

"I think he's already done it." I hesitated, then invited them both back to the kitchen. "I think he'll tell us, when supper's done. Better come eat. My mother won't like it if we don't make a good meal from her work!"

Sarah smiled and nodded to her brother. "Come eat, Franklin."

Without speaking, he lifted himself onto the crutches and started back to the kitchen. We followed him, touching hands for a moment. Sarah, I realized, had as much faith in my father as I had. Our friendship, despite nearly two years apart, held firm.

It took forever to eat and then clear the table. When my mother turned down the lamp a bit and sat again with the rest of us, I dared to ask: "What did you do, Papa?"

Pulling out a pipe and beginning to tamp tobacco into it, my father said, "What would you do if you had the chance, Alice?"

"Stop that man from ever driving another horse," I declared. "But can you do that?"

"Maybe. Or more to the point, maybe Judge McMillan can. You remember him, your mother's cousin?"

How could I forget? The judge had sat in our own parlor, not that long ago, deciding whether my brother had murdered a man—a terrible, bad man, but still, murder was a crime, and punishment would follow. My chest pounded, recalling how frightened I'd been. And how relieved by the decision that William hadn't done wrong.

"Well," my father drawled, "it's a crime to beat a horse like that. It's been a crime for six years now, thanks to the Vermont legislature."

Franklin spoke now, in quiet surprise: "Truly? To beat an animal?"

My father rephrased carefully. "To willfully wound, maim, or disfigure one," he spelled out. "And I think the wounds on that horse qualified. In fact, I'm sure no stable in Upton Center will let a horse to that man, under any circumstances, and I do believe your mother's cousin the judge may have taken the wounded horse into his own custody."

I clapped my hands.

Franklin saw further, though: "So that man's stranded nearby?" His voice cracked with strain, though I could tell he was trying to stay calm.

"Oh, no," my father assured him. "They'll send him east on the stage, which might come in first thing tomorrow. Nobody wants to keep him around. He'll be gone before you know it."

The tension in the room eased. "And the horse?" Concern made Sarah wrinkle her face intently.

"Oh, well. I might have told Judge McMillan that we had an extra stall in the barn if a wounded animal needed time to recover," my father replied, holding back a smile.

"Oh, Papa!" I threw my arms around him a moment, then stepped back and beamed at Sarah and her brother. "What should we name him?"

"He's used to Lame Old Creature," Franklin answered, a hint of a smile at last on his face. "Or Stupid and Slow and Clumsy. You know any name that sounds like that?"

"Mephibosheth," my mother answered promptly. At our incredulous stares, she added, "He was lame. He was the grandson of King Saul, and father of Micah."

"Micah," my father repeated. "Let's see if he'll answer to that. It's different enough from Sam and Ely. And now," he lifted his eyebrows, "seems to me some young people might want to study a Bible verse before tomorrow morning. Or get some sleep."

We three settled for sleep, after choosing a Bible verse for the morning. Sarah chose to keep her brother company for the night, and while I missed her warmth in my own bed, I surely understood.

I said my prayers with a grateful heart and added at the end, "And please bless Micah with healing. Amen."

As I snuggled toward sleep, I thought of Charles and John again, glad I'd at least been able to pray for their safety. Of course, I had no idea of the news that would arrive the next afternoon, or how Franklin himself, quiet though he was, would play a role.

CHAPTER 18

My father offered to drive us all in the sleigh to worship. I knew it must be for Franklin's sake; maneuvering those crutches in the snow would be exhausting. So I said right away, "Oh, Papa, that would be so kind, because I wanted to bring a blanket with us, and it would be hard to carry."

My mother nodded. "A very good idea. Girls, and Franklin, fetch your cloaks. Ephraim, I don't have hot bricks ready, since you didn't caution me ahead of time, but you could take those two warm, dry blankets from behind the stove, if you would."

Though worship service and the Reverend Alexander's sermons often lasted hours longer than my twitching feet and legs appreciated, attending church usually meant learning news about other families, or even insight into why some boy we all knew had behaved so badly. My mother, who'd seen the teacher in me for years, would often nudge me to pay attention to something, whether in the words flowing from the pulpit, or the positions of parent and child. Today, however, we were the focus of all eyes, as we entered with both Sarah and her brother. Did others see beyond the fierce rigidity of Franklin's face, to the embarrassment I could perceive? How terrible to walk into a large group of people who only knew the color of your skin, and your label as "former slave"—and at the same time have to clutch a set of crutches and maneuver into a wooden pew.

My father made sure to sit at one side of Franklin, and Sarah, of course, to the other. So I couldn't even convey a sympathetic touch to his hand, and he didn't see my face; he only gazed at the pulpit. Surely, he wished everyone else would look there, instead of at him. Well, I could do that much.

First came psalms and prayers and such, lasting an hour. Then the sermon, which I hoped would absorb my attention better, as I felt restless and couldn't stop worrying about everything, from the snowy roads north, to my brothers, and to the health of my brother William's wife, Helen. I took a deep breath and tried not to squirm in my skirts.

The minister began with Jesus's teachings in the Book of Matthew: "Think not that I am come to destroy the Law, or the Prophets: I am not come to destroy, but to fulfill." Deftly, he outlined how this charged each of us with taking a stand for Abolition, and he described "nullification": the duty to nullify, or declare invalid, a federal law found to be immoral. I knew he meant the Fugitive Slave Act. It encouraged me to think that most Vermonters agreed. Maybe this answered one of my prayers: a confirmation that Sarah and Franklin would be safe as they traveled north, someday soon.

Then the sermon moved to Temperance—the need to abstain from drinking and drunkenness. The sense of "everyone agreeing" vanished, and I couldn't help but look sideways and forward to where the Clark family occupied a pew: Caroline of course, who'd flashed a smile at me before settling to look only toward the minister, but also Matthew, and Mr. and Mrs. Clark. As if a storm brewed among them, I felt the crackle of anger. Every new call for Temperance threatened their very livelihood, making the management of the inn and its customers so much harder.

When the Reverend Alexander paused to draw breath and re-arrange the pages in front of him, Mr. Clark stood up. His seat on the aisle allowed him to leave the pew without much rearrangement. But he must have felt every eye upon him. Much of his face hid within a full, brown winter beard and lush moustache, but the skin around his eyes showed the red and purple of choler, that most passionate of angers. And he made no effort to hush his boots as he stamped from the church, although habit perhaps made him shut the door quietly behind him.

Now the fullness of our pew, the presence of Sarah and Franklin between me and my father, prevented what I'd ordinarily do: exchange a glance with my father to see which way his sympathies lay. But he only looked forward, and so did my mother. I saw Franklin's eyes were shut, as if witnessing Mr. Clark's anger overflowed his capacity to bear the moment. Sarah's hands, instead of being neatly folded in her lap, gripped his.

The third hour lagged unbearably, but finally the service came to a close for the dinner hour. Those who could invest more in the Sabbath would return for the afternoon's service as well; I doubted our family would do so.

Outside the church door, a number of men lingered, and several shook my father's hand or tapped his shoulder approvingly. I angled around the bottleneck, to accompany Sarah and her brother to the sleigh. In silence, we waited for my parents.

Home again, warm and somehow much safer in the kitchen, I dared to ask: "Mr. Clark knows the law against liquor licensing is a good and moral law, doesn't he, Papa? That can't be what nullification is for, can it?"

My father handed back a question: "Is the Temperance law an immoral federal act?"

"No, of course not!"

"Then, my girl, it's clearly no case for nullification."

Unlike in the church, Franklin now sat alert, wide eyes flickering among us. He asked my father, "Is that why that man left the service? Because he doesn't like the law?"

"And because it's hurting him," my mother cut in, with some compassion. "He owns the tavern, Franklin. And he's a good man, in a bad position right now."

Everyone nodded. Enough said. Dinner took over as the most important task for the time.

At last my father pushed back from his empty plate, complimented my mother on the apple crumble, and announced he'd walk to the store to collect any letters.

Now it was my mother's turn to tense, and I realized Franklin, in his raw new state of freedom, felt every emotion around him. I bent forward and quickly explained, "We're waiting for word from my two oldest brothers. They're late in returning from the California gold fields, and we hope there will be a letter."

Just as my father reached the door, in cloak and boots, a light tapping came against it, and Caroline entered the house. A flurry of introductions ensued, in words and gestures and letters spelled out. With more hands, clearing up from the meal went quickly, and we settled to converse in a rapidly adapting mix of methods.

How much like his sister Franklin was! Quick to understand, gentle in communicating—I watched a bond form readily between him and Caroline, despite her lack of hearing and his understandable fears and uncertainty. They even laughed together over his missing leg somehow. Caroline's laugh came breathy and thin, but merry. If only life could always be so full of friends!

For a moment I wondered whether Almyra, too, would come calling, then realized that since her uncle was the minister, she'd likely be sitting through the afternoon hours at the church. At last, something I didn't envy about her life!

With a bang, the door flew open, and my father hurried into the house, talking before he'd even pulled off his outer garments. "Abigail, they're in Boston. They're on land. Alice, where's your young man this week? Quickly, how can we reach Solomon?"

Caroline and Franklin, each startled and confused in a different way, leapt to their feet. Sarah reassured her brother, and my mother stepped quickly to Caroline, gesturing for her to sit and wait a moment. Which left me to reply to my father: "I don't know! Maybe Matthew can reach him though. He often knows how."

I caught the letter my father had waved in the air, as he raced back out, hastening to the Clarks' inn. Would Matthew be there? Caroline seemed to read our speaking of his name, and she was nodding emphatically and pointing in that direction.

My mother firmly took the letter from my hand, glanced at it, then laid it out flat on the table so we could all peer at the hastily scrawled lines. She read it aloud as she deciphered it, while Caroline eased close to follow the page:

Dearest father and mother, John and I are well, which I know is the news most urgent to convey to you. We are resting in Boston, which we reached yesterday, although I shall not say quite where, as you will understand the need for care and prudence. I trust my earlier letter reached you, with its description of the shocking conditions on the boat we thought to take from California. John and I are traveling with two esteemed friends who have given us much assistance in San Francisco and wished to come east with us. You will understand when I say that they remind us of Sarah and will grasp our situation when we saw the cargo of that ship. We sought a smaller, safer boat, and it took some weeks to find this. Then, in the hands of Providence, we suffered a tediously extended ocean voyage. Little Alice will appreciate that we can now describe to her, of our own knowledge, several South American civilizations and one in the Caribbean Islands.

To our dismay, Boston proves to be nearly as risky for our friends as California had become. We expect to travel north on the railroad, of course, but we would greatly appreciate the sort of travel documents that Mr. Gilman can provide, in two sets, one for an age just a few years out of the schoolroom and the other more mature. Then we will feel assured of safety all around when we board.

Speed is essential. Seek Mr. Gilman's advice on how best to take action. For the time being, I will hope that you can assist directly. We will watch Mr. Gilman's Boston office in hopes of hearing from you there. In haste and with abiding affection,

Your son, Charles.

My mother and I stared at each other in a mix of terror and pride. This letter must mean that my brothers had traveled with two dark-skinned men, friends of theirs from California, on their oceangoing journey. They must have been sure New England would welcome their friends—only to discover the chaos created in the agitated city of Boston, where many an abolitionist and Free Soiler challenged the Fugitive Slave Law daily while some others, we had heard, kidnapped even those who'd never been enslaved, to sell them for wild profit. "Nullification," I remembered, was how most Bostoners treated the new law that they so despised. But could Charles and John and their friends stay truly safe in that city? I thought the risk considerable. We must help them at once.

Sarah explained at length in a low voice to Franklin. Meanwhile, I picked up Caroline's card of hand shapes for letters, and we jumped among words and half sentences and more, as she quickly grasped the situation. She asked me whether Sarah was free, and I said yes; and so was Franklin, also. Was it dangerous for them? Not really. Not here in Vermont, where we all hated slavery as a dreadful sin and a reproach to the liberty prized by the Founding Fathers of our nation. Was it dangerous for—She taught me the gesture for brother, and I let her see the uncertainty and concern in my face. Even though most New Englanders despised the Fugitive Slave Law and did all they could to oppose its effects, it had indeed become the law of the land, and I knew my brothers might land in terrible trouble— and, even more so, their friends, if falsely accused of not being freemen. Caroline put her arms around me and drew my mother, too, into an embrace. Then she taught me a hand gesture for courage. I repeated it several times, determined to follow its lead.

Abruptly, we all felt the thumping of booted feet coming up the cellar stairs. Before I'd even realized who it must be, my mother stepped across and opened the door for the men arriv-ing—my father, of course, and Matthew Clark.

"You used the tunnel!" I had never seen my father pass through it—it had been how Jerushah and I exchanged mes-sages. And Matthew had used it to bring apprenticeship papers for me to give Solomon, to carry south, two years earlier, when so many fugitives from the Slave Power needed every possible document we could provide, to guarantee their freedom and safe travels.

Matthew set an extinguished candle to one side and nodded. "Your father told me he hadn't been in there in years," he said with a half smile. "Good thing we carried some light, or he'd have knocked his head half a dozen times on the ceiling beams."

"But why?"

This time my father answered. "Mr. Clark's in a mighty dark humor just now. We didn't much care to do this in front of him. All the push for Abolition at the same time as the pressure for Temperance—on Tuesday the state legislature votes on a law that will make his business even more difficult."

Mr. Clark kept North Upton's only inn, with a public tavern. I knew the law from two years earlier, banning the sale of spiritous liquor, must have lowered the tavern's revenue. Thinking aloud, I said, "But he can still provide cider, and won't that satisfy most people?"

Laughter in the room around me signaled I'd been naive. "It's mighty hard to get properly drunk on hard cider, no matter how much it may smell of spirits," Matthew pointed out dryly. "And for people like Old Mo, getting drunk is the whole point of drinking." He added, "Cider's also not near as profitable. And the newest law will even reward people who report the intoxicated by paying them from the state's collected funds—funds that tavern owners contribute, to be used against them!"

"So your father's upset?"

"No," Matthew drawled. "Not so's to say upset. Furious and blind enraged might be closer. At any rate, in no mood to see your father and me in conversation. We lucked into a moment to enter the tunnel and counted ourselves fortunate."

He lifted a satchel that rustled with documents.

My father confirmed: "Enough apprenticeship papers left over from last year to provide well for your brothers' two companions, to hold out against anyone who tries to stop them. We have more, which we'll yield to Solomon at the same time, in case there are others in need. Now Matthew shall ride for St. Johnsbury to send a telegram to Solomon, to engage him in what we're doing. We must plan the best way to carry the papers to Boston, to meet Solomon and the others there."

Under my mother's stern glare, I hushed my own impulse to volunteer and waited for what else my father had in mind. But I wasn't the only one who had a notion—Caroline, who'd followed more of the conversation than I expected, tapped my father's arm and began to gesture, first with questions, then with an idea.

As we all turned Caroline's idea around, we formed a plan: she and I and my mother would make a train journey to Boston, to purchase cotton goods for summer skirts and gowns. Solomon, we guessed, could find a way to carefully escort John and Charles and the two friends in their company, by quiet roads, up to Manchester, New Hampshire, where they could join us for the train north, with far less scrutiny than they'd face trying to board in Boston, and less danger than traveling for days in a wagon or coach. Plus Caroline would draw so much attention, as a deaf woman traveling, that we could distract others. We could all add to such fascination by "conversing" with her in public.

The journey should get safer as the train left the cities, and we would escort these friends, Isaiah and Walter—directly to St. Johnsbury, if they wished. "Then," Sarah added, "Franklin and I might take them further north with us to Coventry." We all seemed at once to realize we had no clear notion of why the men were coming to Vermont, though. Just because they liked my brothers? That couldn't be all of it.

"Wait," her brother interjected from the far side of the room. "There's a better direction for them if they don't have something in mind already. I was going to tell you," he said apologetically to Sarah, "but there hasn't been time. I want to go to Woodstock, the Vermont town near the railroad center of White River Junction. I have a job waiting for me there, and I can find two more."

Sarah stared. "How can you have a job there? I am taking you north with me to the Mero farm in Coventry, where you can be safe with me. And we can wait for"—she choked down a sob—"for all the others there." I knew she meant their parents and the rest of the brothers and sisters, whose ransom we had not yet raised.

Matthew and Franklin exchanged speaking glances. My father lowered his gaze to the table, then looked up at my mother. With clear reluctance, he voiced what the men all seemed to know but hadn't been clear to the rest of us: "It's grown more dangerous now in the states in between, like Pennsylvania, where kidnapping of Africans happens daily," he pointed out. "And I'm afraid the price for ransom from slavery is rising, not falling. Slaveholders fear their supply will dwindle. We have no guarantee of bringing the others north." He added swiftly, "Though Thaddeus Stevens tells all of us not to give up hope."

In the moment of silent shock, Franklin resumed explaining: "When I stayed with the Warrens—" he began. I could tell he wasn't accustomed to such a large group of people waiting for his words. Sarah went to him and patted his shoulder.

I realized what he must be getting toward. "Mr. Harris and his friend there," I guessed. "They work with horses. They told you about a position open to you?"

"Yes," Franklin nodded. "There are livery stables in Woodstock and nearby towns that hire Negro men as grooms, coachmen, even more. And Mr. Harris said they have no raids there: a local judge supports the stables and won't brook any interference. I'm sure I can bring two more with me. Already I have a letter giving me work at the forge there," he said with some pride. I thought he deserved to feel very good indeed, to capture employment as a man with only a single leg. The thick muscles of his shoulders and arms, which made his crutches readily useful, must be from past labor, perhaps at a forge in the South. I wanted to ask more but saved my curiosity—we would have time later for such conversation.

My father now firmed up the plans. "Sarah, Franklin, you must not ride into Boston. Even with your papers of liberty, the risk is too high. Franklin, would Mr. Harris escort you to White

River Junction and this nearby town, if the Warrens can spare him for two days?"

"I believe he would," said Sarah's brother.

The realization that she wasn't going to spend much time with her brother after all broke into Sarah's thoughts, and I saw her face crumple in pain. I rushed around the table to the other side, to embrace her. We held each other, and she buried her face in my chest.

"Sarah," I said quietly, "I imagine you could ride along with Franklin, to see him settled, and come back next week on the train yourself. We would find someone to bring you north again." For no young woman, white or black, should take the train without a form of escort, preferably an older woman.

"That could be my task," my mother offered. "When we come north from Boston, I would detour with these others to Hartford, if they're willing, and meet you there, Sarah. You and I will journey the rest of the way together."

It was a complicated set of plans and journeys, and as I laid them out in my thoughts, I saw some weak places. One, very obvious, I asked about right away: "Papa, how will you feed yourself if we are all out and about, conducting these adventures for some days?"

Now the room echoed with laughter again, and Matthew said, "There's something to be said for living across the road from an inn, when your wife's gallivanting about! I'm sure my father will gladly pack up a meal or two, or simply invite you to share his. And now, I'm off to St. Johnsbury, before the light's fully gone from the road."

"Hold, Matthew," my father suggested. "Take William with you. The pair of you will manage the return in darkness much better together, and he's in need of a little time away from his usual routine. Take my two horses. The two of you will make it back by bedtime if you don't linger in town. Alice," he told me, "skip on over to William and Helen's home and fetch your brother." He smiled. "By the heavens, it will be good to have more of your brothers here again."

And so, in a flurry of preparations, everyone scattered—and I was glad to have an outdoor errand, bundled in my cloak and boots, to let my thoughts come into line and face what lay ahead: my first trip to Boston. Oh, Solomon!

I could hardly wait.

CHAPTER 19

Monday the 22nd of November in the year of our Lord eighteen hundred and fifty-two—the beginning of my new life. Or so I savored it, as each of us completed our packing that morning, invigorated by confirmation that Matthew Clark and my brother William had found the telegraph agent the evening before and sent word to Solomon McBride in the city of Boston. They had also telegraphed the Gilman office in that city, to let my older brothers John and Charlie know my family was en route to help them, in many complicated ways.

I kept getting lost in imagined conversations with Solomon, as I gathered the necessary items for travel, like my second skirt, a hair brush, extra hairpins, and, oh, where was my Sunday bonnet? I pictured myself saying to Solomon, "Well, of course we are here to assist in your noble efforts to bring people to safety, whether born free or not." And Solomon would look deep into my eyes the way he had before, except this time he would say, "I always knew you were my soulmate, Alice Sanborn. Will you permit me to come courting, now that you are a grown woman?"

My mother called up to me, "Where is my linen handkerchief, Alice? Did you take it to your chamber by mistake?"

I assured her I didn't have it and saw through my window that my father had started hitching Ely to the sleigh. Sarah, Franklin, my mother, Caroline, me—and, of course, my father to drive us to the station in St. Johnsbury: we would surely be warm enough, with so many tucked together under the woolen blankets and bearskin. What else should I pack for the railroad journey? Did one bring a blanket? Or just a shawl? Spare stockings?

As I wrestled to fit my second collar into the small valise my mother had allocated to me, I heard the downstairs door bang, then Franklin's muffled apology. I raced down the stairs and found him struggling to carry his and Sarah's bundles while maneuvering his crutches. "Let me," I begged, but he declined, his jaw grim with resolve. So I only held the door open, and my mother followed him out to the sleigh. Caroline and Sarah already waited for us; Caroline was rubbing Ely's nose, and Jesse the sheep dog pressed against Sarah, obviously fond of her—or else trying to "herd" her toward the house again. Who could tell? I smiled and surrendered my valise to my father, who was balancing the load of the sleigh with care.

A sudden eruption of barking and the flying snow kicked up by Jesse as he raced down the track toward the main road alerted us all to Almyra's arrival, school bag on her arm. She strode up to the sleigh, nodded casually all around, including a raised eyebrow in the direction of Franklin and Sarah, and addressed me directly: "Aren't you attending school today, Alice? Miss Wilson wonders when you're returning to your studies."

Not that it was Almyra's business, I thought, but I stayed civil and gave a friendly smile. "How thoughtful of you to ask, Almyra. I've left a note with my father that I'm sure he'll deliver to Miss Wilson later, but since you'll see her first, perhaps you'd be so kind as to tell her I'll be out of town again this week. I will surely return to the classroom on Monday next."

"Are all of these people going out of town with you? Are you headed north, perhaps?"

"Just to St. Johnsbury at the moment," I said firmly, and my mother came up next to me to support the statement with a nod. To try to settle the matter, I added, "I'll describe it all to you when I return. Perhaps you could visit with us after school on Friday."

Clearly annoyed, Almyra huffed "It's possible" and turned on her heel to head toward school. My father muttered something behind me; I thought it sounded like "little busybody," but that might have just been my own thoughts. Caroline walked up the track toward us, as Almyra left, and I could guess there'd be considerable gossip wafting around our village today!

But it wasn't going to spoil my own joy in making a journey that would soon reconnect me with Solomon, in the best of ways.

Jesse resumed his duty in the barn, and we drove at a steady pace toward St. Johnsbury. The day's deep cold seemed out of place for the end of November, more like a December day, with a bold blue sky, air as clear as brook water, and the bright clip-clop of Ely's hooves on the hard-packed snow. Caroline and I "conversed" in what was now our accustomed mingling of finger signs, broader hand gestures, and bright emotional play. Snuggled beside us, Franklin and Sarah watched and sometimes laughed. It delighted me to see their faces light up the way I believed young people should. Granted, they had seen much sorrow and pain and still must endure a longer separation from their family—and much doubt about when they would be rejoined—but I wanted them to have a chance to feel happy, even if just for the journey in the sleigh.

For a moment, a dark doubt seized me: Had I yielded to my mother's way of caring, tending to one person's comfort at a time, yet neglecting the wide injustices of our nation? Ah, this topic cried out for discussion with Solomon, whose labors took him to the rooms where the fates of wide swathes of land and peoples were determined. It was a world of men's labors, wasn't it? Almyra, though, seemed to think women should play their part. I thought about her insistence that women should be able to vote, as men did. I doubted women would desire to join the arguments in the chambers of rough and ready male discussion of principles, however.

Caroline reached over to touch my cheek in question. What was I thinking? Could I describe it? I did my best, and the effort did us both good, I think. I had never in my life struggled so hard to follow another person's "words," and perhaps she felt the same about mine. Eventually we silenced our fingers and pulled the blankets closer to our faces. The warmth of the four of us helped, but it still felt like December!

Other conveyances joined us on the road: several smaller sleighs, a large farming sledge, a slow wagon. Two men on horseback cantered past, tipping their hats to my mother. The scent of "town" rose up and greeted us: horse leavings, woodsmoke from kitchen stoves, coal from others. I sat taller, eager to hear the train whistle yet also worried we'd be too late to board.

We arrived at the station in good time, and, while my father tended to Ely, the rest of us unloaded parcels and baggage and paced back and forth, testing whether we could stay warm enough or would need to go inside the station house.

There! The train whistle reached us, thin and reedy at first, and gradually gaining power and volume. Wood smoke from the locomotive hung over the tracks, and the cars rattled along beneath the plume. Flat-roofed yellow passenger cars, a smokestack at each end, pulled up next to us. While loud-voiced men loaded freight, we five—my mother, Caroline, Franklin, Sarah, and I—carried our goods into the nearest car and established ourselves on the wooden benches. We sat close to one of the stoves, but it needed feeding and barely had any coals in it. While my father added fuel and made sure we had a supply of split wood for the next stretch of travel, my mother arranged blankets, gathering us all, with Franklin at the center this time, into a cozy array. A few people stared, as many families divided themselves as women to one rail car, men to another, but my mother's confident smiles seemed to silence any doubts.

The whistle blew its warning, my father leaped out the door to reassure Ely, and, with a rumble and shake, away we went.

At first I could hardly stop staring out the train windows at the speeding landscape. We must be traveling at twice the speed of a rapid sleigh, or more! The track wound down into a narrow route between high banks of snow, interrupted from time to time by wide vistas of the nearby Connecticut River. I began to look around me in earnest, to observe the other passengers, and to wonder at last: What was ahead of us?

All too soon, noon crept close and so did the junction of the various railroads at the White River, with the White River Junction station. Franklin and Sarah gathered their belongings, and we all exchanged embraces, despite the wobbling passenger car.

When the train creaked and squealed to a halt, my mother stepped out with Sarah and her brother, to see them to a coach that would carry them up to Woodstock, some fifteen miles up the White River valley. Caroline and I watched, tense and worried, lest my mother not return in time to our train car. But she did, and moreover a man followed her, carrying a fresh armful of wood for the stove. I saw her press a coin into his hand as he left the car, and then she bent to nurse the stove back to a good flame.

Even these three hours of travel had brought some relief from the bitter cold. Our transit southward and east, across part of New Hampshire, also saw easier temperatures, and more passengers in the rail car, which added to its warmth, if also to the cloying scent of people pressed close together, much like a winter schoolroom could develop.

The mills of Manchester, prodigious in size and built of red brick, with fuming smokestacks and a sea of wagons and sleighs around them, struck me as nearly biblical in their crowded magnificence. Caroline watched without as much surprise. I asked her whether Hartford, her school's city, looked the same, and she hesitated, then expressed to me: not so tall, but just as full of people and conveyances. I marveled.

At the last stop before Boston, two grown women making "finger conversation" entered our car, and I saw a new side to Caroline, confident and sociable, as she established where they were from and why they were going to Boston. If I understood correctly, they were on their way home, to an island off the Boston coast where many other deaf people resided. "Martha's Vineyard," Caroline spelled out to me. I asked my mother whether that was the island name, or the name of a fruit farm there, but she'd become too busy straightening everyone's garments, adjusting hairpins, and making sure our bundles were snugly fastened, and I did not gain any certainty, just amazement—imagine a place where there were so many people like Caroline that she would be ordinary!

Like Sarah and Franklin might be in Woodstock, I suddenly realized. I wondered whether my friend would be willing to leave such a special place, to return to North Upton and then to Coventry.

Then the time for wondering ran out, and instead we hurried along the station platform, looking for a coach for hire. Others with more confidence seemed to reach them first, and we continued down the row.

I heard a familiar voice: "Mrs. Sanborn! This way!"

Solomon, with a tall, dark hat perched on his dark locks of hair, beamed as he strode toward us, then swept his hat off in greeting and gave a half bow to my mother, a gloved hand thrust toward her to take hers a moment and then grasp her valise and the satchel that contained our precious documents for the journey. "I have a buggy for you all," he said with cheer and tipped a wink toward Caroline and me as my mother preceded us along an icy wooden boardwalk. "And if you ladies can wait another hour for your supper, there are some gentlemen awaiting you a half mile away, very eager indeed to see faces from North Upton."

He meant Charles and John! My heart leapt, and I clutched Caroline's arm in excitement. After three long years—my brothers!

How on earth we could reach them with so many conveyances and people all around us, and so many buildings of all sizes, old and new, baffled me. More meekly, I climbed into the waiting buggy, grateful for Solomon's hand on the step, and for my mother's warm if trembling smile. At least someone I knew sat beside me! Realizing that it must be even stranger for Caroline, I turned to place a hand on hers, only to find her calmly smiling and introducing herself—by alphabet card and gestures—to Solomon McBride. I blushed for my own lack of manners and quickly completed the introductions. Solomon's eyes sparkled with delight and curiosity, and after another half bow, he jumped in front of us to take the reins of a fine-looking bay horse, guiding it toward another part of the bustling port city.

How quickly he must have acted, to have located my brothers and be ready to take us there, in a matter of less than a day since the decision to come here! I marveled at more than just my surroundings. The shouts and the creaking of vehicles, the whinnying of distressed horses, the gusts of icy wind, all combined to disorient me, and, for a moment, I envied Caroline's personal silence! So this was Boston.

A lurch of my heart reminded me of what my father had told me two years earlier: that if I set my cap for Solomon, and my heart, I'd be giving up my home for his. A city of strangers, without parents close by, or friends I'd known all my life. An enormous change. Although Solomon hadn't made any clear gesture toward such a romantic connection as yet, I found myself testing the thought: Could I walk away from North Upton and the comforts of my sheltered, safe life there, in order to partner with this man determined to ensure a better moral standing in our nation?

These interesting reflections, which raised a blush to my cheeks, ended abruptly as Solomon pulled the buggy close to the doorway of a structure that must be a rooming house, with some sort of public supper under way. He turned without releasing the reins and asked whether we could dismount without his help: "I need to hold the horse, and I'll take him to the stable down the road," he explained.

So we three entered the Boston rooming house, stepping into a chaos of chatter and the clatter of dishes in a long "front room" crammed with three enormous tables. My mother walked forward while Caroline and I held hands behind her and stared into the crowd.

It was the two dark-faced men I spotted first. There were other Negroes in the crowd, but not as tense and alert as those two, who watched the door while spooning their fish soup, the scent of which pervaded the air. They saw us and spoke to two large, rough-looking men across the table from them, who turned to face us—at which my mother gave a cry of recognition and sped among the many persons, to the only two who mattered to her in that moment.

Yet I thought she must have chosen the wrong faces, for the two men smiling at us looked like railroad laborers—garbed in rugged overalls, bearded, heavily muscled. And old! At least, the sun-browned and creased skin around their eyes spoke for many hours, even years, outdoors, surely more than my brothers Charles and John ever had.

Caroline looked at me questioningly. Then she crooked her

arm through mine, and we walked slowly between the rows of men, most of whom looked up and seemed to smile mostly at her. She wore a small and gentle smile of her own, meeting some gazes with little nods. Looking at her anew, I realized what a striking woman she was, and how much more fashionable her clothing seemed than mine. I resolved to figure out the tucks and darts that made her garb stand out as elegant, instead of workaday. Did city ladies always sew better clothing? Or was it something she learned at her school?

A scrape of chair feet on the floor broke me out of my distraction. The two massive workmen were standing and embracing my mother. She gestured toward me, and they turned to look. One exclaimed, "No! Our Alice?" And the other replied, "She grew up!"

The scent of them as they each wrapped an arm over my shoulders had no connection to my home in North Upton. No horse or sheep scent, no farm aroma. I smelled tobacco and sweat and onions and coffee—and then, just a hint of my father, so that I pulled back and looked more closely into these two faces, and at least could see a similarity to home in that way, even if I couldn't really match them to the brothers I'd known three years earlier.

Minding my manners this time, I drew back and introduced the men to Caroline. *My brothers,* I signaled and spelled out each name. "Our neighbor Caroline Clark," I told them in turn. "Visiting with us."

The brother I realized must be Charles, the older of the pair, lowered his frame into a courtly half bow over Caroline's hand. As he stood tall again, he looked directly into her face and spoke slowly, exaggerating his lips so their motion showed within the rough beard. "I remember you," he told her. "You were a pretty little girl. Now you are a lovely woman." To my surprise, he salted his words with several gestures that looked a bit like ones Caroline used.

She was blushing and clearly understood. She pulled her hand back and gave a pleased nod.

"How did you know how to talk with her?" I asked Charles.

"Plenty of men who've worked in the mines are deaf from the explosions," Charles replied. "And some start that way, which is sometimes an advantage. You can learn a lot if you travel the world, little sister. Speaking of which, welcome to Boston, the home of the bean and the cod." He lifted his bowl of fish soup, offered me a spoonful in fun, then continued to consume it. "It's better if you eat it when it's hot or warm," he mumbled around a mouthful.

Now John introduced the three of us to the men traveling with him and Charles: "This is Isaiah, and here is Walter. Expert miners and staunch friends. Fellows, this is my mother, Mrs. Sanborn, and my little grown-up sister Alice, with her friend Caroline. Would you ladies care to join us for supper?"

Two women in aprons and caps stepped forward as if they'd been waiting for the moment, and my brother set six coins on the table, which were swept into an apron pocket instantly, as men nearby slid chairs over to us. A plate of thick slabs of bread, already buttered, also arrived. I thought, "I am eating my first boardinghouse meal!" And I wondered whether Solomon did this often, as a city resident.

Solomon! He should have arrived by now. I looked anxiously toward the door, then bent toward my brother John. "The man who drove us here," I whispered, "he hasn't come back from stabling the horse."

"Give it time, little sister," he replied with a wink. "If he's a good man, he's rubbing the horse down before he leaves it, or taking time to make sure the groom at the livery stable will do the same. Horses that work in cold weather need special care." He paused, knocked a fist against his own head, and said, "But

153

you must know that already. Papa still has the farm, doesn't he? It's in his letters."

A cheerful discussion of numbers of sheep and the price of wool ensued. Charles meanwhile paid careful attention to including Caroline, and so did my mother. Men around us began to leave the tables, but Charles asked one of the women for one more setting of soup, which arrived just as Solomon himself did.

He carried the precious valise of documents slung across his shoulder and chest and never even set it down while eating his meal. Heads close together, the men outlined the next day's actions. My mother drew Caroline and me together so we could firm up our own plans: We would spend the night at a nearby home for women (this place where we'd dined clearly catered to working men), then shop for fabric and notions. The train north left at seven thirty each morning, so we'd need to spend one more night in the city and board the Wednesday morning train.

Caroline asked, and taught us the gestures at the same time: *May we see the ocean tomorrow?*

The Atlantic Ocean! How could I have forgotten how close we were? I looked eagerly for my mother's response, and after a moment she said, "Purchases first, because that is our reason for being here, should anyone ask us. Then perhaps Solomon will take you to see the water, and the ships, in the afternoon."

Solomon at this point bent toward us and inserted a question into our womanly conversation: "Tell me about Sarah's brother. He arrived safely? Is he on his way to Coventry?"

"No, he already has employment elsewhere." I explained to Solomon about the horse farms and livery stables at Woodstock, and he brightened, turning back to my brothers and adding fresh details to their maneuvers of the next day. I gathered he was proposing that Isaiah and Walter be attired as grooms, and that the party of men would conduct a small group of horses from a livery stable in the city, north into New Hampshire. I wanted to know more, but, with the boardinghouse supper over, we needed to remove ourselves. Isaiah and Walter nodded, rarely speaking, then set off for a staircase toward the boarding rooms, while Solomon, Charles, and John walked us down a rough boardwalk to a nearby brick-faced home where soft lights glowed behind heavy curtains.

"Charles," I said quietly as I pressed closer to him, "I want to know about your friends. Did you say they are miners? Why would they come to Vermont?"

"Hush," Charles whispered in my ear. "Some things shouldn't be talked about, out in the open. There will be time later."

How annoying! Yet at least he hadn't said I was too young to hear—just that, once again, I'd have to wait.

Fatigue swept me all at once, and I looked across and realized Caroline felt the same. In silence, we followed my mother into a warm parlor where she paid for two nights' stay, and we all climbed to a shared bedchamber, where sleep came quickly, after the murmur of good night and amen.

To my disappointment, Solomon did not conduct us the next day for our visits to a fabric emporium and an à-la-mode milliner. He'd left a note for my mother, explaining that the timing meant he and the other men were all headed north before dawn, horses and all. We would meet up with them in Manchester, New Hampshire, if all went well.

A sense of unease hung over me all morning, making it difficult to focus on the ginghams and calicos set before us. Fortunately, between my mother and Caroline, decisions fairly flew. Then we bought fresh bread at the largest bake shop I'd ever seen and took it to our bedchamber to make a noon meal with cheese and apples my mother produced from her bag.

Without Solomon, could we see any sights at all? I begged

permission to seek the landlady's opinion.

"Oh, no," she said bluntly, "young ladies must not go walking near the seaport itself. And not in the neighborhoods, either— the Irish are far too rough; the Italians, very foreign and sometimes dangerous; and now the West End is full of Russian Jews, not a good place at all to walk."

My crestfallen face brought a merry laugh from the well-rounded and aproned lady, clearly very busy with her own affairs. She added, "It's not like taking a walk in the countryside, I'm sure. But you young ladies may walk safely in the public gardens. I'll direct you to the route."

So Caroline and I, arm in arm, arrived at last at a wide stretch of snow-covered landscape where a few fashionably attired pairs of women, and some men on their own or in larger groups, paced the neatly shoveled pathways. To my disappointment, although I could see spaces that might become flower beds some time in the future, the open land felt unimproved, almost abandoned. Caroline and I expressed our bewilderment to each other. Even a Vermont green would be more decorative than this space.

A signboard at the far end of the "gardens" announced meetings in the city. One tacked-up notice in particular set me shivering: It began, "Caution!! Colored People of Boston, One & All," and warned of "Kidnappers and Slave Catchers," adding, "Keep a Sharp Look Out for Kidnappers, and have Top Eye open." What a terrible threat! And this was the reason we'd come to Boston: to make sure my brothers' friends, after so many miles traveled, would not fall prey to any such scheme.

All the people we saw looked to be of English stock: well dressed, with the men in long coats, some in breeches and others in long trousers, the women in wide skirts tiered in ruffles and supported by hoops beneath. In our country clothing, with only layers of petticoats to sustain our skirts, I felt that we looked like poor relations or even servants.

Disappointed, we retraced our steps to the ladies' boarding-house. The calls of birds overhead, which I imagined might be seagulls, drew me further along toward the station where we'd first arrived. Caroline did not object, though I noticed she pulled herself up to seem more formal, and I did likewise. We reached the station house, where freight cars lined up, waiting for a locomotive. Beyond it I saw a mighty bridge across a river, and cautiously, we approached.

The river proved to be filled with ships, a few in motion, most of them moored in some way. And beyond them—I pointed, and Caroline nodded enthusiastically. The sharp scent of salt, old fish, and tarred rope declared the body of water before us to be some part of the mighty ocean that our ancestors once crossed, to become settlers. I laughed in delight.

Shouts from a massive ship slowly gliding ocean-ward drew my attention, and Caroline's gaze followed mine. A smaller boat, attached to the larger by a pair of ropes, hung empty, and a man waving a cudgel climbed more ropes dangling down the side of the ship. "Halt! I have papers of arrest for that fugitive!" he shouted.

I gripped Caroline's arm, and she urged me to explain. I did my best, and we watched in horror as a tussle developed on the wooden deck of the ship: the man who'd climbed the side insisted his papers entitled him to take possession of a black-skinned man in sailor's attire, whose mates appeared to be shielding him.

The interloper began to lay about with his cudgel, making his way toward the Negro, who backed up toward a roofed structure at the center of the desk. A whistle blew sharply several times, from up in the masts of the ship.

Anger surged in the crowd on the deck, and watching the crowd, we could see the emotion heat and focus. Again the whistle blew, and I sensed a pattern to it. The mob on the deck halted in place, and then, all at once, a pair of sailors lifted the invader and tossed him overboard.

I screamed despite my best intent. "He'll drown!"

But, in fact, he rose to the cluttered surface of the water and flung himself back into his small vessel. Even as we witnessed it, the men on the ship cut loose the ropes that held the smaller boat and raised two more wide sails, which caught the wind at once.

For a moment I thought the Negro on the deck looked right at Caroline and me; perhaps he did. But a moment later, he swarmed up a mast and vanished from sight among the tangle of ropes and canvas dangling and changing shape there.

My hands were clenched so tightly on Caroline's that the blood had left them, and the cold wind bit at them. I released my grip and fumbled to shape letters. With my hands, I asked Caroline: *Slave? Fugitive?*

She shrugged her lack of knowledge. *Safe,* she signaled back to me.

For now, I thought. And in that moment, our walk in this dangerous city seemed foolish to me. Our purpose must be to assist Isaiah and Walter to reach the safety of Vermont.

What might my own purpose be, beyond that? A schoolhouse in Barnet seemed a cowardly retreat from the moral wrongs of our time.

I needed to talk with Solomon.

CHAPTER 20

The night's rest, the hurry to the morning train, even the mingling with people on the train, who ranged from two Irish families to a tall man in a furred cap—whom I suspected might be one of those Russian Jews the landlady had mentioned—nothing adequately distracted me from the urge to reach Manchester, New Hampshire, and rejoin my brothers, Solomon, and Isaiah and Walter. Would they be there? Were they safe? I scolded myself—I should have found a way to ride with them, put my skills to use deflecting any unwanted attention.

My mother insisted, of course, on learning what we'd witnessed on our "walk" in the city. I could barely fill in the details; I felt so unsettled. She only nodded and then let me sit with my thoughts and concerns, while she and Caroline sorted through hat ribbons and other notions, smoothing and winding them to prevent damage in their transit.

Absentmindedly, I gazed at the others around me and noticed that the poorest people on the train had huddled most closely to the stoves at either end. Their clothing must not be as warm, I thought, as the garments worn by the group sitting together at about the center of the car. Thick fur coats, a bearskin rug, baskets of provisions. And fur muffs for each of the ladies. Such differences.

One of the group not garbed quite as ostentatiously—her cloak was thick and well made, but it had no fur even as trim, and she used no muff—looked up and met my gaze. I flushed, embarassed to have been found staring. But she smiled and stood, as though she'd been waiting for a reason to stretch and walk. Holding to whatever she could in the jolting car, she wove her way toward us and perched next to Caroline, reaching a slender hand to touch a lush, purple velvet ribbon that Caroline was winding neatly. "So lovely," she said pleasantly. "Boston is the best place for trimmings, I believe. I should have looked for some while I visited."

Caroline looked quickly back and forth between the stranger and my mother. My mother picked up the conversation: "The milliners were so welcoming," she confirmed. "We don't have anything quite this fine in northern Vermont, and our shops lag a bit behind on the styles. My husband doesn't notice much, but I do appreciate a bit of style."

"Mine also, in Maine," the lady replied. "I'm sorry, I should have introduced myself. My name is Harriet. Harriet Stowe."

"Abigail Sanborn," my mother said, nodding. "Are you traveling with family?"

"Friends this time," Mrs. Stowe replied. "They'll see me safely back. And," she held a hand politely to Caroline, "I'm Mrs. Stowe, my dear. Will you tell me your name?"

This time Caroline looked to me, and I came over to take part. "This is my friend Caroline Clark," I told the lady. "And my name is Alice Sanborn."

Caroline, now following the conversation a bit better, gestured, and I translated: "She says your shoes are beautifully made, Mrs. Stowe. She wonders whether they are also from Boston, or from a cobbler in your home town?"

"Ah, what a good eye your friend has," Mrs. Stowe answered. "These were made in Hartford, Connecticut, where I lived before I married."

A smile blossomed on Caroline's face, and she slid one of her feet out from under her skirts, setting her own shoe next to

Mrs. Stowe's. There were differences, but the workmanship clearly matched. The lady showed her delight and, looking directly into Caroline's face, said slowly, "So you have lived in Hartford also, my dear?"

Eagerly, Caroline agreed and again relied on me to interpret a quick series of gestures.

"She says the cobbler is old now but still makes the best shoes in Hartford."

Everyone laughed, especially because Caroline showed such pleasure. Now Mrs. Stowe began a slow and tactful set of questions, curious about the gestures Caroline used and how I knew what she was saying. I explained as best I could, and Caroline pulled out her "alphabet" card to show the finger signs. Our new acquaintance devoured each bit of information, exclaiming over it. "I must write to this place," she declared. "I can tell there are stories to be written about its teachers and students. I hope to shape some pieces for the women's magazines, and this may be a perfect topic."

Oh! She was an author! I asked whether she also wrote books. Her eyes sparkled with mischief. "One or two," she admitted but refused to say more, turning the topic back to the school in Hartford, and then to our destination in Vermont.

"But first," I said without much thought, "we will add the other half of our party in Manchester, when they meet the train there."

"Well then," Mrs. Stowe teased, "you'd best prepare, for I believe the train is slowing for the station even now."

She rose and rejoined her own group, and they gathered their parcels, clearly changing trains to the Maine route. They lingered outside on the platform, as no other trains stood in the station. I stood in the doorway, searching the boardwalks, anxious that Charles and John and the others hadn't yet appeared. My mother and Caroline remained in their seats, intent,

161

as I was, on who might arrive.

A rattle of the wheels back and forth and a puff of smoke from the locomotive suggested we'd soon be leaving the station. Where were my brothers? And Solomon? I stepped up into the train car, still facing the platform, searching for any arriving vehicle. Panic filled my chest.

Just as the train wheels trembled and began to turn forward, a group of men leapt out of a carriage near the road and ran toward us. Four, five . . . yes, it was our men! I called out, "Hurry!" And they accelerated, racing to catch up. Each made the jump into the moving train, but the last one to board, Walter, dropped his bundle as he grabbed for the iron bar to pull himself upward.

Mrs. Stowe darted forward, quick as a young girl, and pitched the bundle into the railroad car, where Walter caught it. "Take good care of each other," she called, "fare well, and guard your freedom!"

Solomon tensed, staring back as we pulled out of the station. "Who was that woman?" he demanded. "Do you know her?"

I interceded, pressing my hands down in a calming gesture. "Just a woman we met this morning," I said. "A Mrs. Stowe, from Maine. A writer."

To my astonishment, Solomon burst into laughter and clapped all the other men on their shoulders. "There's a blessing for you if you like, fellows," he chuckled. "Walter, Isaiah, I dare say you're the first Negroes to reach the free lands of northern New England with a welcome from the woman who's enflamed the passion of Abolition far beyond what Seward or even Daniel Webster himself could have done if he'd been so inclined."

My mother seemed all at once to catch what Solomon meant and clapped her hands to her face. "And we talked about hats and shoes with her," she gasped, half laughing, half shocked.

Caroline and I looked back and forth, still lost. At last my brother Charles stopped laughing for long enough to explain.

"Alice," he announced solemnly, "you've just ridden the rails with the author Harriet Beecher Stowe herself. God bless us all."

I took a long moment to explain to Caroline, whereupon she and I threw our arms around each other and gasped with amazement and merriment. When we finally let go of each other, I turned to look at Solomon. He in turn was watching Isaiah and Walter, who sat side by side, mufflers wrapped around their necks, dark eyes studying the landscape and the wintry mountain peaks with their white, icy summits. Solomon's face had settled to its usual determined look, one that perceived the hardships ahead and saw no easy way around them. For a long moment, I felt I knew his thoughts and hoped that he knew mine. We must, we must, find time to talk.

Oh folly. Oh heart, so readily misled. But still unwounded. I had five more weeks to dream of happy endings.

CHAPTER 21

Railroad passenger cars do not make conversation simple or easy. Most pertinently, they fail to allow conversation between a young woman such as myself, and a man such as Solomon.

In my mother's hands, gleaming knitting needles tapped endlessly as she added inches to a stocking in progress. Caroline struggled to maintain a small book on her lap, and, when I peeked over her shoulder, I realized it was a psalter. Not of interest to me at that moment. If only I had brought a copy of Mrs. Stowe's book with me—what an adventure it would be to again read the chapter of *Uncle Tom's Cabin,* after meeting the very woman who'd written such a powerful treatise.

Though I would have liked to at least become acquainted with the men we were accompanying—Isaiah and Walter—their fixed attention to the route of the railroad and the way they avoided meeting my inquiring gaze did not encourage me to cross the boundaries in the car. For there were clearly boundaries! Even in the small clusters that represented family groups, men perched separately from women.

Solomon, his eyes closed, sat just beyond Walter and Isaiah. And then my older brothers, so strange to my eyes—bulky-shouldered with large, calloused hands and long coats patched with both wool and leather. They slept as though any moment of rest should be used that way, snoring and snorting. A harsh jolt of the wheels tilted Charles, who clung to the end of a bend, and he jerked awake for a moment, took a breath, looked around. He tipped me a sleepy wink and smile and promptly resumed his nap.

Judging by his silence, Solomon wasn't actually asleep. No snoring. No sudden capsizing sideways, though he maintained the other end of the same bench.

My gaze at last must have affected him, for he lifted his face and opened his brown eyes for just a moment and brushed back the dangling lock of hair, a habit I'd often seen. Clean shaven, his lips showed a hint of a smile, but he raised a hand and pressed a quieting finger to them. Then he closed his eyes and once again pretended to sleep. Or so it seemed to me.

How aggravating! I needed to talk with him about my new perceptions, those from seeing the fugitive escaping pursuit on the Boston ship, and my sense that I must, truly must, commit myself to action as an Abolitionist myself. Being Sarah's forever friend did not suffice. I wanted a more potent, active role.

My teeth ground together, and my back began to ache. My own anger, I realized, could thus cripple me. Well then, let me sort through other options. Surely Solomon must be headed to St. Johnsbury once more. Perhaps I could visit Sarah's friend Miss Farrow there, and ask her to help me find a role of my own among those taking steps toward the end of slavery. And Almyra, though I hated to admit it, might have connections I could use. Woman to woman, conversation appeared simpler. Although this sense of being herded to a female side of life, and of railroad cars, also annoyed me.

I stood up, clutching the back of a bench to hold my balance. My mother looked at me. I mimed a stiffness of body, and she nodded. Cautiously, I eased my way along the row of seated passengers, making a small show of discomfort.

The train twitched up and then down, and I nearly tumbled onto Charles's lap. He woke instantly, assisted me to my balance again, and said quietly, "Best to ride sitting down if you can, Alice. Stand when we're at the next station instead." He drew out a pocket watch on a long chain and estimated, "Another half hour to White River Junction."

I nodded and turned. Charles rose and, with an arm under mine, walked me back to my seat.

My mother looked up at my brother, smiling. "It's only a five-minute stop at White River Junction," she said. "Then we'll all be headed the rest of the way north, on Mr. Gilman's line of rail."

"You ladies and John will," Charles corrected. "Solomon and I will visit Woodstock, as we escort our friends." He nodded to the two unspeaking dark-skinned men, who now were listening closely. "We want to meet some people there. Then Isaiah and Walter will ride further."

Startled and not happy with this change of plans, my mother added to the complications: "You know that our Sarah is there with her brother?"

"Yes, Solomon mentioned it, and that you wanted to bring her north with you. But if you haven't yet heard from her that she's ready, you must not leave the train at this point. I'll talk with her and provide that she may return to North Upton with me, if her visit in Woodstock is complete. And if not, I'll at least be able to let you know how she is fixed." He paused and patted our mother's arm. "My business there is important. And it will only delay me another two days, at worst. Tell Papa I'll be there soon."

The slowing of the train and its clanging bell signaled our approach to White River Junction. On impulse, I stuffed my few loose belongings into my valise and said, "I could go with you, Charles. And then keep Sarah company and ride the train north with her."

Charles shook his head. "Let me solve that, Alice. Go with Mama, and see our neighbor Caroline safely back, too." He gave a half bow in her direction, and I realized she'd been intently watching him speak. She nodded, as if she grasped the point of the words. Charles added, "Her presence with you was exactly the needed distraction in Manchester. When our men boarded, everyone's curiosity remained fixed on Caroline, and then on this happy, laughing group. Well done, ladies."

He tipped a smile to each of us, then stepped quickly back to his seat to pick up a small bundle and press a larger one, clearly heavy, close to John, who casually looped a bit of rope through its grip and snugged it to his own pack.

The brakeman raced through our car, setting the brakes on the wheels, then sped to the next one to do the same, and, with much screeching and clatter, we came to a halt at the busy station platform. The four men—Charles, Walter, Isaiah, and Solomon—leapt for the platform, while a knot of Irish workers boarded at the far end of the car.

A rustle in my lap betrayed a crumpled scrap of paper that must have landed as the men swept past. I folded it quickly and hid it in my sleeve. Caroline and my mother, fixed on the departing men, hadn't noticed. But by the knowing glance he gave me, I suspected my brother John, sleepy though he appeared, knew quite well that Solomon had just given me a note.

Between Norwich and Pompanoosuc, I maneuvered myself to hide the message and drew it out to parse. It had only a few words: "Meet me at Miss Farrow's a week from Friday if you can. Bring your reports, if you please. S."

Well! How much like a man, to ignore the important matters and refer only to the reports on the women's reading group of North Upton. I stuffed the scrap back up my sleeve and seethed, teeth gritted together, eyes shut to hide my irritation.

Caroline tapped my shoulder and signed a question: *In pain? Toothache?*

"No," I answered, shaking my head and forcing a smile. "Just tired." But I didn't think she believed me; well, of course, she must have seen me mooning over Solomon and would conclude that he'd ignored me.

My pride objected. I pulled myself together, slid closer to her, and told her, in our strange mix of signal and letter sign and facial emotion, something of Sarah's story, and Franklin's. John watched from his bench, awake but unmoving; my mother continued her knitting, and every few minutes the train stopped again to take on a passenger or some mail or release a few more people into the brisk November afternoon.

When the train reached Wells River, the last major stop before St. Johnsbury, a man leaving the car offered his newspaper to John. He accepted and moved a little closer to us to comment aloud on the news of the week. "I see Mrs. Nichols had her evening before the legislature, telling them a woman needed to own her property with title, not just through her husband. I like her approach, a very motherly sort. But I see the Vermont papers haven't given all of the details. A New York paper last week printed in addition her proposal that women be able to vote in school meetings."

My mother gave a most unladylike snort of disagreement. "Unpleasant and often barbaric, those meetings. None of the women I know would want to be there."

"What about the ones you know, Alice?" John's sparkling eyes made it clear he was teasing.

I groaned. "Almyra, the minister's niece, I imagine she'd want a say. She's all for Temperance, too, as well as Abolition, of course."

"Of course," John chuckled. "Sounds like a fireball. Don't you agree with her?"

I said stiffly, "Of course Abolition is a moral necessity. And Temperance is already under way. I believe our legislature in Vermont holds its balloting tomorrow on a new set of laws to better enforce sobriety. But from what I've heard, voting in meetings is a coarse and unwomanly process."

"Ah, but if women were there to cast their ballots also, perhaps the tone might alter," John pointed out. "I can see we'll have much to discuss at the supper table, little sister."

My mother began to list her supper preparations aloud and to tell me which parts I should help with. I nodded without much attention and told Caroline what John had said. She looked quite surprised and told me that at her school, women always took part in balloting and planning the school's direction. Teachers, she said, were usually very wise. And eager to guide both the students and an overall view of education.

At the far end of the railroad car, a few Irishmen passed a flask back and forth, becoming more noisy by the mile. I cut into my mother's litany of tasks to ask, "Do you think they work for Mr. Gilman?"

"Of course," she said, barely glancing toward the rowdy group. "Probably in the millworks. But he won't thank them for showing up inebriated. They may even be fined."

How were the Clarks managing at their inn, with so much pressure from law and state and town to forsake the traffic in intoxicating beverages? Was hard cider enough to keep their regular customers coming to what once was a bustling tavern? I had no regrets about Temperance—clearly, men who spent their pay on inebriation harmed their families in many ways—but it must terribly complicate the business of keeping an inn.

Perhaps this was prescient on my part. The remainder of our journey passed uneventfully, with my father meeting us at the station and a mostly silent ride home. I could see the powerful bond that my father and John shared, and my own fatigue may have accentuated a rub of that for me, so accustomed to being the center of the household these days. Even so, I realized that Caroline, working so hard to grasp the conversations and changes around her, must be at least as tired as I was, and we snuggled together under the blankets on the back bench of the sleigh, only occasionally awake, while my mother slipped into an easy nap.

The next day, Tuesday, I surprised Almyra by returning to my studies at the schoolhouse, while declining to describe the Boston trip in detail. I said only, "You must come see the ribbons and cloth we brought back, perhaps after the women's meeting on Saturday." If she thought I was guarding secrets, so much the better; she would not press for them in the schoolroom.

It was the Wednesday newspapers that ignited a fury in our village—one I might have predicted, had I followed my thoughts further. But, I confess, my mind was mostly on when Sarah and my brother Charles would return, and on seeing Solomon again soon, and attending another women's meeting first, which would provide material for a fresh report for him. And, of course, though I hadn't said much about it, word circulated quickly from Caroline's description of the trip to her mother, Mrs. Clark: We had met Mrs. Harriet Beecher Stowe herself! What could be more exciting, and impressive, than that?

CHAPTER 22

The return of my older brothers had involved so much tension and crisis, with the escort of Walter and Isaiah, that I'd forgotten to ask what the village neighbors wanted most to know: Had my brothers' years in the gold fields of California made them rich men?

Anyone looking at John in his first days home in North Upton would doubt it. His outer clothing, although made of heavy and well-tanned leather, bore stains and signs of hard work that rubbed the leather shiny in places. His overly large winter beard clearly disturbed my mother, who offered twice to trim it with her sewing scissors. Although I could see him smile from time to time, the sun-browned skin around his eyes and the creases in it reflected time laboring outdoors, and he rarely spoke, except to praise our mother's ample meals. Monday and Tuesday evenings, he wasn't home until late, though I half woke each evening at the sounds of his horse returning to the barn. He slept in his old bed in the "boys' room" over the parlor, rising early to help Papa in the barn and then leaving for all-day absence with Ely, our younger horse. Tuesday he took the small sleigh; Monday, I'd noticed, he simply rode.

Wednesday at last he broke the pattern: After the sheep were fed and examined for any problems, he accompanied our father back into the house for a full breakfast. My mother must have known, or hoped, for she pulled fresh biscuits out of the oven and nodded toward a pan of ham slices at the back of the stove.

"Plates and forks, Alice," she ordered crisply, while also moving a dish of butter and jar of blackberry preserves to the table.

The air of an intentional gathering struck me, and I made a quick decision to be late to the schoolroom today. Or perhaps not attend at all. I bit back my questions until all plates were filled, the four of us seated and forks in our hands.

I began with a simple query: "Do you suppose Charles might arrive on the stage today?"

My father shook his head and forked a second slice of ham onto his biscuit. "There's no sense in riding the stages when the train is so much quicker. I'm expecting them Saturday, if all goes well."

"Why so long?" A sideways look from my mother warned me I shouldn't question this, but I persisted. "You must have heard something from him, Papa. Yes?"

"No," my brother John cut in. "I did, though. At the telegraph office yesterday. In St. Johnsbury."

Ah. That explained, in part, why he'd been gone all day. I took a bite of my own meal, aware that if I asked in the wrong way, the tension among my family members would simply result in "you're not old enough to know," which I could already feel coming. But I tried anyway. "So Walter and Isaiah, they'll be settled by then?"

John pushed back his chair and said to my father, "She always asks questions, does she?"

With a half smile, my father said, "That's how she took off for Canada with Jerushah and Sarah while you were gone. Asks questions but sometimes not quite enough. Makes her own conclusions and takes action."

John choked back a laugh. "Wonder where she got that from." And, while my parents shared a look of both exasperation and fondness, John finally turned in his seat and faced me directly. "Guess I'd better tell you everything, then, to keep your decisions on the level. But I'm not much of a talker these days. So you listen, and I'll tell it all to you once. Only once. Agreed?"

"Oh, yes!" I abandoned my breakfast, clutched my cup of hot tea, and gazed directly at my brother. "I want to know everything!"

"Not enough time for everything," he pointed out. "Here are the main points. Charles and I—You don't know about the rough life of mining, and you don't need to. Enough to say that Charles and I found our way to the gold fields, discovered how uncertain the return was for most of the miners, and turned our skills to supplies instead. Sifter frames, shovels, sacks, tins, even sometimes wagons. For every miner making a thousand dollars, we made near a hundred ourselves. We did," he concluded with emphasis, "very well indeed. Well enough to pay attention to how many fellows were robbed before they'd even left California, or reached home. So."

He paused to swallow more tea and take another bite of biscuit. "Mama, you'd be a wealthy woman out there, with the way you turn flour and lard to exceptional sustenance. So, Alice, Charles and I wrote to Mr. Gilman, being as he was the only man of wealth we knew well enough to ask. And he in turn connected us to a legislator in Washington, Mr. Thaddeus Stevens."

"Wait! I know him! I mean, I know of him. He was the one, from Pennsylvania, who helped Sarah come north with Miss Farrow. Born in Upton Center, too; people in Upton Center still talk about him, and his mother still lives in Peacham," I finished proudly.

John nodded his approval. "Good. Yes, that's the fellow. He and Mr. Gilman are both railroad men, you see. And he knows the men in California who are planning the railroads there." He turned to our father. "Mr. Stevens says the way the North and South are fighting, the commerce of a railroad across the country may be the only way to hold them together, for the sake of prosperity."

My father snorted. "He's not paying attention to the chaos in Illinois, then, is he? And he didn't stop the Compromise two years back. The way he and his kind are letting slavery leak into the Territories is a sin. Almighty God above knows it."

All of us nodded this time. John picked up his story again. "So Charles and I, we're more interested in an investment for the long term. And we figure where Mr. Gilman and Mr. Stevens put their investment is where we should place ours. So," he ended abruptly, "we sank our profits into the railroad that's forming out West and took ship for home to settle back to a productive life here. We always meant to come back, you see."

I was awestruck. "You and Charles put all your earnings into a railroad that isn't built yet?"

John smiled through his beard. "Sharp question. No, we kept a portion to bring home and invest right here, in the family farm. We always meant to," he repeated.

"So then, when you went to board the ship," I prompted him, "you said you saw the black men all chained and shackled, being transported to the Slave Power in the South."

My father looked down at his hands, clearly disturbed. My mother patted John's shoulder. She spoke softly. "You did the right thing."

"What? What do you mean, Mama?"

My mother looked at John, who shrugged, and she turned back to me: "Before your brothers left California, they went to see John Bigler, the new governor of the state. Mr. Bigler already took action to restrict Chinese from work there and to tax the ones who do work. But California this spring enacted her own fugitive slave act, even more punitive than the federal one. Mr. Bigler went along with it. So your brothers went to speak the truth to him: that such support of slavery, especially in that

Free Soil state, made a mockery of justice." She hesitated, then finished: "Your brothers took a beating for such arrogance, yet Providence sent to them two Free Black men they'd done business with. The men hauled them out of danger and took them away to recover."

I whispered, "Isaiah. Walter." Now it all made sense. "They are miners, you said?"

"Not quite."

I could see John come close to saying that I wouldn't understand, and I scowled at him. "You said you would explain."

He sighed. "Alice, this can't be discussed beyond our kitchen, and you're not to address it with Solomon, even. This is business, and there's significant money at risk. My money, and Charles's."

I leaned forward, agreeing eagerly, wanting to know all of it.

"Walter carries out assays of metals in ore. Isaiah maps the veins of metal. They've done well in California for the larger mining companies. But they have a better offer—here in Vermont."

"Gold in Vermont!" I could scarcely believe it. "They've come to mine gold here?"

"Not at all." John leaned close, as though there could be listening ears even in our kitchen. "Copper. Vermont has copper, the railroads and telegraph companies need it, and a sizable mine will develop within two years, not far from White River Junction. And that, little nosy sister, is where Charles and I have invested much of what we brought home to Vermont, after all." He looked sideways and added, "Papa said he didn't need it here yet, so we thought we'd double it once or twice before bringing it back to him."

We all laughed, with my father laughing the most of all. "Providence moves in strange ways," he announced.

John capped this with a pleased smile: "And, with Walter and

Isaiah on the site . . . well, that leaves Charles and me free to go a-roaming."

Which meant I had one more question, considering I would soon have to face the inquisitive minds of the village, at Saturday's women's meeting if not sooner. "So, you aren't a rich man for the moment, John? And neither is Charles? What will you do?"

"Ah. There you have it, little sister. What should we do?" He'd phrased it just differently enough for me to realize this was the discussion of the moment, the reason he'd come to sit with our parents at the table instead of heading out to whatever business he had to do in town again.

My mother answered first. "You should do what's right," she said simply.

This prompted another snort from my father, but John answered quietly. "That's what Charles and I believe. And from what we've seen, that means we're headed to the Territories, first to Uncle Martin in Illinois or Kansas, and then to sink what money we have left—yes, Alice, we kept a bit—into a homestead and a plow out there. A man who owns land is more than just a man. He's a vote."

"No!" I hadn't meant to wail. But these two brothers had only just come home, and we hadn't yet had a proper family dinner with William and Helen, or even all gone to church together. "You can't go away again!"

"It's what we should do," John repeated gently. "The time's coming, Alice. Slavery and the greed of the cotton plantations have lit a blaze that could destroy the Union and will surely damn us before God if we take no action. Charles and I, we're action men. We'll fight fire with fire. That is, we'll head west," he pronounced with an apologetic glance at my mother, "ten days after Charles gets back here. He'll not be bringing your friend back with him, though," he added. "It appears young

Sarah will stay a while yet. Seems between them, Woodstock and Hartland have quite a few Africans settling."

The scrape of my father's chair as he pushed back from the table signaled the end of the meal—one I'd never have guessed would end this way. I scrubbed a hand against my eyes, took a deep breath, and chose to follow the example of my mother, who rose without complaint and lifted the plates from the table.

She said to John, "Be sure to bring me all your mending so I can make sure your socks and such are fit for the journey."

What could I add? I fumbled and said at last, "I'm doing something here, in the village. Solomon asked me to help. Mama and me, that is."

John's massive left hand lifted to brush my chin affectionately. "I know you are, chickadee," he said quietly. "We men who take the action can do so, because of the women who keep the home fires lit for us." He looked around the room and said, "I'm off to Upton Center, just a short ride this afternoon. I'll be in the barn if you need me. Might be I'll have to take Old Sam this time and give Ely a break."

My father nodded and picked up a piece of harness to repair as he settled closer to the stove. Mama opened her dough box to check the rising bread, and I tried to decide what to do next. And how I felt.

Losing my brothers so soon after they'd finally come home: I felt bereft. But also darkly sure that they were right in their choice.

Was I right in mine? Oh, if only Solomon were here to assure me that he needed me and the home fires I could provide.

A strange small thought arrived as I packed my school papers for a mid-morning trek to the schoolhouse. I wondered, thinking of Almyra, who'd surely want to know what had delayed my arrival: Would Almyra keep the home fires lit for someone? Or was she going to race into the battle for Abolition, Temperance, and votes for women, with all her city brashness and air of certainty?

I didn't like the way that made me feel. Yet I had no further time to consider it, for a door slammed and boots thudded into our house, with Mr. Clark's agitated voice shouting, "Ephraim! By God, Ephraim! Look what they've gone and done!"

He waved a telegram in front of my father, and I thought it must be news of a death in his family—another death (oh, Jerushah)—for there were tears on his reddened cheeks, and his voice cracked with pain. Then he roared again, and I realized I'd misunderstood: not pain, but anger. Rage, even. "Ninety-one votes to ninety. All the state newspapers will have the news tomorrow. What use is Gilman as governor, if he can't save us from these idiots in the legislature? Ephraim! What's to be done!"

My father finally laid hold of the paper and parsed the broken phrases on it. "It's the Maine bill," he said grimly. "No traffic in intoxicating liquors, and no licenses. But it won't take effect until next March at the soonest. There's to be a roll call on whether March or November of next year."

Mr. Clark seized a chair and thumped it on the floor. My mother pointedly left the room, and I realized I should do the same. But, I wanted to know more, so I tiptoed partway up the stairs toward my chamber and listened, leaning against the wooden wall.

"Exception for wine for the Lord's supper," my father continued. "You know it doesn't ban cider, the hard cider most of the village drinks."

"Are you sure?"

"Positive. I've read the Maine bill through over and over, and the version for New Hampshire. Beer, liquor, anything with added sugar, so all of the liquors, even apple whiskey. But not cider."

A silence. Then the thud of a body dropping onto a chair. "Ephraim, I can't keep the tavern afloat on only cider. People will make their own liquor if they have to. Can you imagine Mo Cook, struck sober? Or half the travelers for that matter. They won't even pass through here. They'll go to St. Johnsbury, where someone will know someone who makes their own. You know that. I can't endure full-on Temperance and keep an inn. Ephraim, what can I do?"

I heard my father settle likewise into a chair. He sighed. At last he said, "I believe I'll be forgetting there was ever a tunnel between your house and mine. In fact, I'll make sure the door at this end vanishes into history. If you need to place some item in the other end of the tunnel—you'll place it, and I won't know about it."

"You'd do that for me?"

"Only," my father's voice grew deep and strong, "only if the courts don't take the law to be against the Constitution before March. Courage, man. With God, all things are possible. And you do have the governor on your side, I'm convinced."

Scuffles and slapped shoulders and boots thumping—I knew Mr. Clark had left, and I waited a moment for my mother to be the first to return to the room. Then I crept down the stairs, hesitating before showing myself. Yet that was not quite honest. So I stepped forward into the room and met my mother's gaze.

"They fit together," she said matter-of-factly. "Temperance and Abolition. And, with each, there will be losses as well as gains. But we know what's right."

A grunt from my father could have meant either yes or no—I wasn't sure, and, considering what he'd just offered to do for his neighbor, I didn't want to push for an answer. I didn't think Mr. Clark's tavern contributed to impoverishment of families, to husbands beating their wives and children, to men unable to work for their living. But, who could deny the role of liquor in all that?

I only knew I carried the death of Mr. Clark's daughter Jerushah always on my shoulders and in my heart. I would not want to harm him further, in any way. How hard it was to see the right thing to do, after all.

My father cleared his throat. "The post must have come. I'll go to the store."

"And I'm off to the school," I confirmed. To study for my teaching certificate would be so much easier than to think about the confusions in my home.

CHAPTER 23

Saturday morning dawned clear and cold, but with a northwest wind that suggested the weather would soon shift. I spent the morning inside, and at an hour past noon I stepped into the yard to taste the air. If it didn't snow too heavily, my other brother, William, and his wife, Helen, would come for Sunday dinner. Helen's continued uncertain health and dark moods often kept them home, but if they didn't attend church services soon, they'd face a letter of rebuke from the congregation. There had barely been time for me to think about them, let alone pay a visit. But I should.

John finished hitching Ely to the larger sleigh. "You're sure you don't want to come to the station with me?" he teased. "Wouldn't you rather take a nice cold ride for an hour or so and wait around for a train that might run hours behind, instead of spending time indoors over some musty old book with a bunch of girls and gossips?"

I giggled. "You're not to say that about them, John. Besides, it's Mrs. Stowe's book, *Uncle Tom's Cabin,* we're reading together. That's hardly musty!"

Pretending to whisper across the yard, John commented, "But very, very Christian. You'll think you've started your Sabbath a day early!"

"Go away," I laughed. "Fetch Charles promptly, and I might forgive you."

I skipped back inside to finish packing a tin of molasses cookies to bring to the gathering. My mother looked up from a newspaper spread across the table. "Mr. Clark was right," she told me. "The law passed on Tuesday is sure to hurt his trade and cost him profit. Perhaps he'll consider adding some other items. I wonder whether Mrs. Clark might offer meat pies for the public. Or something like it. And look here." She pointed to a story on an inner page. "News from California of an earthquake so enormous, it drained a lake by San Francisco. The waters ran out, clear to the sea." She shuddered. "Thank heaven your brothers aren't out there now. I'd be worried sick."

"Won't you worry when they go to the Territories, Mama? Life out there sounds so rough and raw still."

"Nonsense. You've only to read the paper to see how the churches and schools are thriving there. Why, the railroad even serves Chicago and has for years. I dare say there are more trains per day than in St. Johnsbury. Letters from Charles and John will reach here in days, instead of weeks or months. I have no doubt." She turned to the final page, running a finger down the text to speed up her reading. "Look, there is even mention of a school for the deaf in Illinois, in Jacksonville. We'll have to show this to Caroline this evening. Fetch your shawl and cloak, Alice, and mine also, if you please. I'll be ready to walk with you in a moment."

Somehow I doubted the Territories were as well served as the thriving city of Chicago. More to the point, the issue of slavery in the Territories compelled each moral individual to take a stand, did it not? Oh dear. I mustn't start an internal discussion of such issues. Wait for supper, when there would be ample voices and minds to reflect on the news of the day and the rapid changes west of Chicago. Thirty-one states in the Union now with California added, and a wild undeveloped land of possible abundance in between.

How strange to feel as though I knew more than Mama about

something. But perhaps I was more ready to see this new world than she could be. We donned our shawls and cloaks and started down the track toward the rolled road, slipping a bit in the ruts left by the sleigh runners. My mother's boots might have been less secure than mine, but we linked arms and managed.

As we reached the road, we had full sight of the Clark family inn and its tavern, with the rutted route to the stables around the side. Two people stood there talking, and it took me a moment to realize who they were: Matthew Clark, not working at the Gilman Mill today, and Almyra. I called out hello to them, and Matthew waved cheerfully, then headed toward the stables. Almyra tugged her cloak tighter around her as she hurried to meet my mother and me.

"I was just out this way and thought I might join you on your way to the meeting," she announced cheerfully. "Caroline and her mother have already walked ahead. Alice, you said you'd tell me all about your Boston trip, but you've been so busy. I'm thirsty for excitement from the city. And you know, if you had told me where you were going, I could have sent a parcel to my mother with you."

Instantly, guilt struck me. I'd been thoughtless, hadn't I? "I'm so sorry, Almyra. There was so little time to think, the errand came up all at once. You must really miss your mother, too. Will she come here to visit you soon, or might you ride the train to Boston yourself at Christmas? Mother and I were impressed with how quick and simple it was, directly from St. Johnsbury."

My mother, hearing that mention, gave a nod and said, "I believe I'll walk up ahead, girls; I'd like to catch Mrs. Clark and Caroline." On the rolled road, her worn boots didn't seem to disadvantage her, so I released her arm and looked to Almyra for an answer to my questions.

To my surprise, Almyra shrugged. Her eyes twinkled, a

mischievous smile peeping out of her shawl, and I realized I must be missing something. But she only said, "My mother's so busy, you know. She is physically frail, but she has enormous strength of purpose. With my father in Philadelphia, she is practically seeing to all the details of his church. She even instructs the supplied pastor of the month in making calls on the sick and such. And I," she giggled, "I am really quite happy to be here in North Upton."

Oh, no. Now I realized what that look meant. Almyra felt infatuated—no surprise, considering she was on the verge of young womanhood. But who . . . Oh no, oh no, not Matthew! That would be impossible. He was nearly twenty, and so serious, especially since Jerushah's death. She'd been his closest sister. Besides, if he wanted another sister, well, Caroline had come home; shouldn't he be getting to know her better? How annoying of Almyra to intervene at such a moment.

My thoughts must have crossed my face too clearly, for Almyra burst out laughing. "You're not the only young lady in North Upton who feels alive and wants to share it," she pointed out. "What did you think I'd do here, just learn my lessons and sew a fine seam? Alice, you've been country-bred for way too long. Let's get to the women's meeting, at least there's plenty of merriment there, and it's too cold to stand outside swapping stories. Except," she added as we both sped up toward the far end of the village, "I do want to hear about your Solomon, and I daresay you won't talk about that with the ladies' gathering. You must have seen him in Boston. Is he coming to North Upton soon? Everyone talks about him, and I'm longing to meet him in person."

"He's not quite 'my' Solomon," I cautioned. "He helped Jerushah and Sarah and me, but he's really a friend of my brother William, and Jerushah's brother Matthew."

"Ah, but Matthew says he's a friend of yours," Almyra

responded knowingly. "He says you're the one Solomon really comes to see now, despite doing business nearby."

Well! It would be nice if Solomon could say that to me, outright, instead of this awkward way of hearing Almyra say that Matthew said that Solomon—oh, what folly! With a shake of my head, I came back to myself and said crisply, "That's idle gossip, Almyra, and hasn't much to recommend it. What do you hear from your father?"

Now she turned grave and pulled down her shawl to speak more clearly and quietly. "He is in despair over the presidential election. Franklin Pierce, that dreadful doughboy. It's clear the cause of Abolition will not prosper in his hands. Father asked me whether Mother and I might visit Mrs. Pierce together, but of course the distance to Concord, in New Hampshire, is not easily crossed on the train from St. Johnsbury. I declined. Mother is sending one of the deacons there, however, to see what can be done. You know Mrs. Pierce tends to hysteria, and those children . . . oh, my."

I gaped. At Almyra's young age, how did she know such things about a president and his family? I pulled myself together and asked, "Has your family been long acquainted with the Pierce family? I would not have guessed."

"Not deeply," Almyra admitted, "but Mrs. Pierce is so strongly committed to the Temperance cause that she has written to my father and endeavored to support his work in Boston and beyond."

It seemed she meant financial support, by the way she pursed her lips and cocked her head to one side. I asked the only thing I could think of: "If Mrs. Pierce is so strongly in favor of Temperance, how can her husband not be strong for Abolition?"

"Promises made," Almyra said grimly, and in my opinion with far too much of an air of sophistication. "My father says Senator King of Alabama tipped the balance to have Mr. Pierce nominated. And you know what that means."

We'd reached the schoolhouse, so I was saved from sounding ignorant with any reply to this astonishing statement. News of the nation and the world of course came to my home, through my father and brothers and the occasional newspapers they brought from the store. But such statements as tripped lightly from Almyra shocked me. I wondered, too, whether the objection to women voting that said they'd become coarse and manlike might have something to it. Almyra's statements rang far differently from the tenderness of womanly habits.

Looking around the gathering, I wondered whether the stranger was Almyra, or myself: Who else among the neighbors I'd known so long would judge the issues and make bold statements upon them? Surely not Miss Wilson. Or her mother. But now that I thought in this direction, I could see that many of the older women of the village spoke their minds clearly and might assess the new president harshly. Under our shirtwaists, our hearts beat with pity and anger at the plight of Sarah's family and so many more.

Mrs. Alexander called the group to order and pointed out the chapter of *Uncle Tom's Cabin* for the day's discussion: the one where Miss Ophelia is strongly advised to whip young Topsy, for the child's misunderstanding of truth and lies.

"But she resisted," Mrs. Warren pointed out. "And that stands as the difference between Miss Ophelia and Simon Legree, for he drew close to evil in his passion to punish and demean." Whereupon the nodding heads all around revealed that nearly every woman and girl in the room had already pressed through the entire book to its tearful conclusion and the author's own statements about her mission.

And, of course, they'd learned about Mama and me, meeting Mrs. Stowe on the train out of Boston. "Do tell us," Miss Wilson asked Mama, while the others hushed and listened avidly, "what was she like? And what did you talk about with her? Is she writing another volume?"

"If she is, she didn't talk about it with us," Mama admitted. "She is a pleasant woman with no airs, and modest attire, though she must be a wealthy one by now. But a person might never guess. We spoke of shopping for ribbons and other notions, and," she turned to Caroline, "shoes! Mrs. Stowe and our Caroline have shoes from the same shoemaker in Hartford, Connecticut!"

This caused quite a stir, and Mrs. Alexander and Miss Wilson allowed the exclamations and shoe comparisons to continue for several minutes. Then Miss Wilson firmly called the room to order, as if the women before her were students in her classroom, and she asked: "Ladies, if Mrs. Sanborn will be so kind as to establish the direction of Mrs. Stowe's post, shall we write to her our appreciation for her work?"

Applause and acclamation rattled the room with noise. When it subsided, my mother caught Miss Wilson's eye and rose to make a short statement: "I know you have mostly all met Sarah Johnson when she lived with the Clark family for some time." I did my best to signal to Caroline how the conversation had shifted, while listening intently. "And perhaps you're aware, as Mrs. Warren is, that circumstances conspired to allow the ransom from bondage of Sarah's brother Franklin in this past month."

Not all knew this, and much excitement rose. My mother explained briefly about the loss of Franklin's leg making his price so much lower. Any slave owner who'd stepped into the room at that moment would have little chance to survive the tide of horror and anger among the listeners, who alternated between gasps of "that poor boy!" and fury that good Yankee money had rewarded the "owner," even for so worthy a cause.

My mother cut back in. "But it is the assessment of Mr.

Thaddeus Stevens, late of this town and now in the legislature in Washington, that we have little chance of meeting the price for the rest of Sarah's family. The South fears a shortfall, and most slavers now refuse any paid release of the people they claim to own."

"Then what should we do?" Mrs. Clark, despite her friction with my family, wanted only the best for Sarah. "How can we help?"

"With our voices and our strength. Fortunately, Mrs. Alexander here"—my mother gestured toward Almyra's aunt—"can ensure that our letters reach the highest in the land, through the connections of her husband's brother. I suggest that we make the most of this fortunate channel and begin the labor of directing the newly elected president of the nation: no more compromises, no more expansion of slavery, and, at the very least, gradual emancipation of all. At best, immediate laws to outlaw slavery across the nation."

Why did I have no warning of this plan? I stared at my mother, baffled that she'd create this route with Mrs. Alexander and Almyra—for clearly, by the satisfied nods Almyra was giving, she, too, was in the loop of action here. But not I.

I caught Caroline reading my face and tried to reshape my expression. But too late—I could tell she'd seen and understood. She gave a sympathetic nod and tilted her head toward her own mother, as if to say, *It happens to me, too.*

Nonetheless, in that moment I felt my life moving from simple and predictable arrangements, into a wilder and more jagged, even pointed, assembly of edges. It occurred to me that ever since I'd seen the men on the boat in Boston Harbor, I'd lost my balance. Or broken open in some odd way, with something new growing.

A touch on my shoulder woke me to Caroline's change of seat. She reached for my teacup and refilled it.

Impulsively, for the sake of changing the topic and not feeling sorry for myself, I asked her about what I'd heard my mother say earlier in the day: "Do you know about a school for the deaf in Illinois, not close to Chicago, but near the frontier city of Springfield?"

Her brown eyes lit with interest, so much like Jerushah's that it caused me a pang, but still we flashed our hands and fingers to each other, testing the topic.

"I would like to go West," she told me.

Amazing myself, I replied, "I would like to go there, too."

189

CHAPTER 24

While the second round of tea and cookies circulated the room to the twenty-five or so women and daughters present, with enthusiasm lighting their faces, the world beyond the schoolhouse windows had darkened.

Mrs. Warren said her goodbyes, as she had the farthest to travel; her husband, who'd lingered at the store during our gathering, met her at the door to drive her home. I gave her a quick embrace and asked her to mention to Mr. Harris that Charles would arrive with word this evening on Walter and Isaiah's comfort at the horse farms in Woodstock. She promised to let him know.

At least some things could settle and improve. And Charles would tell me, I was sure, about Franklin and Sarah. How reassuring it must be for them, to find so many dark faces around them here in Vermont. Still, I hoped Sarah would come back to me soon. New friendship with Caroline delighted me, but I wanted Sarah, too.

Snow began to fall outside. I stepped to the window and saw several other sleighs lined up, ready to leave for back-road farms. And someone running toward us, boots slipping in the powdery fluff. Almyra, at my side, said, "That's Matthew!"

She stepped quickly across the room and opened the front door, which tugged against her in a sharp gust of northwest wind. I could see Matthew beyond her. He shook his head to something she'd asked and called out instead, "Mother!"

Mrs. Clark flew to her son. "What? What is it?"

Into her ear he whispered, and I heard her give a soft moan of concern. She gestured to Caroline. The two of them donned their outdoor garments and each linked an arm with Matthew for extra balance as they sped toward their home and inn at the other end of the village.

Almyra stared across at me. My mother intervened, firmly shutting the door and saying to all, "The storm's here. We'd best all be on our way home."

The swiftest cleaning I'd ever seen followed, so that dishes could be packed up. Mrs. Alexander's husband, the minister, arrived to ensure the stove baffles were shut tight, its coals left to fade out but not hazardous to the building. As he quenched the last lamp, my mother and I and Almyra waited near the door with Mrs. Alexander.

The two women exchanged hasty plans, and, in a trice, Almyra had joined my mother and me, trudging against the wind toward our home, while her aunt and uncle headed in the other direction to the manse.

"I'm going to help you and your mother with meals tonight and tomorrow," Almyra explained, leaning close to me. "You have so many men to feed for the next few days at least. And my aunt says she appreciates me more when she spends an occasional evening without me."

"Is your father really going to take letters from us to the president?" That seemed far more important to me than meals.

"Of course. Your mother actually suggested the idea when the election news arrived, and I wrote to him. It's simple enough." She changed the topic. "Why do you think Matthew wanted his mother to come home right away?"

Ah, so he hadn't told her in that moment at the door. That, in itself, was interesting. I shrugged, then said aloud, "I have no idea. Perhaps we'll see a hint as we go past the inn."

Indeed, we did, though I had no idea what to make of it: The windows of the tavern room glowed in the stormy twilight, as if a crowd were there, but no signs of horses or vehicles showed in front of the structure. Nor was the path to the inn door shoveled recently.

The icy wind and the pellets of hard snow in our faces made it impossible to discuss this further, so we took the turn up the track toward the house. My mother, I saw, set her basket just inside the door, closed it again, and detoured to the barn, no doubt to talk with my father. As Almyra and I passed in, I gathered that basket along with mine, and we floundered out of the roar of weather, into the chilled kitchen. The harsh wind made the stovepipe damper bang and scrape, and, as soon as I'd shed my cloak, I bent to tend the remains of the noon coals in the firebox, adding some splits of wood but shutting the vents and damper most of the way. The wind could turn a fire into a devouring thing, consuming wood and blazing too hot; the skill was in moderation.

Behind me, Almyra was opening and closing dishes, inspecting the preparations for supper. I turned just as she reached for the lid of the dough box, and stopped her from lifting it: "Don't! Not until the kitchen's warm again, or you'll stop the rise."

Instead she raised the cloth that covered a plate of biscuits. "Is all this for tonight? Biscuits, soup with so much meat in it, pickled beans, and even fresh bread?"

"And a raisin pudding," I added. She looked so surprised. "Don't you eat the same way at your aunt's home?"

"Not at all. We have a cream soup and crackers for supper. My aunt's not a baker, but on Sundays the Wilsons usually give us a loaf, and on Wednesday, Mrs. Palmer does the same. She's your grandmother, isn't she?"

I agreed and marveled. "Doesn't your uncle expect more than that?"

"He might." She shook her head doubtfully. "He often takes supper with a church member if he's out visiting. Most of his dinners, too, so Aunt and I don't fuss much on our own. And, of course, Sunday dinner is almost always at someone else's home, because people nearly quarrel over the chance. Mostly he expects my aunt to plan classes for the children and pick out the psalms and take charity baskets, too." Almyra hurried to assure me, "My aunt makes some of the soups for those, of course. But there are always people dropping things off with her, like cakes and such, to put in the baskets."

I marveled. "So what do you help her to prepare, then?"

"Oh, porridge and Indian pudding and more soup," Almyra said dolefully. We both began to laugh.

"Well, you should come here when you need a change from all that soup," I told her. For a moment, she didn't seem so city-bred; she mostly seemed hungry! "Take a biscuit. Those are from breakfast, and Mama won't mind. She'll be making more tomorrow."

The scrape of wind-blown ice against the window and a sharp draft in the room spoke to the continued force of weather outside. I wondered aloud, "Will the train be late arriving? It might be a hard drive back from town, too. John has gone to pick up Charles at the station in St. Johnsbury."

"And Solomon, too? You know I haven't even met him yet!"

"No, he travels on his own. He works for Mr. Seward, you know, and he's often in a hurry to the next location."

"Mr. Seward? The senator from New York? The *Caledonian* printed one of his speeches last week. I'm sure my papa must meet with him. They are both such strong voices for Abolition. Do you know Mrs. Seward, whose name is Frances? My mother insisted on a tea for her, of course, when she visited in Boston."

There it was again, that city attitude. My irritation flamed like coals blown on, though I tried not to show it. I swept up some biscuit crumbs from the sideboard and asked, "Don't you want to go back to Boston before the spring? Your mother must miss you."

"She does," Almyra admitted. "But I have two older sisters engaged to be married, and they're all very busy making two different trousseaus and planning everything. Plus there are two homes to furnish. I'd rather be here, where I can study when I want to. Or read a novel in peace. I have almost finished *Moby-Dick*, by Mr. Melville. Have you read it?"

"No," I admitted. "I thought it was for boys. Isn't it about whaling?"

"It's about Christian life, and the effects of blasphemy, and the nature of God's grace," Almyra said primly. She laughed at my appalled face. "And, yes, chasing a whale and adventure and the wild ocean. Never mind; you don't have to like it, Alice. But you must have read *The Scarlet Letter*, Mr. Hawthorne's tragic romance. Don't you just feel faint at the parts where her passion rises for Mr. Dimmesdale? I should love to write romances, but I need to acquire more experience first."

This statement so amazed me that I had no words with which to respond. Fortunately, the door banged open at that moment, and my mother, stamping snow off her boots and shaking her cloak, said, "I can't imagine how we managed before that collie. He can even smell the difference if a ewe's been bred successfully. Your father says there are just a few left to breed, so we should have an excellent lambing session ahead." She looked around her kitchen, came over to the stove to test the heat, and moved a large pot over onto a hotter ring. "I hope you enjoy a good soup, Almyra?"

At which Almyra and I fell into giggles that entirely incapacitated us. My mother smiled indulgently for the first minute, then prompted, "Why don't the two of you go to the attic and bring me back half a bushel of pie apples? We shouldn't use the dried ones yet. We'll bake after supper and be partly ready for tomorrow."

"But Mama, does Papa know when Charles and John will be here?"

"It's hard to say," my mother admitted. "In this weather, who knows? But we'll have enough to feed them, and we can always keep something waiting for later."

"Like soup," Almyra said helpfully. We fell again into girlish giggles, then managed to ascend to the attic.

The one attic window gave almost no light, and we fumbled our way to the bushel baskets along the edge of the rough-wood floor. Removing some of its apples to stash in other containers, we worked one basket down to half full and shared the labor of carrying it down the narrow stairs. I felt the door thump, as we hurried to the kitchen.

It was my father, with Jesse at his heels. The dog circled over to his mat and lay down, eying Almyra anxiously. She asked, "Is he tame? May I touch him?"

My father helped introduce the pair, and soon she perched on a chair next to the dog's mat, so she could continue stroking the soft fur of his head and neck without rubbing her skirt on the floor. Unlike his usual habit, the dog didn't go to sleep; like the four of us, he kept looking toward the door at each thump of the storm.

"I hope Charles and John had the sense to stay in town for the night," said my father. "Ely's not as smart in a storm as Old Sam would be, either." He eyed my mother in concern. "I could take Old Sam down the road a ways to see whether they've come close."

"No, you shall not," my mother replied. "Ely may not be all that experienced, but Charles and John are men who've worked hard outdoors for years. They know what they are doing."

"I suppose you're correct."

I finally remembered to ask: "Mama, do you know why Matthew came to fetch Mrs. Clark? Was something wrong?"

"I'm sure she was needed at home. It's not our business, Alice."

"But if her husband is hurt or ill?"

My parents exchanged glances. My father said, "I'll go check after supper. You must have something I can take to them?"

"The rolls are baking," she agreed. "There are plenty. And some jam."

After we'd enjoyed our meal, and Almyra had praised the substantial soup several times (to the point where I thought I wouldn't be able to refrain from another set of giggles), my father rose, lit a storm lantern, and eased back into layers of outer clothes. "Take the dog with you," my mother urged. "He'll keep you on the path if need be."

Even just opening the door to leave meant a gust of snow, all the way into the kitchen. As my father stepped into the snowstorm, the anxiety for John and Charles sat in the room with the rest of us as if it had its own chair. We tackled cleaning everything in reach for distraction and then took out the family Bible to learn a verse for the next day. I noticed that Almyra did this quickly, "sharp as a tack."

"Will you want to teach school someday?" I wondered how she saw her possible choices ahead and braced for an outrageous and entertaining reply. But I was mistaken.

"I doubt it. I like parsing the text, figuring its deeper meaning. My father said that maybe—" She blushed and stopped.

I leaned toward her. "What? What did he say?"

She dropped her voice, although we three sat around one table and could hear each other clearly. "He may have just been teasing. But he said I might set my gaze on a seminary education. To be a minister myself," she clarified. "Surely that is a powerful role toward good. Perhaps you have heard of Clarissa Danforth?"

"I have," my mother confirmed. "From Weathersfield, Vermont. Could you still marry and have children?" The question went straight to the heart.

"I think so. It might depend on who I married, of course. When Miss Danforth married, she mostly stopped preaching, my father said. But I could try to, anyway."

"Of course," my mother confirmed. "Although there would be likely some limits, a struggle. But, for each loss, some gain, perhaps."

What would that mean? And how could a woman preach the Gospel? I tried to imagine a woman's voice in the pulpit and failed utterly.

With a thumping of the door and stomping of boots, my father's return cut off this interesting speculation. He spoke directly to my mother. "Inebriated," he said, biting the word off in his teeth. "Stubborn fool. Worked himself back into a panic again over the new law, then tried to calm down with too much of something from his cellar. Old Mo was there, drinking with him all afternoon. But Matthew's got his father to bed, and Old Mo is out in the stables, probably offending the horses with his reek."

Almyra stared, bewildered, and I tried to explain about the old farmer who'd become everyone's burden now. My mother inserted, "The Lord only knows how he pays for his drink."

With a completely solemn face, Almyra said, "He might need some soup." And thus she plunged the two of us into a new fit of giggles, and my mother announced that it was time for bed.

"But what about John and Charles?"

"Most likely they were sensible and stopped somewhere," my father said. "And if they do come in tonight, you girls have sharp ears and may be the first to hear them. Now, get some sleep. I'll expect you in the barn at seven."

I laughed at Almyra's expression. "He doesn't mean it. He just wants some soup!"

My mother shook her head and pushed us toward the steps to my chamber. "And here's a wrapped brick to set in the bed. Shoo!"

We curled together under the blankets, which warmed around us, and the heat from cooking lingered in the chamber. I thought we might whisper long into the night but fell asleep myself in the pleasant warmth of a second body, which I had not experienced since Sarah's departure.

An hour or so later, I woke, chilled, and struggled to sort the blankets around me. Had they slipped off the two of us? Oh! Almyra wasn't there. I whispered her name, thinking perhaps she'd risen to use the chamber pot, but there was no reply. Pulling a shawl around me, I tiptoed down the steps. "Almyra? Almyra!"

My parents' chamber door stood closed. A faint red glow from the coals in the cookstove lit the kitchen a little, and I looked around, then peered into the chilled parlor. No Almyra.

Back in the kitchen I noticed that one of the candles from the table setting seemed missing. I took the second, lit it carefully from the stove, and, with suspicion and dread, opened the door to the cellar steps, just far enough to pass through and ease down a few feet.

Sure enough, just what I'd dreaded: The door to the cold, wet tunnel that linked our cellar to the cellar of the Clarks' inn showed a dark gap, and half a brick prevented it from closing.

How had Almyra known about the tunnel? And why had she entered it, in the darkness of night—without me?

CHAPTER 25

I dreaded entering the tunnel. Not only was it dark and wet and cold, often with water on the floor at the lowest point along the route—but it also stood for Jerushah's death. Our exchange of messages via this underground route had played a role in the fall that left her motionless and chilled, with mortal illness ensuing.

But how could I not? Again I asked myself: Why would Almyra do something so desperate? And—who had told her about the tunnel?

Only one person could have: Matthew.

Distraught, I returned to the kitchen and silently slid my stockinged feet into a pair of boots. I pulled my cloak around me, and, careful not to let the candle flame stray near my garments, I tiptoed back to the cellar steps and began to descend.

Halfway down them, a sudden draft from the tunnel entry blew out my candle. I froze in place, waiting for my eyes to adjust. When I could follow the faint glow from the kitchen, I turned cautiously and gripped the door frame, pulling myself back to safety. Kneeling by the stove, I lit my candle again and heard my father snort loudly, muted though it was by the chamber door.

This time, the candle blew out before I'd even started down the steps. To my enormous relief, the reason was Almyra's reappearance. Skirt and petticoats rolled up to a scandalous degree, she emerged from the tunnel, a lit candle in one hand, the other patting her hair and probably extracting spider webbing. She turned, and I could see the bright glow of a kerosene lamp beyond her. Someone had "walked her home." Matthew, no doubt.

In an instant, my worry and fear transformed to fury, and when she waved a cheerful farewell and moved the half brick out of the way to close the tunnel door, I finally spoke, though I hissed a whisper, unwilling to wake my parents. "Almyra. What in heaven's name have you done?"

"Hush," she hissed in return, with a beaming smile totally inappropriate to the moment. "I'll tell you everything in bed. Hush, hush."

I shook with anger. But the presence of my sleeping father and mother constrained me. We extinguished our candles, took off our boots, and tiptoed to my chamber, where Almyra dropped her skirt and petticoats and leapt under the covers. "Come on," she whispered. "I have a message for you."

"Where?" Was it a note from Solomon, via Matthew? I would need a candle again. I thrust my hand out, expecting a folded piece of paper.

But no, it seemed the message was something she wanted to whisper to me. Stiffly, not wanting to even brush against her, I angled under the blankets, pulling them to form a ridge between us. She leaned forward and said, "Matthew said to tell you he heard from Solomon, and he's still planning to meet you where and when he said before. Does that make sense to you? I hope so."

I nodded. Almyra extended a hand and cautiously touched my shoulder. "I'm sorry," she whispered. "But I didn't want to wake you, and I suddenly knew I had to check on Matthew. He's so worried about his father. You know all about it, I'm sure."

Biting out the words, I asked, "So you just went visiting a

young man in the middle of the night? Don't you think that's a bit fast? And for someone intending to become a minister, at that?"

Almyra looked scandalized. "Oh, no. I didn't go to visit Matthew himself; I went to see Caroline and ask her. She sleeps in the chamber off the kitchen, you know. I can't understand her as well as you do, but enough to ask that much. I would never visit Matthew in the middle of the night!"

"Then how did you have a message from him?" I didn't believe her.

"Caroline knew he wanted to tell you something, so she went up to see him. He wrote it down, and she brought the note to me so I could read it for you. I left the note there, of course."

"Of course." Bitterly, I thought of how, once again, I had no loving letter from Solomon, no reassurance: just a confirmation of a meeting to which I should bring a report on the ladies' gathering. Well then, a report I would write, and present it formally at Miss Farrow's house on Friday, as requested.

Still angry, and unwilling to discuss it further, I rolled away from Almyra, to face out into the chamber. It was cold, with the winds blowing outside and slapping the house, and the precious evening heat now dissipated. I tugged a corner of the blanket up over my head and fiercely ignored the smaller body lying behind me.

In the chill darkness, I felt Almyra wriggle on the bed, then crouch on her knees under the blanket and whisper: "Our Father, who art in heaven, hallow-ed be thy name."

Against my will, but knowing I must, I bent my head as best I could and followed along, whispering the "amen" with her. And closed my eyes, and prayed for sleep to come quickly, and then morning, so I could rid myself of this annoying Almyra.

Yet the bed was still warmer for the sake of two in it rather than one, and, when I woke in the faint, gray light to a continuation of the night's storm, I felt two slender arms wrapped around me, and a mop of warm, curly hair pressed to my shoulder, as Almyra sighed and snuggled closer in her continued dreams.

I would have liked to throw off the blankets and let her gasp at the shock of cold air. But I wasn't quite that mean, even as annoyed as I still felt. So, instead, I eased out, doing my best to trap the warmth under the bedcovers for her, and pawed through the clothing on the chair to find my own.

At the kitchen stove, my mother already had a good fire blazing, and porridge bubbling. She nodded and said a terse "good morning," and for a moment I wondered whether she'd found out about Almyra's nighttime escapade.

But it was more serious than that. She looked over and me and confirmed: "John and Charles did not reach home last night. Your father's taken Old Sam and the other sleigh to try to find them. Alice, you must have forgotten to braid your hair last night. Go fetch the brush from my chest of drawers, and a comb, and let's see what we can do."

As I passed the table, I nudged the candles closer to the center, and asked without turning around, "Does Papa need me to tend to the sheep?"

"He's already done so," my mother answered. "And he left the dog to keep them company in the barn. Fetch the brush and comb, Alice, I don't have all day. And it will take longer than usual to walk to the church, you know. Where's your friend Almyra?"

"Still sleeping. I'll wake her after my hair's braided." I sensed my mother realized something out of place, but I didn't wish to discuss it. In fact, as she drew her ivory comb through my tangled tresses and carefully arranged my freshly braided hair into a neat coil, finished with a modest ribbon that met the quiet standards of the Sabbath day, I felt my anger ease at last.

Truth to tell, it wasn't really Almyra who'd earned my fury. It was my own hopes for how Solomon regarded me, and whether his regard for me included what a woman wishes for from the man she most respects and admires. And enjoys. I sighed, and my mother kindly asked nothing but offered to lend me her brooch to fasten my Sunday lace collar.

Was I not pretty enough to catch Solomon's fancy? Would a city girl like Almyra, flirtatious and bold, draw his attention? If so . . . well, so be it. I reminded myself of the glances of admiration I'd drawn in town at Dr. Jewett's, and in the Scottish district of neighboring Barnet, as well.

It occurred to me that this sort of distress did not arise when I spent time with Caroline, and I resolved to adjust my days ahead, to do more of the one, less of the other. Almyra somehow rubbed me wrong. Thank goodness we'd had our evening of laughter and "soup" remarks, and I could say I enjoyed her company in some ways.

But I couldn't afford to doubt myself further. I slipped upstairs and woke the "pretty girl," as I now thought of her, and after assuring her she hadn't missed breakfast, I descended with dignity to the kitchen, determined to spend my day of rest regaining my own peace of heart.

More simple to do, of course, in the relative silence of the worship service than in the flurry of cooking at the house at noon, with Almyra eager to assist my mother in any way, and all of us looking to the windows and door twice a minute, anxious for the men to return. In a way, my father's continued absence meant good news, for if he'd found no sign of my brothers, he'd be home by now—or so we told each other. He must be helping to dig them out of a snowbank somewhere, or perhaps, in the irritating way of men who forget that someone is waiting at home, they might have stopped someplace to visit.

Still, when just the three of us sat down to dinner, our appetites shriveled. My mother agreed we'd stay home the rest of the day, and I made two trips through blowing snow to the barn to replenish feed and water and make sure all the sheep seemed quiet enough. Jesse paced and whined softly while I was there, but he made no effort to come back to the house; clearly he knew his post. I drew him some water also and gave him scraps from our meal.

At last, in the faint remaining light around four in the afternoon, a man came wrestling through the snowdrifts, stomping his way in the snow. My mother raced to the door, while Almyra and I clung to a patch of window we'd breathed on, to make a circle to see out. The door slammed, the wind gusted—and my mother said, "Why, Mr. Clark. What brings you this way, in such terrible weather?"

Mr. Clark tugged a thick, knitted hat off his hair; his eyebrows were crusted with snow, and his beard hung frosted like a white nest. "I told the minister after services that I'd bring a message on behalf of his wife. She says if you're willing to keep their niece here 'til the end of the storm, that would be safest. Walking the length of the village just now is a fool's errand. There are six-foot-deep drifts across the road, and more."

Almyra squealed in pleasure, and my mother nodded assent. Her arms wrapped around her chest, she asked, "You've heard nothing from my sons or husband, then? Have any conveyances reached the village from St. Johnsbury today?"

"None at all." Mr. Clark's swollen, weary face showed the ravages of the day before, I thought—and, as he spoke, he held his head very still, as if it ached. "I saw Ephraim leave this morning. They're weather-wise men, your boys and Ephraim. I'm sure they're under cover 'til the storm blows itself out, Abigail." He looked behind him toward the barn. "I'm not much for sheep, but if you need something hauled while I'm here . . ."

I spoke up. "I can manage the evening feeding, Mr. Clark.

I've done it before. Thank you though." I wondered whether to suggest that he return to the inn via the tunnel, and I could see Almyra twitching with the same notion.

Perhaps he guessed what I was about to say, for he pulled his hat back on and said only, "Make sure you tie a rope to the house and hold it as you cross to the barn, then. Best to be safe. Now I'll follow my own boot tracks back to the inn, before the wind fills them in and sets me an extra drift to cross. If you do need help, Matthew or I can come."

"Thank you for such a kind offer," my mother responded. She watched him leave and stood a moment at the door before the icy wind forced her to close it. Turning back from the doorway, she confronted me, with a side glance to Almyra. "I noticed one table candle burnt down more than the other this morning. I don't want to know further, but, if I see it happen again, I'll tell your father to fasten that cellar door for good. Now, it's still the Sabbath. You two may go to the barn and water the sheep—mind that you tie the rope as Mr. Clark suggested. Then I think young ladies might find an improving book to read." She pursed her lips in finality and moved back to the stove to tend the firebox.

Silently, and with much guilt, Almyra and I rolled up our skirts by a couple of inches to save them from the barn's soiling and donned our cloaks and boots. I took a coil of rope from a shelf near the door. There was already a loop in the free end, and, once outside, I dropped the loop over a post next to the steps. "Come on," I confirmed. "We'll unroll it as we walk to the barn, and we'll tie it there. Mr. Clark was right. In this kind of drifting snow, it's safer."

Our heads down into the wind, the rope sliding through our fists, we reached the barn and scrambled gratefully inside. Almyra pushed her shawl back from her face and stared at the crowd of animals examining us. "There are so many," she exclaimed. "There must be a hundred or more of them!"

"One hundred forty-six," I confirmed with pride. "Papa says we shall exceed two hundred this spring, after lambing."

"And you have to take water to each one of them?" Almyra gasped. "That could take hours!"

"No, only to the troughs." I showed her the pails my father had left outside each pen, filled with water and ready to tip over the rails into the water troughs. I gave her a stick. "You can break the ice on each one for me, and I'll follow behind and empty them."

Now Jesse padded close to Almyra, and I wondered whether he planned to herd her in some direction. Indeed, he seemed to know that she should walk the entire row of pails, and, each time she hesitated, he moved to nudge her. Still, she seemed unaware that the dog was "working" and accepted instead the pressure of his shoulder as a reminder to stroke his fur.

It certainly saved time to have the two of them prepare the pails, a relief in the damp chill of the barn. Despite the heat of the many ovine forms, the wind whistled across the pens. Every few minutes it slammed against the side of the barn. The roof creaked. The animals had plenty of hay. I didn't dare add oats to their feed, since they might already have all their due for the day. Better a bit short than overly filled with grain, I knew.

With every pail I emptied, my muscles spoke their own language of concern: Where were my brothers? Why was my father delayed? Were they all safe?

We left the rope in place and followed it back to the house. My mother questioned us, and we made a report on the animals and our actions. "Well done," she pronounced. "And now a bit of Sabbath reading, ladies, if you please."

I offered our copy of *Uncle Tom's Cabin* to Almyra, but, like most of the others in the village, she'd finished reading it and declined. "I'll take *Pilgrim's Progress,* if you're not reading that one," she decided.

If Papa had been there, I might have dared to read some of the newspaper. But with only Mama to judge, and her warning from earlier, I humbly opened a psalter and contemplated King David's youth among the flocks.

My mind wandered to Sarah and Franklin and the livery stables and increasing dark-skinned community around them. I asked aloud, "Mama, do the Gilmans have papers they can send for women fleeing north?"

"No, Alice. There's little work for women at the Gilman mills, and, even at the big homes the family owns, the kitchen labor's likely Irish."

"Why Irish?"

Mama shrugged. "They're trained for it, arriving off the docks in the cities and taking employment in the many kitchens there. But women fleeing the Slave Power are just as likely to have labored outdoors rather than in kitchens. And those who've been trained as cooks and maids and such in the South, they likely have children they can't bear to leave behind. It's different for a man."

Almyra, of course, must add her observations. "It's always been different," she agreed. "And that, too, confirms we must have the vote for women, so we can speak to what we need. Men cannot always speak for us. Did you read Mrs. Clarina Nichols's remarks in *The Freeman*?"

At my clear confusion, she continued: "*The Freeman* was the only paper in Vermont willing to print her remarks on women and the need for them to own their own property. She spoke before the legislature at the start of this month. She spoke also on the vote, especially for women at school meetings, but no editor would print that part."

My mother clicked her tongue in distress. "I can't imagine a woman stepping into that rowdy and boisterous room of rough men," she pointed out. "I hope they were at least respectful of her presence. For school meetings, where women must know the needs of the students, perhaps their vote is justified. I'll bring that up with the ladies next Saturday for discussion."

"We have our reports to draft also," I reminded her. "Mother, I have word that Solomon will visit Miss Farrow in St. Johnsbury on Friday. May I take our reports to him in person?"

Almyra looked up in excitement. "I want to meet this Solomon. Won't he come to North Upton this time?"

"I doubt it. Or why would he ask for the reports to be sent to Miss Farrow's house?" I wanted to press Almyra away from her unseemly eagerness to meet the man who, most certainly, had captured my own interest already. "And I doubt he'll be there long. There are many calls for his travels."

"Oh! Must he go to France to meet with the new emperor there, Louis Napoleon? Or to China, where the rebellion is being fought? How exciting! I wish women might take part in such efforts!"

This dizzied me, for such events found only short mention in the region's newspapers, and I rarely paid them much attention. Our own struggles as a nation took far more importance. I struggled to cap Almyra's comments with some in another direction: "I only know that he works for Mr. Seward, trying to line up the votes toward Abolition and all the laws that must change. And, since Mr. Webster's death, all of New England must rearrange its political lines, to press forward on the matter."

An approving nod from my mother assured me I'd taken a good direction. Still, I had no further chance to press my advantage, for she rose and summoned us to the kitchen to prepare our supper, which we consumed in worried silence. Every added hour without Papa's return, and that of Charles and John, added to our concern. The clock in the parlor ticked "trouble, trouble, trouble."

By eight in the evening, there seemed little point in expecting any arrival. Almyra asked my mother, "Will you leave a lamp burning to guide them home?"

"Oh, my dear child, not in such wind and weather. What if the lamp should topple and light the house afire? Besides, Ephraim and the others won't be outside in all this wind and snow after dark. Mind that you say your prayers before you sleep, and we'll trust to Providence to bring them home, come daylight."

"From bears and storm, from cold and hunger, from all peril, may the Lord above protect and preserve them," I whispered under the covers.

Almyra, her tousled head of curls so close to mine, added, "Amen."

Hours later, waking near midnight, I thought a sound had startled me, and I reached to be sure Almyra hadn't left the bed. She slept soundly. I lay awake a moment, trying to hear it again, and realized: What woke me was the silence. The wind had ceased its roar and clatter. I whispered another prayer, for Sarah and her brother Franklin, and drifted back to sleep, knowing I'd have to rise at dawn for barn tasks, if the men hadn't returned.

With the dawn, however, came the arrival of my brother William, to feed and water the animals. And, as Almyra and I laid out a hearty hot breakfast to share with him after his labors, the first disastrous news arrived.

CHAPTER 26

At first it seemed good news: Mr. Hatch, rolling the road from Upton Center to North Upton, spent some of his time, and that of his horses, rolling our track from the main road. This unusual action, a gift because word circulated about my father and the others still being gone, would make it much easier to walk the horses and sleighs to the barn. Long deep drifts became flattened stretches under the roller.

William observed this from the kitchen, shoveled the last of his hot meal into his mouth all at once, and tugged on his half-dry boots. Almyra and I tried to watch from the window, but my mother shooed us into activity at the table instead, clearing the plates and cups and wrapping the bread.

When William came back to the house, he stood in the doorway, unwilling to remove his boots and cloak. "Mother," he said in a formal tone that signaled us all, "Mr. Hatch told me— That is, he said no persons were injured, except the conductor, but still, the train was forced to wait for two hours for a poor man's . . . ahem . . . he fell from the platform between the cars, and the wheels passed over him."

"Who was it?" My mother gripped the back of a chair and braced to hear a familiar name.

"Mr. Fitzgerald, I think that's the name. From Springfield."

We three, my mother and Almyra and I, exhaled in guilty relief. My mother noted, "So Charles's train ran late. By two hours or so?"

"No, later than that, because the first delay put them head-on into the storm, and they also had to keep stopping to make sure no delayed freight train would come around a bend. They didn't make St. Johnsbury 'til close to midnight."

"So, of course, Charles and John would stay in town," I said right away. "And then with the roads drifted . . . ."

"That's right, Alice. And Mr. Hatch says some of the roads are open now, but the direct one from St. Johnsbury to North Upton is always later to be rolled."

We looked at each other. William scuffed his feet. "Mother, if you can spare me, I should go back to Helen. She's still uneasy when I'm off and away. I've filled the pails with water again, for this afternoon. Can Alice manage those, if Father comes late?"

"Of course, and thank you. I'm sure your father will be here soon. I'll send a message to let you know, one way or another, later."

William nodded and ducked out the door. I asked Almyra, "Now that the road's rolled, do you want to go home? I could walk with you."

"Oh, not yet, if you'll permit me to stay 'til the afternoon," she said, turning toward my mother for permission. "I'm sure the school's not in session, and I'd love to learn how you make your bread. Perhaps I can do that for my aunt. She's not adept in baking, you see."

There could be no swifter, surer way to my mother's approval than the attempt to learn and be helpful. In minutes she had Almyra and me making notes of amounts for her recipe, which, of course, lay only in her hands, not on paper. As we counted cupfuls and stirred, I realized Almyra kept checking the window, angled for a view of the track to the house and barn.

How could I not tease? I told her, "We won't draw other guests until the aroma of the bread reaches the village. Right, Mama?"

"Don't be foolish, Alice. When you and Almyra have kneaded the dough enough, set it in the box to rise. I believe you have a letter to draft to Sarah, and a report to write on the ladies' gathering for Solomon, haven't you?"

Almyra pushed back her sleeves further and struggled to press and fold the stiff dough. "Why are you writing to Solomon about the ladies?"

"Mama is writing also, aren't you, Mama? Solomon's curious to know how the passion for Abolition is enflaming, and how the feelings part out among the ladies here. He said it could help Mr. Seward in his thinking on how to move aside the fugitive slave laws."

"Oh! May I also write him a letter on that aspect? I wish to help!"

My mother blessed us with an indulgent smile and agreed.

An hour later, she gathered our pages along with hers and folded them up for Solomon. "Wait and see how the roads are by the end of the week," she told me. "We can send these on the Thursday stage if Friday's travel doesn't appeal."

I consented but of course promised myself I'd reach the town on Friday no matter what. It was well past time for me to meet with Solomon, and my irritation of a few days before lingered: I wanted to know with certainty whether he felt for me as I did for him. Bearing in mind what Caroline and I had said to each other at the ladies' meeting, I pictured saying to Solomon, "We could go West, you and I, together!" A vision of a Conestoga wagon drawn by a team of matched horses teased me into smiling.

As my mother inked Solomon's name onto the exterior of our bundle of pages, Almyra leaned across and wrinkled her nose in puzzlement. "McBride? Solomon McBride? You never told me his surname before, Alice. From Boston?"

A rapping at the door interrupted this and shot Almyra from

her seat, to straighten her skirts and fluff her curls. I smoothed my braided tresses just in case, while my mother called, "Come in!" as she hurried across the room.

Sunlight streamed through the open doorway, and I blinked, then realized it was Matthew. Almyra beamed. My mother asked, "Matthew, is your family all well? Oh, Caroline, too—how nice to see you both. Come in, come in!"

Caroline promptly seated herself at the furthest location possible from Almyra, which confirmed my thoughts from earlier: such different sorts of hearts and minds in these two! Though I'd rather be spending the next hour or more with just Caroline, I understood my role and offered to make a fresh pot of tea for all.

At the door, Matthew was shaking his head and exchanging quiet words with my mother. I heard the name of Doctor Jewett, and an Upton Center physician, Doctor Ayer. Almyra, too, must have overheard that much, for she rose from her chair, agitated, and, after a moment's hesitation, approached Matthew. "Who is ill?" she inquired, her voice trembling slightly.

Caroline looked to me for explanation, and I gestured for her as quickly and accurately as I could, though I was still trying to spell out the doctor's name as Matthew responded: "No person whom you know, Almyra. Sit down with the girls. I'm sure Mrs. Sanborn will tell you all about it in a bit."

Almyra drew herself up to her not very great height, but the intensity of her gaze and voice made her seem taller and older. "None of us here are girls, Matthew," she said sharply. "We are young women and prepared to act as needed. Now please inform me, who is ill?"

My mother turned to confront Almyra's interruption but must have seen the same thing I did. Instead of scolding, she gave a crisp explanation: "John and Charles brought a man north with them. Older than the others. They found him hiding

213

on the train; he ran from Hartford, Connecticut, where things are not yet as settled as they are here. They're worried for his safety. There's no good way to move him north to Coventry, so he'll go to the Warren horse farm for now. Doctor Ayer will visit there, in the evening. The man has been burned in a fire and should take some time to heal before he moves to Hardwick and from there to . . . to a safer route across the northern border, if that's what he requires."

Having delivered this all at once, she turned back to Matthew. "So Ephraim is taking him to the Warren farm?"

"Yes, but not directly. There's been talk of someone in Upton Center with a grudge against the Warrens, and we don't want to be obvious. I don't think Mr. Sanborn will reach home before tomorrow noon, at the earliest."

"We'll manage," my mother confirmed. "What more, Matthew?"

"If you'll allow me, ma'am, it would be helpful if I walked Miss Alexander to her aunt's home later, when I come to fetch Caroline home. Then I'll have good reason for stopping to visit the minister, and he's another who needs to know about the fellow, for he can alert the minister in Hardwick and set more preparations under way."

"Of course. The girls—that is, the young ladies—will need to manage watering the sheep while it's still light. I'm sure Alice can show them all what to do. And I'll have fresh bread ready at five, which you and Almyra can carry to her aunt and uncle's home. A little extra setting of the scene, so to speak."

"Thank you, ma'am." He tipped his head in all seriousness toward the three of us and said, "Young ladies, your obedient," as he exited.

My mother immediately gestured to Almyra. "Let's shape our loaves and set them in the pans to rise. Alice, you can explain to Caroline all that's transpired. By the time you finish, Almyra will be ready to see to the sheep with you."

It almost felt like second nature now, to show Caroline a conversation with my hands and my expressions. Surprisingly, what she wanted most to know was the name of the man on the run from Hartford, Connecticut. I disappointed her by not knowing. Of course, she'd lived there for so long—perhaps she'd know the man? She asked also about his burns: *House fire? Or from a train explosion? Not tar and feathers? Body or face?*

I knew so little. I repeated what I could and promised I'd find out the answers for her. She told me that, if she could, she'd go herself to the Warren farm and meet the man. Then she asked me whether I still thought I'd like to go West.

Yes, I signaled back to her, *but I need to talk with Solomon about it first.*

Is he your sweetheart? Her question stopped me cold, and once again I thought about all the things Solomon never quite responded to, never quite answered. I replied that I wasn't sure. A political man, though. Someone who fought for what was right. For the end of enslavement and brutality. I did not mention the warmth of his hand on mine, or the way I felt his eyes soften when they met my gaze.

She could tell I'd held something back and waited a moment. Then she asked me, *Does he work for Abolition?*

Always, I signed back to her. She approved.

Soon the three of us were rolling up our skirts in preparation for our visit to the sheep. I signed to Caroline: *Many sheep; the horses are gone right now; one dog.* That was all I had time to say. I thrust the small pail of dinner scraps into her hands and signed, *for the dog.* She nodded.

More snow had fallen, thick and light, a fluffy addition of several inches on top of the mostly rolled track. We all held to the rope so as not to slip. I struggled with the catch on the barn door, and Almyra helped me dislodge the snow packed into it so we could enter.

It seemed the experience of being gazed at by more than a hundred sheep did not fit with what Caroline expected from her years in Hartford. She hung back by the closed door, eyes wide and hands clutched to her chest, with the pail of food for Jesse dangling. He stepped to her gently and sat at her feet, wide, brown eyes imploring, and finally she bent to his need, locating his dish and emptying the scraps into it. He paused in a mannerly fashion until she rose from the task, then hurriedly consumed his portion.

Meanwhile, Almyra and I repeated the routine we'd created the day before: she broke the ice on each pail of water, and I emptied them into the troughs. The sheep seemed to accuse me of not being my father or not being generous enough, but, again, I hesitated to spread grain for them. William, more in tune with our father's routine in the barn, must have given them their share in the morning, or else he would have measured some out for me.

From her stance at the door, Caroline gazed at the flock and finally stepped forward to peer into more of the pens. As Almyra and I reached the end of the row, she beckoned and pointed out the two rams, solo in their own box stalls. *Boys?* Her smile and touch to the imagined men's cap made me smile in return. *Boys,* I confirmed. *No babies? Not yet. In the spring.* She gestured to the muck underfoot in the box stalls and pinched her nose shut. I laughed, and Almyra and I tossed straw into each box for drier footing and bedding. *Good,* I signed back. Almyra, picking up the conversation to some degree, repeated the sign for "good" and beamed at Caroline. I could see there was hope for more connection between the two and wasn't sure whether to feel pleased or a touch envious.

Jesse darted to the barn door with a sharp bark. Caroline must have felt the vibrations of horses' hoofs, realizing that a sleigh had pulled up to the barn, and she tugged at my arm urgently. The three of us hurried to discover who'd arrived.

It was my father, with the larger sleigh and Old Sam. And a passenger.

"Ladies, this is Mr. Benson. Would you kindly assist him into the house, Alice and Caroline? And, Almyra, perhaps you'd help me a moment, holding the horse while I set him loose from the shafts?"

This very quick assignment of duties showed how rapidly my father could see and adapt to faces in front of him, for Almyra's showed dismay and a hint of fear at the man stepping carefully out of the sleigh. His skin, far darker than most of the men I'd seen before, shone nearly black in the soft light of dusk and snowfall; his beard was long and well laced with white, obviously covering a set of old scars to his face, and one eyelid hung nearly closed. His cloak hung crooked, as his left arm, encased in bandages and a sling, set him off balance. I reached politely to take his right hand—and fell back, as Caroline abruptly pressed in front of me and reached to embrace the old man's sound shoulder. Dear Lord in heaven, she knew this man!

Under my father's unspoken but urgent instruction, I pressed them both toward the house. "We need to go inside," I said aloud, and the man, Mr. Benson, must have been able to hear, for he choked back a sob of recognition and pulled Caroline with him toward the door. Jesse, having darted out the barn door with us, saw the need for his skills and herded us all toward the warmth.

In the small kitchen, the presence of so many people and so much emotion astonished me, especially once my father and Almyra entered as well. Almyra settled uncertainly into a chair, trying not to look at the man's disfigured face, yet drawn to it anyway. Caroline assisted him, while flashing gestures in both directions at once: to the man, who, once he'd given up his cloak, clearly was quite elderly, and to me, expressing *friend* and *school* over and again. And my mother, catching the same scent I had already noted—the smell of infection and fever—swept into action to make a poultice as well as tea, and to administer a few drops of laudanum in a kindly but firmly offered teaspoon.

Over this chaos, my father began quietly to explain: as all of us already knew or guessed, Mr. Benson worked at the school for the deaf in Hartford. Confronted by a visiting parent from Georgia, he'd panicked and leapt onto a northbound train. The conductor for the first stretch north ignored him, confused by a larger group. At White River Junction, though, the change of crew led to a man challenging him for his ticket and chasing him behind one of the rickety woodstoves in a passenger car. My brother Charles, having boarded one stop earlier, intervened and paid the man's fare. But he'd already sustained a bad burn, and the railroad conductor feared being blamed for it, especially when the snowstorm delay raised everyone's irritation.

"When they reached St. Johnsbury, John took the conductor aside and gave him both carrot and stick," my father added, "while Charlie persuaded Mr. Benson he could safely ride to the Warren farm and spend time with Mr. Harris and others. They stopped to see Doctor Jewett first and get the burn treated. That's where I found them on Sunday afternoon." He hesitated, then admitted, "It took quite a while for me to reach town. The roads were worse than I expected."

I wondered whether Caroline would persuade Mr. Benson to return to the school with her, when he recovered somewhat. Meanwhile, I could see that the Warren farm might put him at his ease, more than feeling out of place in North Upton.

"Then why didn't you take him to the Warrens?" I asked my father. The best road to West Upton would not come through our village at all.

"Charlie and John felt a ne'er-do-well from the shantytown

had an eye on our Mr. Benson," my father confessed. "So we did a bit of switching, and I do believe a certain money-grubbing Paddy may find himself having followed a perfectly ordinary sleigh of local men to a horse farm where he'll be greeted with an old-fashioned scolding of sorts." At my mother's cross expression, he added, "Nothing terrible, Abigail, just something to remember. We can't let a man like that think he can hunt others, no matter what the new legislation says." If he had been at the store or outside, my father clearly would have spat for emphasis. But not in my mother's kitchen.

We'd all lost track of time, so the quick knock and hesitant opening of the door made most of us startle in place—all but Almyra, who called out, "I'll be ready in a moment, Matthew." She gestured to Caroline, who was supposed to walk along with them as Matthew escorted them both through the village. But Caroline, of course, wanted to stay with Mr. Benson and help him settle for the evening. So, after a quick explanation, my mother recalled her guarantee to William to let him know my father'd come home. She handed a storm lantern to my father and suggested that he and I walk the length of the village to take Almyra to her aunt and uncle, then circle past the mill to let William know all was well. "By the time you return, Caroline and I will have Mr. Benson comfortable, and supper ready."

So four of us went out the door, into the gentle evening with only a few snowflakes drifting down. At the inn, Matthew bade us goodnight, and my father and I walked on with Almyra, encouraging her to speak her mind about seeing an injured man, and her first serious injury at that.

As we stepped toward the parsonage, Mrs. Alexander rushed out the door and threw her arms around Almyra. "Oh my dear child, my dear child," she sobbed.

My father and I stared. She'd only been at our house and was quite safe. What was the fuss?

Then we realized a large, ornate carriage stood outside the parsonage barn, and we looked through into the lamplit drawing room where more people waited anxiously: a couple, and a man.

We followed Almyra and her aunt into the warmth, closing the door snugly behind us, and I turned to gain an explanation of all this emotion.

And in that moment, I realized who the man was. It was Solomon.

CHAPTER 27

Almyra extricated herself from her aunt's wet and emotional embrace, saying firmly, "Aunt, I am neither a child nor poor. Please compose yourself." She turned, set down her cloak on a chair, and began calm introductions. "Alice, Mr. Sanborn, I believe you are already acquainted with Mr. Solomon McBride of Boston and parts west. So, may I introduce to you his parents, Mr. Duncan McBride and Mrs. Jean McBride, also of Boston. Mr. and Mrs. McBride, these are my neighbors here in North Upton, Miss Alice Sanborn and her father, Mr. Sanborn."

While the men exchanged handshakes and I bent at the waist to give a shallow curtsey to Solomon's mother, my mind raced, and my heart pounded. Something was terribly wrong. More wrong even than Mrs. Alexander's sobbing could suggest.

I asked the only simple question I could think of: "And your uncle, Almyra?"

Solomon interjected. "He's seeing to the horses. He'll be back in a moment." He paused, looked at everyone except me, and added, "Almyra, I drove my parents here for your benefit, but I think this news comes best from your aunt."

Mrs. Alexander dabbed at her face with a damp handkerchief and, with remarkably little grace for a minister's wife, announced, "Almyra, your mother died on Saturday night, when her heart ceased. May the angels welcome her to heaven. Oh, my poor child," she said again, resuming her sobs.

Almyra stood perfectly still for a long moment, eyes closed as if in prayer. Then abruptly she opened them and touched Mrs. Alexander's shoulder. "It's not such a surprise," she said softly. "She's been ill for many years. I've always marveled at how she managed for so long. Heaven will surely sing praise with another angel now." She gestured to the drawing room. "Shall we all be seated? And perhaps, Alice, if you would be so kind, would you pour the tea and bring it on that tray? I see the kettle's nicely at the boil."

My father nodded to me and lingered beside me in the kitchen to help place the teapot and a set of perfectly matched cups onto a tray already laid out. His clenched jaw signaled to me that he, too, had a disturbing guess at the presence of this set of individuals. But it can't be, I told myself: Solomon can't possibly have an understanding with Almyra. She's far too young! And flirtatious!

A lengthy absence of conversation followed, broken only by Mrs. Alexander's sniffling, the rustle of garments as people settled, and then the kitchen door opened again. The minister, Mr. Alexander, stepped inside, brushed some snow off his garments, and shook my father's hand. He took the tray from me and carried it to the drawing room, and my father and I followed. I accepted a stiff brocaded chair near a lukewarm potbelly stove, while my father and Mr. Alexander took seats at a table, and Mrs. Alexander finally pulled herself together enough to pour and pass the cups of tea. She added a piece of maple sugar to each, without asking anyone's preference. I thought her behavior odd, but, then again, the entire room seemed something out of a dream. Or nightmare.

Almyra again took control. She thanked her uncle for passing her a cup of tea and for his hastily expressed condolences. Then she turned to me and finally explained: "Alice, I believe I mentioned two of my sisters are to be married during the Christmas season. A Mr. Robertson from Chelsea is marrying my eldest sister, Louisa. My sister Janet is one year younger than Louisa, and hence five years older than I, and is to marry Mr. McBride."

I could feel the blood drain from my face. Such a fool I had been, to think that the brush of a hand and some kind statements and sparkling eyes meant something beyond the text of Solomon's polite correspondence. In this room, only my father knew for sure how I'd pinned my hopes on the affections of Solomon McBride. But others might guess, for I'd been teased about him often enough. And from the shamed curve of his shoulders and the way his gaze remained on his own feet, I felt quite sure that Solomon knew it, too. For a hard, crushing moment, I saw myself as he must have seen me: a young woman whose admiring expectations could be allowed to flicker and flame, for the sake of a greater cause.

My father reached toward me; I shook my head slightly, and he pulled back. I drew a deep breath, straightened my spine, and returned Almyra's direct gaze: "That certainly explains a great deal. Thank you, Almyra. I am so sorry for your mother's passing. How may I be of assistance to you?"

Now Almyra turned back to her uncle. "Has my father been informed?"

"He has," Mr. Alexander replied, nodding. "His telegram says he'll take the train directly from Philadelphia and should arrive in Boston by midday on Wednesday. You have time enough to meet him if you ride with Mr. and Mrs. McBride, who have brought their carriage." None of us commented on the folly of driving in the snow with a city carriage, but it seemed quite obvious to me, and I thought even less of Solomon for allowing a pair of horses to struggle with a wheeled conveyance in this wintry weather.

"Thank you, but no." Almyra took a long moment to examine the people who had driven to bring her the news of her mother's

death, then again sought her uncle's attention. "I would prefer
to take the train. Perhaps my aunt would be so kind as to accompany me. I expect to return to North Upton immediately
after the funeral, if you'll allow me to continue to make my
home here. I anticipate attending the academy nearby, and I
will be glad to discuss my further plans with you and my aunt,
after I have a moment to share them with my father in Boston."

Everyone looked both startled and shocked. In spite of my
humiliation and fury at my own situation, I began to be
impressed with Almyra. She continued, "I have envisioned my
future, and it requires both peace of mind and an excellent
education. I have no liking for Boston, my sisters do not depend
upon me, and I am sure that my father, when he has heard my
decision, will respect it."

Did the Alexanders already know something of Almyra's
strength of purpose? Had she told them her aspiration to study
for the ministry, as she'd recently revealed to me? I thought
surely the answer was yes, for husband and wife exchanged the
sort of speaking glance that my own parents often did, and Mr.
Alexander said calmly, "If your father is willing, we would be
very glad for you to continue to reside here for your schooling."

Mrs. Alexander nodded and swallowed her next "poor child"
comment in order to say, "I wholeheartedly concur. Almyra, we
welcome your continued presence. Perhaps you'll want to pack
some items this evening, however, for your trip to Boston." She
wiped her face one last time and turned to her Boston guests.
"As you can imagine, we are not prepared for the comfort of
guests, but our village boasts an excellent inn just down the
road, and I am sure there is a good meal waiting there, with
warm beds."

Her husband added, "I'll walk with you; it's just a few houses
away, and your horses can rest for the night."

Mrs. McBride clearly didn't grasp half of what had just

transpired. She turned to her own husband and said, "I must say, I'd prefer to take the train myself, if we're not gathering up all of Almyra's belongings yet. Can't Solomon drive the carriage back, so we can both return in comfort?"

"Aye, of a surety." Mr. McBride's voice surprised me, with its soft Scottish burr. His Boston-raised son had none of that; I would have noticed long since. "And, though mayhap I'm not the best one to say it, as I'm no parent of Miss Alexander here, I do thank you all for making her so welcome."

My father nodded, and I forced a half smile. Then I turned and said formally, "Father, I believe we're expected at William's and then at home. Shall we depart?" My father nodded, rising, and, as I did the same, I said to Almyra, "We'll be looking for your return next week, then. If you notify us in advance, I'm sure someone can meet the train to bring you home to North Upton."

At the word *home*, Almyra blinked a tear for the first time and stood to briefly embrace me. "Until next week, then," she agreed.

Gratefully, with our re-lit lantern, my father and I escaped the room and walked out into silvery moonlight on fresh powdery snow, and a baffling contrast of peace and bright, spare beauty.

All the way around the mill pond, past the lumber mill and to William and Helen's small, neat home with its glowing kitchen window, we said nothing to each other. I felt the pieces of emotion settle in me as if they, too, could tumble into place with intricate pointed designs, then form a blanket of under-standing and intent.

At William's, we spoke in the doorway, assuring him all was well and suggesting that he bring Helen for the noon dinner the next day, if she felt up to it. She had already gone to bed, early though it was, and I wondered how long it was going to take her to heal—or whether she'd ever be the person she had been, before her baby's death.

This, too, my father and I refrained from discussing. As we circled back through the village, curtains blocked the windows of the parsonage. I hoped Almyra would take time for grief, since I had no doubt she felt it, even if she didn't wish to expose it. Then we strode past the lit windows of the inn, where the unexpected presence of three paying guests should be cheering Mr. Clark. I wondered what he'd serve them for beverage—surely Boston folk expected the best. Then I set those thoughts aside and straightened my shoulders, ready to walk into our own kitchen and help with Mr. Benson and what he needed.

My father's hand on my shoulder stopped me at the door. "Do you want to tell your mother, yourself? Or shall I let her know, later?"

"You may let her know at any point you choose," I replied. "You'll have her to yourself later in the evening. And I have better things to think about."

"That's my girl," he told me as he opened the door.

What an unusual supper gathering at our table! But perhaps the unusual could become commonplace, with enough experience. Surely the gentle calm of the evening and quiet conversation, over our biscuits and gravy, gave comfort to me and to our newest guest. Mr. Benson sat between Caroline and my father. At first I found it hard to look into his damaged face, and a whiff of infected tissue lingered in the air. But Caroline's obvious friendship with this man assisted me in learning to meet his gaze and make him welcome.

So, too, did my task at the table. "Talking" with Caroline came so easily to me now, but not to the others, especially my father. Tales of each one's travels and labors needed sharing. First, of course, was Caroline's explanation on behalf of Mr. Benson: No reason for any Southerner to "capture" him existed.

He'd grown up in Rhode Island, where all persons had been free for many years, and he and his wife worked at the school Caroline attended in Hartford, Connecticut. But the panic all who shared his skin color must now feel about the Fugitive Slave Act and the perfidious slave hunters coming from the South had pressed him into his ill-chosen leap onto the train.

Would it be possible, Caroline asked my father, with me interpreting, *to send a telegram in the morning to the school, assuring them that Mr. Benson will return safely next week, after some time to recuperate?*

"Of course," my father agreed. It meant a trip to St. Johnsbury, for the nearest telegraph office, but he'd add other tasks to accomplish and make the most of it.

My mother inquired about nursing care at the school, already possessive of her patient and unwilling to let him travel back unless his welfare was assured. Caroline and Mr. Benson both responded to that, with some pride.

Almyra's situation and loss needed to be conveyed. Everyone marveled that she'd choose to live in North Upton rather than Boston. With my new insight into her family and choices, I offered, "She feels at home here."

My mother wept at that and said she'd make sure Almyra felt part of our family, as well as the Alexander household.

Explaining about the McBrides turned out to be beyond what I could provide at that moment. Instead, my father outlined their presence and the reason they'd arrived in our village. I took advantage of the need to clear the table, in order to not feel my mother and Caroline's unspoken sympathy for me. I didn't want to soften, especially in front of Mr. Benson, who should experience calm and safety, in order to recover. Besides, the pain of self-pity didn't appeal to me—give me the steady heat of a justified anger at being so betrayed, and then a fresh focus instead on work to be done.

Next summer's classroom labor seemed far away. I wondered what I might put into action sooner and began to think about Dr. Jewett and Mr. Gilman and their network of resistance. And Miss Farrow, of course, anchoring their purpose in St. Johnsbury as someone who'd known slavery herself. Which made me think of Sarah and Franklin and start to worry about them.

"Alice, we need you here at the table." My mother interrupted my flitting thoughts, calling me back to the need for finger talk and explanations.

Matthew's arrival once again, to collect Caroline, signaled the end of our evening. We sorted out where Mr. Benson would feel most comfortable resting: a bed made up in the kitchen near the warm stove seemed wise, considering that my mother wished to check on any fever during the night. Caroline made sure her friend knew she'd be just down the road and would return after breakfast, and, one lamp and candle at a time, the room settled to the hushed sounds of a low fire in the stove, and "good night" all around, with layers of compassion in every direction.

I thought the past hours of distress and reconsideration would keep me wakeful. Instead, I fell instantly into near-dreamless sleep, waking again to the clatter of pans and dishes in the kitchen. Peering out my chamber's window, I saw deep snow, furrowed by my father's path to the barn. You could feel December about to arrive, in the midst of this week of change and rearrangement.

Stepping down to the kitchen, I realized a new freedom for myself. Without Solomon to consider, I could make different choices. I almost smiled.

CHAPTER 28

Three persons and word from Almyra all arrived at my home on the morning of the first of December. After a dull few hours at the schoolhouse, completing the last tasks of teacher preparation, I came home for our noon dinner to find my mother in a tizzy, steaming thinly sliced potatoes and carrots to add to her venison stew, to extend it further.

"Alice, there's biscuit dough in the bowl. Quickly, please, pat and cut it to bake. If we slice the bread a little thinner than usual and set out the biscuits and jam . . . Oh, fetch the rhubarb jam from the shelf as soon as you have the biscuits in. Never mind, here's Caroline; she can get the jam and open some pickled beets, too. Alice, tell her what I need, please." Steam and pans hissed and clattered on the stove.

"Who's coming to dinner, Mama?" She seemed too distracted to respond. When Caroline had her boots and cloak set aside and could face me, I flashed my mother's requests to her, then hurried the biscuits onto a pan and waited for Mama to test the oven temperature. At her nod, I slipped them into the heat and turned back to Caroline.

Where is Mr. Benson? I asked it with the symbol we'd happily assigned to him earlier in the week, a snip of the fingers such as a barber might apply to a man's hair.

In the barn, she gestured back, *with your father and your brothers.*

"Mama! You might have told me—are John and Charlie

back?" If I'd been paying attention, instead of thinking about when I'd have my teaching certificate, I should have noticed extra sleigh marks on the track from the main road. "When did they get here?"

"Just a few minutes ago," my mother said, without ceasing her swift preparations. "I sent them to see your father, as they fill half the kitchen, the two of them plus their friend."

"Who did they bring? Someone from the Warren farm?" I wondered immediately whether they'd brought a fugitive or other person in need of assistance.

"No, someone from Massachusetts." She noticed my sharp intake and breath and assured me, "Not a McBride. Not from Boston, either. No, this man's a bit older, and he's from Worcester, where he has a school. A college for women."

"Is he here to meet Almyra?"

My mother looked confused. "No, I wouldn't think so. She's far from ready for college, Alice, though I confess she's astonishingly bright. It has something to do with politics, I believe. They mentioned him in a letter once. Eli Thayer is his name."

"What a shame Almyra isn't back yet. A college for women, and politics, too . . . she'll want to meet him and hear all about it."

Caroline grasped some of the meaning, especially since, by habit now, I gestured with at least half of what my mother and I said aloud. Some words I couldn't put into the hand language quickly—there were probably gestures for them, but I didn't know enough and would have to finger-spell the words instead, usually too slow to try in the midst of a spoken interaction. But we had a symbol for Almyra already: the closed fist of *A* swept down the cheek with a bouncing curl movement. It fitted the subject perfectly and made me smile. How my feelings for Almyra had shifted, witnessing her independence and courage—and learning of her loss.

What Caroline told me now was, her father had a telegram from Almyra earlier, since his inn enjoyed the best conveyances for collecting someone from the train station. Mrs. Clark and Matthew would collect Almyra after four o'clock this afternoon, adding a few errands to help make the journey worth the effort.

"Let's ask her to visit with us after supper," I suggested, and Mama looked up from her cooking. "We can make popcorn and catch up."

"If the men aren't having their own gathering," she warned. "Mr. Thayer is staying at the inn tonight, but I don't yet know enough of what John has in mind."

A gust of cold air and the banging door announced the men coming in from the barn. My mother gained a few minutes by sternly directing them all to wash their hands before the meal, while I checked the biscuits. Almost ready.

Mr. Benson seemed a whole new person compared to when he'd arrived. Quick to throw off the infection and begin healing his burned arm with the aid of my mother's care, plenty of rest, and Caroline's devoted attention, he even laughed at something Charlie muttered, while waiting his turn to wash up in a pail of warm water near the door.

The gleaming darkness of his skin reminded me of Mr. Hayes up north, the blacksmith whose family had become hosts to my friend Sarah when it seemed danger threatened her here in North Upton. I marveled at the range of colors I'd already witnessed, all called "blacks" in men's hasty talk, but hinting to me of a wider world and making me wonder about Africa.

My mother's crisp directions took me out of my daydream, and I pulled out the biscuits, gathered them into a basket, and began handing plates to my mother, to be filled with stew at the stove. Clattering spoons and forks replaced chatter, as everyone began their meal.

Like my mother, I took only a small portion, so I could watch for what others needed. Besides, it seemed that I needed to "meet" my much-older brothers anew, in their larger, stronger version as men who'd traveled, labored, taken such risks.

Charlie caught me eyeing him and grinned, then dabbed at his short beard with his handkerchief. "Gravy in my moustache, little sister?"

"No, but keep on trying," I teased.

John, whose mustache curled to either side in a waxed point, laughed and added, "Told you my way is better, Charles."

Mr. Thayer paused to check his beard before speaking up. "Better a bit of gravy now and then, than a scraped-bare dough-face like Franklin Pierce," he said bluntly.

My father perked up, pushing back from his nearly cleared plate to ask, "What news can you add to the newspapers this week? Any word from Washington?"

I watched Mr. Thayer's face, so long and expressive. I guessed his age at thirty-three or so, and his small, soft hands spoke to his scholarly profession. "Washington's mostly obsessed with Europe, watching the friction between Russia and Britain, France and the Ottomans. I daresay armed conflict will erupt before the next year's end. Only the winter weather's holding it back now, I believe."

"But what about at home? What's the balance for Abolition? How goes the wrangling over the Territories and their future?"

All the men set their forks down, the better to pay attention. Our guest examined the intent circle around him for a moment before answering. "Webster's death has cost us dear," he admitted. "Scott never had a chance in the election. When I meet with the senators and congressmen of the Commonwealth of Massachusetts, we talk about what measure may provoke action at last. But, in my opinion, the place that will spark a second revolution, one that finally banishes slavery from this nation, is Ohio."

Caroline, sitting across the table from Mr. Thayer, watched him closely. When she couldn't tell what he'd just said, she glanced toward me, and I'd try to finger-spell it swiftly. Now she spelled to me in confirmation: *O-H-I-O?*

I nodded, then leaned forward and asked, "Not Illinois? It's closer to the Territories."

An eagle-sharp stare from above the beard caught and pinned me. "I thought perhaps only Boston women paid close attention to politics. It would appear I was mistaken."

My brothers laughed, and I blushed but persisted: "I've read that's where the railroad negotiations are most intense. There's a railroad lawyer there, Abraham Lincoln, who gave the eulogy for Henry Clay last summer."

John cut in. "Clay never went further than to stand for gradual Abolition. And that can't be a choice now. If we can't get even the Whigs to step forward—you saw what happened with Thaddeus Stevens, the man's not even in office this coming year—then we'll have to form a new party."

"It's possible," Mr. Thayer mused. "Yet that will take passions and energy best spent directly on the cause." He looked sideways at me again and added, "I've a hankering to ride the rails to Ohio and then Illinois, to get a more direct feel. But the rising tide of sectionalism, with each region of the nation declaring its own stand, will only enflame the underlying conflict, you know."

John leaned forward. I could see his younger self in the passion he put forth. He gripped his hands together and declared, "Nearly every Vermonter would hold for Abolition now, Eli. You must bring our strength into the Territories somehow. I daresay you could say the same for the men of the Commonwealth of Massachusetts."

"I could," our guest confirmed.

My mother held up a hand to announce an apple crisp, and I

poured more coffee for those who'd emptied their cups.

Mr. Thayer gave a contented sigh and said he wasn't sure he'd saved room for more. Mr. Benson, though, looked eager, in more ways than one. He addressed Mr. Thayer in a low voice that trembled: "Don't forget the freedman and the slave, sir, when you're planning that second revolution. It's our backs that bear the cost of King Cotton, and our children who weep for their parents in separation. We have reason to join any and every battle on behalf of Abolition."

Next to him, Caroline clapped her hands together in appreciation, and Charlie looked over at my father. "Had word last night from Woodstock," he drawled. "Our fellows enjoyed their stay there and have left for the mountain ore sites now. Those two youngsters you sent along, Sarah and Franklin? It seems they're secure for the winter. Letters will follow to Alice," he nodded my way, "and to our mother. Compliments from all."

"There's some good news, then," my father confirmed. He asked Charlie, "Have you and John worked up a safe route for Mr. Benson here to make his return to Connecticut?"

I asked, "Isn't he safe enough to just ride the train?"

Heads around me emphasized the "No" that each man uttered. Charlie explained: "Once the train passes out of Vermont, he'll be more at risk. Massachusetts is filled with scoundrels and traitors of one sort or another. Begging your pardon, Mr. Thayer, and present company excepted. And in Connecticut slavery was only abolished four years ago, so there's still mixed feelings. No, he'll need company on the journey."

Caroline signaled her willingness, and I said I could go, too; she could not travel without another lady, surely. But this did not solve the issue, since many times the train cars separated men and women. The issue of race would also be against us. One of the other men needed to be present.

My mother intervened. "Caroline," she said, mixing a few hand gestures with slow words so her face would be easy enough to follow, "are you staying in North Upton for the next year? Or returning to Connecticut to teach the children?"

The men stirred and began to talk in low voices with each other, while Caroline gestured at length to me, asking me to say the words aloud to Mama. I reported, "She's thinking of fetching her things from Connecticut and bringing them here. But she's not staying long. She hasn't told her family yet. She had planned to teach this winter in Hartford again but has changed her views. By spring, if they'll hire her, she wants to teach in the school for the deaf in Springfield, Illinois."

John looked back at us "ladies" with new interest. "Alice, ask her if she'd like to go sooner. We're headed to Illinois after the first of the year."

My mother gasped, and he apologized. "I didn't mean to spring that on you all at once, Mama. Bear in mind you'll have Charlie and me for another month. But we've a hankering to see the railroad being built, and to bring Vermont common sense to the region. Maybe do some profitable business along our way."

In a ladylike manner, Caroline indicated she'd discuss this with her mother over the next few weeks. A flame of eagerness in her face told me it was a discussion in name only: My new friend would go West soon, no matter what. I recalled when she'd signed *I want to go West* at the schoolhouse, and my own quick reply: "I want to go, too."

Now, if I really wanted to, I could. There would be no Solomon in my life to negotiate with. I could have an escort from my brothers. My teaching job, if offered, wasn't due to start until next June. All I had to do—no small task!—was convince my mother to let me go West instead.

At the other end of the table, meanwhile, a plan had emerged.

Mr. Thayer must like it a great deal, for he was chuckling and patting Mr. Benson on his unbandaged arm. "This will suit admirably," he said. "And I'll telegraph Garrison in the morning."

Passing the apple crisp along, I asked, "Garrison? Do you mean William Lloyd Garrison, the great anti-slavery publisher? I don't understand!"

Charlie was still laughing. I realized he'd lost several teeth in California and determined to ask him how, if I could draw him aside later. He took a deep breath and explained: "Judge McMillan's due to bring that horse you rescued, probably tomorrow if the weather holds. We'll ask him to ride with Mr. Benson and me on a scenic railroad trip to northern Massachusetts. And there, if Mr. Thayer's plan works out, we'll exchange the judge so he can return home, replacing him with Mr. Garrison. He's an old friend of Eli's, you see. It will give us all a chance to exchange views along the remainder of the route, and John has a business proposition for Mr. Garrison as well. Can you picture it? Anyone taking offense at Mr. Benson would have to deal with two strong Gold-Rush men, one state judge, and the most notorious newspaperman of the age! Not a chance of any interference at all."

Mr. Benson didn't quite understand yet, so John sat down to review the plan with him. Meanwhile, I carried on a silent conversation with Caroline, my lips moving when I needed to form a word that way, but otherwise quiet enough to be just the two of us. "When should we fetch your things?" I asked her. "Who should go with us? How will you tell your mother?"

At length we found that the demands of kindness and courtesy constrained us to pace this more slowly, with more conversation, especially at Caroline's home, than Mr. Benson's planned return trip could allow. In the meantime, he could assure the school that Caroline flourished, and that she'd correspond.

"Don't tell your mother that I'll travel with you," I warned Caroline. "It would be one more wound for her. Maybe she would want to be your escort to the school in Hartford instead. Think about it."

We'd lingered so long that my mother finally ejected the menfolk, directing Mr. Benson to take a nap, and sending the rest of them to the store and fetch any letters, while we females restored the kitchen to order and began preparations for supper.

"And for Almyra to visit later," I added hopefully. Caroline gave a cautious nod, and I realized she still held some reservations about Almyra. So did I, in truth, but I'd decided to move beyond these and see what might come in better days ahead.

While my mother and Caroline began to assemble cornbread and a well-seasoned pot of beans, I stepped out to the woodshed to fetch more split wood for the kitchen stove. The clear air and bright, snow-covered landscape delighted me. For the first time I wondered, would I feel this same sense of joy in other places? What would it be like to travel West? Who might we meet along the way?

It took two trips to the shed to fetch enough wood, and, as long as I had my boots and cloak on, I accepted the scraps from the noon dinner, to take to the barn for Jesse. The dog pressed up against me affectionately, half herding, half eager for the meal I'd brought. I poured it out for him and stroked the long, soft fur of his back a moment. When I turned to leave, his ears pricked up, he raised his head, and he gave a sharp bark. A farewell to me? No—a reaction to an arrival outside.

I shut the dog carefully inside the barn, making sure the latch held firmly, and turned to see who was coming up the track. It was John, in quite a hurry.

"It's a letter from Uncle Martin, to you," he told me as he passed me an envelope. "Matthew's at the store, and he said you'd want it right away, so I offered to come back. It's tucked inside a longer one, to Papa and all. Papa's already looked at it, so take it to Mama."

Curious, I eased the thin paper open and withdrew a brief note: "I understand you are close to your teacher certification. Would you consider teaching in Springfield, in Illinois, for a season? I believe I have a task that may suit you. Write back immediately."

I looked up to ask John what he thought it meant, only to realize he'd spun around and tramped halfway down the track to the main road already. He waved an arm over his head and called, "See you at supper!"

Men in, men out. Caroline back and forth. Almyra to arrive in a few hours.

This felt like a complicated railroad schedule. I bounced on my toes. If Uncle Martin had a task for me, it related to Abolition, no doubt. I could taste adventure in the air.

Most importantly, it appeared I'd have an ally in persuading my parents to bless my own journey west. Could that be?

Now I knew I had true friends in my life—I could tell, because all I wanted at this moment, more than anything, was to draw Caroline aside for an hour and explore this idea with her. Almost as satisfying, I realized, might be a conversation with Almyra.

Oh, dear heavens. I'd been so wrapped up in my own adventure, I'd forgotten why she'd traveled to Boston. I headed toward the kitchen, a sudden notion in mind that would need both Caroline and my mother to accomplish.

CHAPTER 29

Supper's cornbread baked quickly, and soon a pan of stewed fruit sat fragrant and warm at the back of the woodstove. My mother and Caroline consulted with each other over whether to make something more for Mr. Benson, whose health must be supported. With the two cows dried off for the winter, milk toast, the usual invalid meal, was not an option. At last my mother chose to add frizzled beef to her preparations.

As she carved a chunk of dried beef into paper-thin shreds, I offered my notion: "Almyra wants to feel that this is her home now. But she also has just lost her mother, and it must be hard. Could we make an autograph album for her? I have some silk scraps toward a decorative cover, and if we go to town next week, we could buy a few sheets of heavy paper. Mama, perhaps you would paint a small watercolor border for each page? And Caroline and I could stitch them together? We'll make a pocket or two where she can keep a token of her mother perhaps, and some pages for autographs from others in the village. What do you think?"

Mama beamed, and Caroline bounced with pleasure, telling us she had some spare bits of ribbon to contribute. Then she told us she needed to go back to the inn to help her father finish chores and lay out supper there. She gestured deftly: *My mother will be cold and tired when she brings Almyra back from the station, and if I feed the younger ones before she arrives, she will have some peace.*

Of course, Mama insisted that Caroline take one of the pans of cornbread with her. We bundled into our outer clothing (with mine still damp from earlier) and walked together down the track, until there was just the main road for Caroline to cross to the inn. With Caroline's hands occupied, we didn't "talk" but smiled warmly at each other. I waited on my side of the road until she'd entered her family's home, then walked back in the gathering twilight.

Supper without Caroline felt subdued to me, though the men kept up a slow discussion of the demand for Washington to assist the growth of the railroads. "It's the only way to hold the states together in one prosperous Union," my father declared, and Mr. Thayer and my brothers clearly agreed. Mr. Benson, who said he hadn't thought about it much, asked excellent questions. And he told us about having met Mr. Garrison, at a talk given in Hartford, not long after *The Liberator* began to be published.

"I imagine you'll be glad to meet him again in a few days," I suggested, smiling.

"I hope I recognize him again," Mr. Benson chuckled. "It's got to be more than twenty years ago."

So much had happened so quickly that I realized we knew very little about Mr. Benson himself. He answered my questions willingly, telling us how he and his wife had found jobs at the school in Hartford, and described his grown children and young grandchildren. "I don't know how I'll tell them why I ran onto the train," he admitted. "It seems such a foolish action now."

My father, overhearing this part, inserted, "The most foolish things I've ever done took place when I was frightened. You're in good company on that!"

I would have asked what some of those things were but saw my mother's shake of the head just in time. Perhaps Papa would tell me a few, out in the quiet of the barn someday. I hoped he might.

In the parlor, the potbelly stove creaked with heat, making the room much cozier than its custom. Mama shooed us all out of the kitchen.

Just as we'd all settled around the room, a gust of cold air swept through, and I dashed to the kitchen to welcome Almyra and Caroline. To my surprise, however, the arrivals were Almyra and Matthew and Mrs. Clark. Matthew immediately angled past into the parlor to join the other men.

It was the first time Mrs. Clark had come calling in the past two years, since Jerushah's death. My tongue seized in my mouth. Thank goodness, my mother's grace covered my fault, for she swept in front of me and embraced Mrs. Clark.

"You must be half frozen after riding to town and back, and then walking over," she said. "Girls, why don't you go upstairs and have a cozy visit, while Mrs. Clark and I enjoy our tea."

I started to ask about the popcorn we'd planned, but a sharp glare sent me scurrying to the steps to my chamber. I said, "Almyra, won't you come visit with me? Come tell me about your trip to Boston and back, and I will show you a book I've borrowed from Miss Wilson." Almyra's hand slipped into mine, and we scrambled for safety.

The heat of the kitchen warmed my chamber, and we sprawled atop the featherbed, exchanging details of the past few days. When she heard my older brothers had arrived, Almyra, of course, wanted to go downstairs immediately. But I persuaded her to wait a bit, and coaxed her to reveal some of the Boston tidbits—not about her mother's funeral, which seemed too sad to mention, but about her sisters and their wedding plans.

"I suppose I shall have to attend, as a bridesmaid," she sighed. "But that is in late March, so I have time to just stay home and study."

She checked my response to that, examining my face. I wrapped my arms around her in an embrace and said, "I am so glad you are home. Tell me about the Christmases you've known. You know it's a scant three weeks away!"

Downstairs a set of thumps and thuds indicated someone departing. Almyra and I rubbed the frost from the window pane and peered into the darkness. Two people, I thought: men, both of them. We could find out more later. I wanted to first give my mother time to ease Mrs. Clark's discomfort, before reappearing in the kitchen.

Coaxed into describing Christmas trees and presents and visits from elderly relatives and small children, Almyra revealed a far wider holiday celebration than I'd ever experienced. "Our minister, your uncle, tells us it's a sacred time, not to be frivolous at all in the church," I explained. "He allows a pine wreath for the doorway, nothing more."

Almyra said, "That may be the case at the church. But at home, I plan to encourage a festive holiday for my aunt and uncle if I can. Perhaps not a decorated tree, but at least some cut evergreens and bright ribbons. And I brought back a gift for each of them from Boston!"

She reported also that her father planned to stay in Boston until the spring, which I said must be a great relief to his church congregation. Apparently I misunderstood, however: Almyra laughed and declared they'd surely miss the parade of supply ministers who'd raised a host of question, religious and otherwise. "They already know my father's positions on everything from Paul's Epistles to the immorality of slavery," she pointed out. "The only thing that could enliven them will be gossip about who he'll marry next."

Shocked, I said, "He won't really, would he? He must have loved your mother far too much to simply take a new wife so quickly."

With a sigh, my friend pointed out how long her mother had been ill: seven years at least of heart ailments and intermittent bed rest. "I'm sure he'll grieve," she admitted, "but he must also experience enormous relief. Be assured," she added, "this is not a topic for discussion between my father and me. But I fancy I know the way of men a little bit. They do not care to live alone, but prefer to have their needs and their comfort seen to. By the time my sisters are both married, I am sure he'll have made a choice."

Now it was even clearer why Almyra preferred to live in North Upton. Who would want to watch their father in the midst of such decisions? I could not imagine it.

I took my turn to narrate events, of which quite a few had passed since Almyra's departure. She gasped over the story of Mr. Benson, and she paid intense attention to every detail of the politics discussed. She declared that she must meet Mr. Thayer as soon as possible and added pensively, "I wonder whether your brother's notion about Vermonters heading to the Territories might provide a vital plan for the future."

We listened for a moment to the quiet voices in the kitchen and finally decided to risk going downstairs. I did my best to look humble and penitent as we stepped into the kitchen, and Mrs. Clark seemed willing to ignore me. Almyra said she wanted to speak with my brothers briefly, and permission was granted, more or less: "It's a cold night, Almyra, and I'm tired. My daughter's waiting for me." Mrs. Clark said this with a bit of a sharp edge, and I thought perhaps she meant my mother to hear the "my" part especially. We had hosted Caroline for more hours than Mrs. Clark wished.

However, Almyra apologized prettily and thanked Mrs. Clark again for bringing her back from the station. Then she turned to my mother. "I wonder whether Mr. Sanborn could see me home to my aunt's house later? Then dear Mrs. Clark won't feel she needs to stay." With quick agreement on this point, especially since I said I'd accompany Almyra, too, my mother then rose to walk with Mrs. Clark to the main road, saying she could use a bit of fresh air and peace. They headed out the door, storm lantern in hand.

Almyra and I slid into the parlor and caught a few words about surveying, in a discussion centered on President Polk's past campaign and the Oregon Territory.

I blurted out, "But Great Britain has nothing to do with the Territories now, isn't that so? I thought she was fully involved in European squabbling."

Mr. Thayer nodded agreement. "Still, never forget she's the sovereign nation with the most interest on this continent. Whatever takes place in the cotton industry involves England as well. Keep learning, young lady. You're asking good questions."

While I blushed and stammered a thank-you, Almyra pressed the hand of my brother John, as well as Mr. Thayer himself and Mr. Benson. Her twinkling girlish challenge to each of them seemed to wake them in a new way, and their appreciation glowed. I doubted I could ever do what Almyra did so naturally and brightly!

"And where is the other brother I've heard about? And Matthew?"

"Across at the inn," John replied. "Matthew had some work to do, and Charles kept him company."

I could guess the work: making sure Mr. Clark was sober and functioning. Poor Matthew.

My mother entered the parlor with Charles at her side. More trains in and out of the station? I stopped myself firmly from giggling. Around me, the men began to talk about an early night. Mr. Thayer would bed down with John and Charles; William's old bed sat available, and the parlor stove would already have warmed that chamber nicely.

Bundled into cloaks, my father and I waited for Almyra to embrace my mother, who held her for an extra moment. Then, after re-lighting the still-warm lantern, one more stroll through the village followed.

We didn't talk much this time. My father asked whether Almyra knew how to ride, and she said she did. He suggested that she come visit tomorrow, to meet Micah, the rescued horse that would arrive around mid-morning. I hoped he meant to test her skills and consider assisting her transport for her further schooling, which would be at the academy some five miles away. The sparkle in his eye suggested as much to me!

At the parsonage, Almyra and I embraced, and I whispered, "I'm glad you're home." With our lantern, Papa and I stood at the road until the door opened, and we watched her step into warmth and comfort. It felt very satisfying.

Barely a whisker of moon accompanied the December sparkle of stars. As we walked, we located Orion, the hunter, whose constellation only rises in the cold months. Then, as we made the turn from the main road toward our house and barn, my father gripped my arm. "Ssh."

I froze, afraid the bear we'd seen a month before might stand between us and safety. A moment later, my nose isolated what my father's already had: skunk. We stood still a bit longer, and the black and white furry creature strolled down a bank of snow, walking in front of us as if we were a parade. We held back until it reached the barn and began a ramble along the further side; then we hurried to the house, laughing as we hadn't in a long time.

"Papa?"

"Alice?"

"It's all working out well, isn't it?"

Just inside the door, in the quiet, darkened house with a single candle on the table and Mr. Benson softly breathing, all bundled within his blanketed bed by the stove, my father and I paused to look at each other. I thought for a moment his eyes sparkled with something more like sorrow than joy.

"We'll talk about it in the morning," he told me. "Your uncle Martin's letter, I mean. Never pray for guidance at night, chickadee; only give thanks. Tomorrow we'll consider all of it. Tonight, we count our blessings."

I did just that, curled in bed, missing the warmth of Almyra or Caroline while counting each of them as a blessing, saying my prayers and trusting in my Shepherd.

None of my dreams involved flame, or fire. But when I woke, the scent of smoke hovered in my chamber. It came, I was sure, from cracks around the window, not from the stairway to the kitchen. In just my waist and woolen petticoat, I stumbled sleepily toward the leaky window to rub a circle in the frost and peer out.

I screamed to the kitchen, "Mama! Papa! The inn's afire!"

CHAPTER 30

My mother shouted back to say Papa and Mr. Benson were in the barn, and she'd fetch them. I heard the door slam. I scrambled for my skirt and stockings and hurried into outer clothing, with a shawl wrapped over my bonnet and around my throat. From the icy feel of the kitchen floor, I knew it must be fiercely cold outside, so, after I found boots, I dug for mitts and a second woolen shawl.

The terrible screams of horses erupted as my parents and I ran down the track toward the main road, with Mr. Benson following at a distance, still cautious when running on snow and ice. Harsh air bit at my throat while I ran, gasping and shouting: "Caroline! Matthew!"

As soon as we could see the inn, flames leaped abruptly higher. But they did not rise from the structure that housed the family and its business, or the attached low-roofed tavern. Instead, they crackled and smoked wildly from the stables just beyond the inn. More screams from the horses tore through me.

Someone seized my arm. My mother! She gestured toward a knot of people holding each other and shouting toward the fire.

"Caroline!" I called again, and then my thoughts woke up all at once and realized she would not hear me. I hurried close, and, as she swung her view back toward the three children clinging to her skirt and sobbing, she saw me.

Her quick gestures of *help children* made complete sense. She could not take the younger ones back inside, for fear the flames could catch the inn itself on fire. I turned and found my mother beside me. She leaned close. "Take them to our house," she shouted to me, above the riotous sounds of fire and men's stamping feet and horses. "Feed them and make sweet tea. Take Caroline, too. Go!"

I tugged at Caroline's arm and gestured up the track, with an arm's sweep to indicate the children and what we must do. One, Peter, had no boots on, only stockings. I crouched next to him and urged him to climb onto my shoulders as he whimpered in pain from the cold. Caroline swept Polly and Nancy ahead of her, and we rushed across the road together. The track to the house had never seemed so cold, or so slippery. I dreaded the notion that I might drop Peter, as my arms strained to hold his legs in place and his clutching hands tore at my shawls and my hair. Forward, forward.

Suddenly my legs banged against the doorstep. Caroline, next to me, seized the door and shoved it open, and we lifted the children into the half-warm kitchen. While she comforted them as best she could and pulled off Peter's wet, icy stockings to rub his blue-white toes, I thrust split wood into the stove's firebox and re-set the vents for more heat.

In the relative quiet of the kitchen, I tried to calm my face and hands, understanding that the children needed to be soothed—their feelings must be a mix of terror and desperation. "Where is Mama? I want Mama," Peter whimpered, and Polly, too, began to weep.

Caroline threw a quick look at me and gestured above the head of the child clinging to her: *Matthew ran to fight the fire*, she told me.

"Your mother, too?"

Yes.

"Your father?"

She shuddered and conveyed with her hands and her face: *We don't know. He didn't answer when we shouted.*

Fire in very cold weather is unstoppable. Water can't be found to pump with a hose, and if it did enter a hose it would freeze in place. I knew the only way to stop the fire from reaching the inn, and then perhaps spreading to more of the village, depended on the men to cut the structure down as quickly as possible, tumble the burning walls and roof into a dense bonfire, and then control any flying sparks. Every man and woman would contribute what strength they could.

My stomach felt ill as the echoes of the horses' screams came back to me. This was no time to collapse for any reason, though. I started water heating and fumbled for mint leaves for stomach tea, as well as ordinary tea leaves. And maple sugar: I gave each child a lump to suck on right away, which quieted their sobs a bit. Aloud, I repeated to Peter, Polly, and dark-haired Nancy, who, like Caroline, resembled Jerushah closely: "They will be here soon. Your mama and papa are fighting the fire, but they will come soon."

Mr. Benson's bedding and bed, neatly set aside, sat over in the corner. I dragged it back to its usual nighttime location in front of the woodstove, then a little ways back, so I could have space to walk between and tend the firebox and any pans. Porridge seemed a good idea and might need to stretch for many people; I started more water heating, while Caroline followed my suggestion and bundled the children onto the bed, a blanket tucked around the three of them at once.

What would Mama do about Peter's feet? I shuffled bowls until I found some lard and coaxed him into letting me rub it into the skin. A rosy pink color where I rubbed convinced me he'd no serious frostbite. But I went up to the "boys' chamber" and found a pair of wool socks to pull over the small toes. Too large, of course, but, in this case, a good fit for the cause.

Together, Caroline and I managed to get a bit of hot tea into each youngster. I handed them buttered biscuits next. As they quieted, she and I returned to sharing what information we could. I explained about the village ways to take down a fire. And she, about waking to the acrid, thick smoke filling the house all at once, and her mother's desperate confirmation that Mr. Clark wasn't in the house.

Then she added, *I saw a man.*

"Your father?"

No. A stranger. I don't think he lives here. He was running from the stables. He wore a long coat, hanging open. Like wings.

Could it be? No. And yet—the minute Caroline described the stranger in that way, I thought of the other stranger from weeks before, the one who'd abused his horse near Upton Center. The mean one, with the whip.

I asked Caroline, "Can you manage the stove and start the porridge?"

Of course, she signaled back. *Where are you going?*

"To tell my father about the man," I confirmed. "I'll come back right away. But they need to know."

I raced back toward the fire. In the new light of the day, it seemed more smoke than blaze, a hopeful sign. But, as I searched for my father, I saw fresh tongues of flame rise from the collapsed hay loft.

My mother, her face smudged with ash and her skirt wet and dragging, pushed toward me from the group raking the sizzling embers and tossing snow onto them. "What is it? Are Caroline and the children in trouble?"

"They're safe and warm," I reported. "But Caroline saw a man run from the stables. I need to tell Papa."

Without argument, Mama plunged back into the chaos, and I saw her circle toward the rear of the structure. I stamped my feet, trying to keep them warm enough. The snow nearby had melted, and black rivulets of icy water flowed everywhere.

Papa seized my arm suddenly. "Caroline saw someone? Who did she see?"

"Papa, she said it was a stranger in a long coat, open, so that it flapped around him as he ran. Like wings, she said."

His face registered the same moment of impatience and then incredulity that I'd felt. "The one who whipped the horse so brutally? You think that's who it was?"

I said urgently, "I've never seen anyone else around here who wore a long coat without fastening it. Could it be?"

At that moment Matthew ran toward us. "Mr. Sanborn, we think we've found him. My father. Can you come help?"

"Papa," I called as he hurried away, "where are John and Charles? And Mr. Thayer?"

"They headed to Upton Center very early, to fetch Judge McMillan!" he shouted back. "Go home, Alice, and stay safe!"

Almyra, garbed in a thick cloak with an enormous furred bonnet and muff, hurried toward me. "Alice, is everyone safe? What can we do?"

I told her where Caroline and the children were, then pulled her away from the noise so I could share the urgent news: "I think it may be arson." She gasped in horror. I nodded urgently. "Caroline may have seen the man who lit the fire. I think I might know who it is. And he might still be in the village. But the others are all needed to fight the fire. I want to look for him. Will you help me?"

"Of course," she replied. "But wait a moment." She searched the ground and found a half brick, scorched and wet. Without hesitation, she stuffed it into her muff. "Best to be prepared," she said with a half smile. "Now, where should we start?"

I had a notion of searching for footprints, but the trampled snow around us made that impossible. The man must have used a horse or sleigh to reach the village. If he remained here to see his conflagration erupt, his horse must have shelter someplace. Clearly not in our own barn, since Papa had been tending the sheep when the flames rose. He would have noticed an extra horse in our stalls. But the notion held up, and I told Almyra: "Every barn and shed. Let's start at the far end of the village and work in this direction."

We tramped in haste down the main road, to the end of the village where the route to Upton Center began. My brother William greeted us as he hurried from his mill. "Whose fire?"

"The Clarks' stables," I called back to him. "Take an iron pry bar or two if you have them," I suggested. He nodded and ran back into the mill to fetch what he could.

William's horses stayed at the next farm down, so he had no stables with his house and mill. I saw Helen peering from her house window as we raced past, and I waved. Her face pale and gaunt, she lifted a hand in greeting but did not come out.

Almyra followed me to the first barn, the Wilsons' one, and we rushed toward it. "Almyra," I called. "Look down." In the fresh snow there were no prints at all, neither man nor horse nor the deep runner marks of a sleigh. We turned on the spot and angled toward Grammy Palmer's place. Her barn showed a few tracks outside, so Almyra and I eased toward the door. She reached for the latch, but I whispered, "Wait."

A gap between the sagging doors let us peer into the near darkness. Only one horse, quiet and dry in a box stall.

"Let's go back to the road by the same angle, or else my grandmother will see us nearby and come out to talk," I warned.

Almyra asked, "Do we look in the carriage shed at the schoolhouse, too?"

Grimly, I said, "I think we'd better."

But the pupils hadn't arrived, and the teacher must be on foot, for again the fresh snowfall told us there'd been no entry to the shed as yet.

"Next, your uncle's barn," I said.

Almyra shook her head. "There's no room. He has his horse there, and two sleighs and various carriages. He has to be able to go out quickly when someone needs him."

I nodded. But we still walked up to the horse barn doors and inspected the ground as we approached. "That's odd," Almyra commented. "Someone's scuffed out most of the prints here."

"Hush, then." Biting my lip, I eased up to the door frame and squinted into the structure. "I can't see enough," I admitted.

Almyra pulled one hand out of her muff to tug at the latch, and, as the door creaked open, she dipped back into the muff to seize her half brick.

No persons stood in the dim barn. But Almyra gasped. "There's a second horse here. Saddled and wet. You were right, Alice."

I turned to face the village, uncertain where a threat might come from. Surely the rider must be nearby. Staring at the double row of widely spaced houses and small barns, the front porch of the Blake house caught my attention. I set a finger to my lips, then pointed. Almyra's eyes narrowed. She whispered, "From here, we can go around the back first and surprise him."

A simple plan, but effective. As we sidestepped cautiously around the building, half crouched so the porch itself could hide us from view, we heard a thump as if a booted leg had shifted. Teeth gritted, brick in her fist, Almyra half rose, and I stood up next to her to see.

The man standing half hidden by the porch columns had eyes only for the fire he'd probably started. We could hear his heavy breathing. To my horror, he laughed, as the crash of more of the stable collapsing echoed down the road.

Almyra held up a hand to me to stay still, and, carefully, she edged up closer to the steps. The man must have heard

something, for he swung around, the wide flaps of his coat
swinging as he turned. I shouted, "Over here!" to draw his attention, and I pulled myself up and over the railing. Almyra
leaped up the final steps to the porch and swung her brick with
fury.

Not hard enough, though. Growling like a beast and cursing
aloud, the stranger leapt away from Almyra and toward me,
both arms thrust out, gloved hands reaching for my shoulders
or throat. I screamed.

And Almyra, that city girl now home in North Upton, lifted a
shovel left behind by the last person to clear a path, swung it
mightily, and struck the man's back so hard that he fell, gasping, at my feet.

In an instant, I tore down a length of clothesline from the
back of the porch and improvised fastenings for the horrible
man's legs, then, with Almyra's help, for his flailing arms. For
good measure, we tied a further loop around his wrists, and I
cinched it hard.

"He could have injured you," I croaked to Almyra, pulling
her into a thankful embrace.

"Or killed either of us," she agreed. "Can you tell, Alice, is
this the man who beat his horse that day?"

There was no need for my confirmation: He'd found his voice
again and began shouting at us, dreadful names, and also laughing, saying, "You'll learn not to take a man's horse again, won't
you, you stupid girls. Tell that to your high and mighty father,
why don't you? No stables left for my horse, right? Serves you
all right!"

Finally the door of the house opened with difficulty, snagging
on a braided rug and scraping the floor. Elderly Mr. Blake
peered out at us. He held an antique pistol that he flourished
far too carelessly for my taste. I dodged backward and begged
him to lower the weapon. After a moment, he did. "Why are

you at this door? We never use this door in winter," he said plaintively. "Only the kitchen door."

I couldn't help laughing, nor could Almyra. We laughed for too long, of course, and Mr. Blake stared at us, then stepped out to look at our captive.

"Why is this man on my porch?"

That sobered us. I said, "He set the fire."

"Fire?" Mr. Blake sniffed, then turned and faced the smoking heap. "Well I'll be darned. Seems like this past October I did a fine job fitting the kitchen door. Never smelled a thing. You want some tea while you're here?"

"No, thank you," I said politely, as Almyra stifled a giggle behind me. "I think we need to find someone to remove this man."

"All right," Mr. Blake agreed. "Come back again to visit, young ladies. Bring me some cakes." He closed the door, and we heard the latches snap back onto place.

Almyra asked, "Who stays here, and who goes to fetch the men?"

I offered, "I can run for them. Are you willing to stay? It shouldn't take long."

She picked up the half brick again and perched near our foul-mouthed prisoner. "I'd prefer an opportunity to hit him again. If he's too noisy, I will."

The curses muted to a malicious hiss. I checked that our knots looked tight, nodded, and began to run as quickly as I could toward the knot of neighbors, calling for help.

Two young and slender farmers rushed back with me to the Blake house, then fetched a small sleigh and rolled the bound man into it. "Tell your father we'll take him to the schoolhouse, and the county sheriff can collect him," one of them said to me, while the other asked Almyra her name, with great curiosity about where she lived. I saw her perk up into her usual flirtatious self, and felt relieved.

Arm in arm, Almyra and I returned to the gathering by the smouldering wreckage of the horse barn. Women still worked at the boundary between the smoky heap and the inn, piling snow onto embers and catching blown bits before they went far. But no men were there. Nor was my mother. So we walked further, to where we could see the tangle of larger forms, struggling to lever up a beam at the back of the hot mound of broken timbers and half-ashed hay. At least there were no more screams from horses—although I feared that meant they'd been shot to stop their misery.

Triumph leaked away from us as we edged closer to watch. Matthew and my father seemed the directors of the action, and warning shouts filled the air as each man tackled his share. A pair of onlookers turned—my mother and Mrs. Clark, each drenched and soiled. I released Almyra's arm and stepped toward them.

"Will you come to the house to get warm and see the children?" I asked.

"Not now, Alice," my mother replied in a cracked and shaking voice. "It's Mr. Clark under there, and the men are trying to pull him out."

CHAPTER 31

A sleigh pulled up to the side of the road, and John and Charles and Mr. Thayer leapt out, with Judge McMillan following. They strode forward to add their strength to the crew struggling up ahead.

I pressed close to my mother, afraid to watch, afraid not to. Almyra stood next to me, and we held hands, tucked inside her muff for warmth. Likewise, my mother gripped Mrs. Clark's shoulders. A series of small moans and whimpers came from Mrs. Clark, as if her heart could only spill out this dark rhythm of fear. The grating crunch of a beam scraping against another told us the heap of timbers must give way to the dozen men straining and heaving. Smoke spun occasionally on a whirling gust of wind, into our faces. My eyes streamed, and I had no certainty on whether I wept from anguish or from ashes. Almyra wept plainly, sniffing occasionally. I heard her murmur at one point, "How could he do this?"

Sarah's shocked face hovered in my thoughts: her quick recognition of the cruelty of the man who struck his horse violently, in direct parallel to men who whipped people, made in the image of God, if darker of skin than the whip-holders. I shook in a fresh torrent of grief, thinking what she and her family, and so many like her, had endured. And I knew, from Mrs. Stowe's novel and the many newspaper reports that followed its printing, that for hordes in the Deep South the torment increased daily, in the loss of their family members. Was Mrs.

Clark about to lose a second of her own?

I closed my eyes. Prayer outside of church, prayer not spoken by the minister, who knew whether the Lord God heard it clearly? But I could try.

When I opened my eyes while another shriek of lifted timber echoed, I realized our small line of watchers had grown: Mr. Alexander, our minister and Almyra's uncle, stood at her other side, his hands clasped together, his lips reciting the twenty-third psalm: "Yea, though I walk through the valley of the shadow of death, I will fear no evil: for thou art with me; thy rod and thy staff they comfort me."

The next lines came to me, but I found them little comfort: "Thou preparest a table before me in the presence of mine enemies: thou anointest my head with oil; my cup runneth over. Surely goodness and mercy shall follow me all the days of my life: and I will dwell in the house of the Lord for ever."

Goodness? Mercy? A shiver of dread passed among us all, as the corps of men bent forward and lifted, together, a blackened something that was not a beam, was not a timber, was not (though I wished it could be) a horse or other ordinary inhabitant of a barn.

Mrs. Clark ran forward, a terrible cry rising from her throat, and, to my astonishment, my mother turned to run behind us all. She returned in a moment with a blanket. Even the men around her wept, as they rolled the wet and ash-covered form into the coarse woolen covering.

Almyra and I turned to each other and sobbed, until a thought seemed to come to both of us at the same moment: Caroline.

Mrs. Clark and, I saw now, Matthew walked together beside the bundle from which life had been so cruelly extinguished. Mr. Alexander stepped up and walked alongside them, still murmuring a prayer.

And Almyra and I, with my mother suddenly alongside us, trudged across the road and up the track to the barn and house, to meet Caroline and the little ones with news that their father had perished.

I stopped a moment and looked into Almyra's face. "Your mother?"

A strange question, or a strange way to ask it. But she only nodded and said, "With the angels. This is not the same kind of passing, Alice. It will take more from everyone."

And she was entirely correct.

For the next two weeks, it seemed that, over and over again, I said goodbye or stood with others saying their own farewells. The funeral for Mr. Clark took place on Saturday at our church; I assisted with the dinner afterward, working as vigorously as I could, in hopes of becoming tired enough to escape nightmares. Not until a few days later, after school had let out for the season, did I realize Almyra, too, found the nights torn by violence and fear in her dreams. With readily gained permission from my mother, I invited her to stay with us until Christmas Eve. Sharing the bed under the eaves, keeping each other comforted and warm, we found some relief.

With my mother's encouragement, we knitted for hours, making mitts and socks for the Clark children. Sometimes Caroline joined us by the fire in the evening, or for a cup of tea at midmorning. But mostly she cared for her mother, who rarely had the strength to climb out of bed, in spite of the small children's needs. My mother often invited Polly and Nancy to her kitchen, to make Christmas breads and cookies. They always took a portion home. Sometimes Peter came to the barn to sit while my father cared for the sheep. But it would be another two months at least until lambing began, and the grown sheep in their uncaring cycle of eating and resting did not interest him. However,

Jesse seemed to understand that here, too, was some sort of lamb; I often saw the dog leaning against the child, the boy's fingers snug in the long fur.

There was one welcome arrival at our farm: Micah the horse came with Judge McMillan, later on the day of the fire. A person could be forgiven for thinking the animal had always lived with Old Sam and Ely, for they sighed and snorted and sometimes whinnied in chorus, and it was an easy change to everyone's habits, to include Micah in any plan. Judge McMillan confessed he'd grown fond of the horse during the animal's recovery, and the judge stayed a night at our home, before returning to hold court in Upton Center and send the coat-flapping stranger, whose name turned out to be Barton Watson, off to trial on murder charges. The judge assured us that, when the time came right, he'd be happy to meet Mr. Benson at the St. Johnsbury train station to be an escort on the railroad. A letter to Mr. Garrison gained similar assurances for the last leg of the planned journey.

Mr. Benson, of course, required a few more days of rest, after exerting himself with the rest of the men of the village. I noted that all the men made him welcome, in their ways, at firesides and at the funeral. When he left, with my brothers and Judge McMillan to keep him company for a safe return to Connecticut, he gave me a set of polished wooden buttons he'd whittled, and he set a new pair of spoons in my mother's drawer. He also offered to see that Caroline's trunks were sent north to her, but she declined his kind effort. We had other ideas in mind, she and I.

Charles assured me he and John would return by Christmas Eve. "I'd say we'd be home sooner, but we both have a hankering to spend a day or two talking with Garrison," he confessed. "You know what we're aiming to do, and we feel he'll give us good guidance. Also, we may need his alliance in the future."

I leaned forward against his wide chest, the scent of wood and sawdust mingling with sheep in the leather of his coat. I whispered, "If you see Solomon, I don't want to know."

His massive hand rubbed my back. The rumble of his voice through his chest comforted me, as he replied, "We don't expect to. And, if we do, he'd best be going in the opposite direction."

I gave a wet giggle and pulled back to wipe my eyes.

"Come back soon," I urged.

"We will."

Neither of us had begun the hard conversation with my mother that we knew lay ahead of us. By unspoken agreement, we set it aside, for after Christmas, in the hollow final days of the old year.

I did hear from Sarah at last, by letter. It arrived on the morning of Christmas Eve, and Almyra and Caroline, both in the kitchen finishing the wrapping of gifts for the children, paused to read over my shoulder:

Dearest Friend and Sister Alice,

May I call you that? It seems so right, after we have seen such adventures and changes together. I miss you every day. Your letter about the fire and the tragedy shook me deeply. I thought of Charles Hayes, up north, and sent him a note asking him to hold you in prayer, and the same for Caroline. Such loss, and such pain, only Heaven's healing touch can minister to. I know you must walk the day-after-day journey of grief again, and I think also of Jerushah and how much she meant to us all.

You would be surprised, I think, to see how Franklin has settled here. He has what they call the "touch" for horses who've been mistreated, and he sits with them sometimes until they are ready to accept kindness from other hands. His work at the forge amazes all who observe the many tools and other items he makes there. His crutches somehow never hinder him in these labors, and I rejoice to see him becoming a man who both works and comforts, with only the rarest hint of bitterness or anger.

I heard from my mother last month, a letter conveyed via that good Mr. Thaddeus Stevens, to whom I owe so much. She and my father remain in good health, for which we all praise the Lord Above. She says two of my sisters are marrying, so I suppose the time is past for hoping for their presence here: Even if the master were willing to lower their prices, most likely they would choose to stay with their husbands. I don't know whether to weep for them or be grateful. My other three brothers remain safe, although of course I must fear for them. And with each month further into manhood, the price to ransom them from the Slave Power rises. Yet Mr. Stevens tells me to hold onto hope, and I try.

Please give my warm greetings to your mother especially, and to the others in your family. I must write a small further piece that I hope you will help them to understand. Alice, I have decided to stay here in Woodstock for the time being. I miss Mrs. Hayes, of course, as well as all of you in North Upton. But, at the Hayes home, I can always see the hope in Mrs. Hayes's eyes, that somehow I will develop warm feelings for one of her sons and become the daughter she desires, by marriage. Though I like them well enough, such expectations daunt me.

Here in Woodstock, however, among so many Africans like Franklin and me, I feel free to care or not care, to choose companions, to choose where to pledge my heart and my future. Can you imagine how remarkable a gift I have found here? This broad possibility of choice is new to me, and entirely welcome. I feel I must treasure it, and that means I will remain exactly in this place, where you and your family have enabled me to find a home for my heart.

Still, a part of that heart remains with you, whether in North Upton or elsewhere. I await your next letter with much delight.

Your friend and sister always,

Sarah.

"So those are the words for it," Almyra commented. "I do know what she means. If I hadn't left Boston, though, I wouldn't."

Caroline nodded. She commented with her hands, *She writes it well, doesn't she?* She reached out and lifted my chin, so that our eyes locked in understanding.

I nodded and said aloud, so that Almyra could grasp it, too, "We are so fortunate to make some choices together, aren't we?"

Almyra sighed. "You're still determined to leave at the New Year?"

Caroline and I nodded at once. I added, "But say nothing yet, Almyra. It won't be easy for Caroline's mother, or for mine. When John and Charles return from Connecticut, we'll start to make our plans."

CHAPTER 32

Mrs. Alexander paid a call at our home in the afternoon of Christmas Eve. She had walked from the parsonage. My mother and I exchanged looks of surprise when we responded to the knock at the door and found her there. Caroline and Almyra had both gone home after the noon meal, and, like every other woman in the village, Mama and I were completing our baking and stewing, laboring to ensure the next day's family gathering would be sweet, after Mr. Alexander's morning worship service.

I drew chairs to the table and followed my mother's direction to fill a pot with tea and set out a plate of small cakes. Abundance called for sharing, and we'd sent bundles of treats home with both Almyra and Caroline. But we could spare a few more, to be sociable.

It didn't take long for Mrs. Alexander to come to her point, and it was addressed to me, not Mama: "I wonder whether you and Caroline Clark might be able to stop in at the parsonage tomorrow in mid afternoon. I'm sure you'll have family around you, and Almyra will have her uncle and me, but I know she must miss her mother at this time, painfully. As well as her father, I'm sure. The two of you have become her close friends. Would you pay a visit and have tea with us, to help her feel there's some pleasure to the afternoon? I've persuaded Mr. Alexander that friendship is not the same as frivolity," she added firmly.

"Of course," I replied. "And I'm sure Caroline will want to

be there also. Would you like me to speak with her?"

"Yes, if you'd be so kind." Mrs. Alexander sighed and turned to my mother. "I always wanted a daughter, of course, and now it appears I have one. But the years of slowly gained experience are lacking. I didn't realize until this morning that I needed to provide for the Christmas spirit for Almyra."

My mother laid a hand on Mrs. Alexander's. "It's clear she's gained much peace of heart in your home, Sylvia. And keep in mind: the true spirit of Christmas is to give to others, in the name of the birth of Christ. I'll be very surprised if Almyra has not prepared for that part of the holy day's custom. She's a very giving person at heart, don't you think?"

"Oh! I hadn't considered it in that way, Abigail. I'm sure you're right. And I do hope she'll feel appreciated, in the gifts I have for her. They're not fancy the way her Boston family might have provided. Just," she blushed, "a quilted silk pouch to keep her bracelet and ring. And a muffler that I knitted." She added hastily, "From very soft wool, truly. In a deep-rose color."

"How lovely," I exclaimed. "Mrs. Alexander, I am convinced she'll treasure those. You have found exactly the right gifts for someone who's nearly a young lady and eager for affection. May I ask," I hesitated, then finished my uncomfortable question, "did her Boston family not send any gifts to her?"

"None. Only a note wishing her a Merry Christmas and saying they were far too busy with wedding preparations to send anything more."

A shared passion took flame among us in that moment, quite tangibly. I almost expected the candles on the table to spring into light in witness to such injustice, that such a sweet and smart young woman's family with so much wealth would treat her so shabbily. I promised again, "I'll be there tomorrow. About three?"

"Perfect," Mrs. Alexander declared. She drained her cup of

tea, thanked us, and bustled back to whatever preparations she still needed to make. For Almyra's sake, I hoped it was more than soup.

After I'd tucked a final pie crust into place for baking, I asked permission to walk across to the inn and convey Mrs. Alexander's request to Caroline. "Of course," my mother said. "But don't stay long. Now there's supper to put together."

The day had been mild and sunny, yet a slice of cold air trailed along the snowy ground. Already the sun had dropped beneath the horizon, and, in fifteen minutes or so, it would be dark. As I hurried along the track, I wished I'd taken a lantern with me. Let that be an incentive to be quick, I urged myself, and briskly stepped to the house door of the Clarks' structure. The sour smell of wet burned wood lingered in the air, and I remembered this was a house of mourning.

Peter came to the door, and shouted over his shoulder, "Polly, tell Car'line! It's Alice. Come on!"

He ran back into the kitchen, leaving me on the doorstep. Caroline arrived a moment later and gestured, *It's not a good time to visit, Alice.*

"Yes, I'm sorry," I apologized. "I don't mean to interrupt your Christmas Eve. I've just brought a message from Mrs. Alexander." I explained briefly.

Caroline, her face pale and damp, signaled, *I don't know. I can't say yet. Ask me tomorrow in church.*

Thinking she was ill, or her mother's condition had worsened, I apologized again and assured my friend that I'd see her in the morning, at worship.

She suddenly fell forward against me. I held her until she pulled back far enough to show me her hands and explain: *We're leaving the day after Christmas. My grandparents are coming to take us to their farm in Rutland,* she gestured rapidly, spelling out the city name. *My mother can't bear it here any longer.*

I was horrified. I flashed back to her, *Do the children know? What about Matthew? What about you?*

She looked behind her, in a panic. She must have felt the tremble of the floor as someone came toward her. I saw the apology in her gaze, and then she shut the door firmly between us. I stumbled down from the step, my heart in pain, my thoughts a-whirl. What of our dreams, our plans, to head west for the work we both had in mind? What of our deep friendship, which had grown so rapidly and strongly as we labored to communicate with each other? What could I do?

I raced home and unburdened my heart to my mother, who said only, "I'm not surprised. Give me some time, Alice. I need to talk with your father."

At that moment, my brothers John and Charles pulled into the yard, loose snow flying from the runners of their sleigh, whooping "Western style" as they leapt from the bench. I ran out to greet them and carried their parcels into the house while they stabled Ely. I heard the other horses nicker to him in greeting, after the several-days absence. Jesse ran in and out of the barn in excitement, and my father's laugh rang out from among the sheep.

How could I be so fortunate, and Almyra and Caroline not? I ached to fix everything for them and to repair the wounds around us. This was not the meaning of Christmas that I wished to ponder.

I lit the candles for family supper, still distressed, but counting my blessings. Tomorrow Helen and William would join us after church, and we'd all share the noon dinner. Almost without thinking, a notion formed in my mind. After the pleasures of hot oyster stew and fresh bread came my brothers' stories from Connecticut, which included a wild welcome home for Mr. Benson and a fascinating day meeting the Abolitionists of the city with Mr. Garrison as host. My father added a proud anecdote of Jesse singling out a sheep for him that was suffering, perhaps from a blockage he thought, and my mother listed the delights in store for the next day's meals.

When I could, I caught my mother for a moment's conversation at the dry sink. "May I invite Caroline and Matthew to spend Christmas afternoon with us?"

She eyed me speculatively and said, "I haven't talked with your father yet."

"I know. I only mean for the afternoon. Please?"

She pursed her lips and weighed the possibilities. At last she nodded. "Yes, you may. But no tracking through the tunnel tonight. If Mrs. Clark knew you'd used it to take a message there again, she'd never forgive that. You will have to wait until the church service. But," she gave way a little bit, "you may linger outside the church this time and give them each a note of invitation, instead of having to wait until the service ends."

Such a challenge to patience! "Never pray for patience," my Grammy Palmer once told me, "or you'll be given opportunities to practice it." This seemed such an occasion. I wondered whether there was any shortcut to the long night of worry ahead, but my mother perhaps read my thoughts. She swept the tin of sulfur matches from the candle shelf into her apron pocket.

"I said, not the tunnel. Will you give me your word, Alice?"

Ruefully, but feeling loved, I agreed.

Still, sleep refused to come, as I worried. Would my mother see the choice I hoped she'd make? To invite Caroline and Matthew to stay with us, so Caroline and I could launch our westward adventure together in the new year? Perhaps, I proposed in my agitated reflections, perhaps Matthew might wish to work for my father. It was so unfair for Mrs. Clark to drag them to her parents' farm, more than a hundred miles away. Besides, I recalled how unpleasant at least one of the older Clark relatives could be, from a long visit she'd once made when Jerushah had been ill.

Like touching an empty place in the gum with the tongue, feeling the absence of a childhood tooth as if there were an enormous gap in its place, I'd been holding unhealed the hole in my heart that belonged to Jerushah, for more than a year. Lying under the eaves awake, I realized the gap no longer existed the same way. Yes, I would always miss Jerushah, and always feel in part responsible for the illness that killed her. But between them, Caroline and Almyra had filled something in a way that I needed. Filled it enough that, like Sarah, I felt ready to make a very strong choice.

After a while, still restless, I tiptoed down to the kitchen, thinking to perhaps break off a piece of biscuit to settle my stomach. Or perhaps reconsider the tunnel and taking a note across to Caroline. Not Jerushah, I reminded myself.

Reaching the bottom step, I felt with my toes in the near darkness and realized Jesse lay at the foot of the stairs. Did this mean my father, too, had taken action to keep me home on this long Christmas Eve night? I tried to step across the sleeping animal, but he stood immediately, facing me, and let loose a low, sorrowful whimper.

From behind my parents' chamber door, my father called out in response: "Good dog, Jesse. Alice, go back to bed!"

So I did.

Come morning, I raced into my clothes, regretting that I'd failed to brush my skirt the night before. I did the best I could and hurried to help in the kitchen, where my brother John already sat yawning over a cup of tea and my mother poked the fire up hotter.

"Papa's in the barn, but he's not staying long," John informed me. "Charles is helping. So you can stay in your womanly role and assist Mama. Which means handing me a hot buttered scone as soon as possible, you know."

"Pooh!" I returned. "Fetch your own. And a merry Christmas to you, just the same."

Laughter and good aromas filled the room. With Papa and Charles a few minutes later, we all appreciated hot porridge and fresh raisin scones, and each place had a small gift in front of it. I knew what the men would find, since I'd helped Mama complete their slippers, with knitted tops and soft leather soles. Each of us had provided a fresh new handkerchief for Mama, which Papa tucked inside an embroidered reticule he'd brought back from Hartford for her. And my own gift within its twist of paper turned out to be similar, though the reticule was a bit smaller and less ornate. Still, I thought it a lovely addition to my possessions, and most of all appreciated being seen as a young woman, not a child.

My mother's eyes seemed red-rimmed, and I worried that Papa had refused to offer a place to Matthew and Caroline. But that was not the case—I received full permission to invite them for the afternoon, and an understanding that Papa would then make a proposal to the two of them. Perhaps she'd slept poorly, as I had? Or the ash from the stove had blown back into her face while getting the breakfast started?

Just to be sure, I took the opportunity to embrace my mother when we finished putting away the breakfast things and waited together in the kitchen for the men to come back from "just one more quick check on the barn."

Mama held me tightly, for twice as long as usual, and I grew suspicious. When she released her grip she said, "Merry Christmas, Alice. Know that I'm proud of the fine moral choices that you're making."

I met her gaze and was sure of it: "Papa told you what I want to do at the New Year, didn't he?"

"He did. We have a week to fill with goodness, and then I must suppose your letter-writing skills will improve with steady use," she mock-scolded.

Our new handkerchiefs found their first use. I assured her, "I will write every day."

"So will I," she agreed. "And though it's remakable to say it, I shall rely on Caroline to see that you're safe and wise as you spread your wings."

A call from outside drew us to the others, and the comfort of a mostly silent family walk through light snow, to meet the rest of the village at the church.

A young lady does not bounce in her shoes on the church steps, no matter how chilled she becomes. But I came close to that, and I felt great relief when Matthew and Caroline approached the church, among the last to arrive. I shook Matthew's hand, saying "Merry Christmas," and pressed my prepared note into his fist; with Caroline, a quick embrace served to do the same. I peered over their shoulders, looking for their family, and was glad to know the quick gestures to ask them discreetly: *Your mother? The little ones?*

Clearly Matthew now grasped much of such conversation, for he said in a low voice, "Mama says they are coming down with colds, and she's keeping them home."

On Christmas? I didn't need to say it, aloud or with a hand; we three shared a look of incredulity. Then we hastened to our pews and drew our psalters out, in preparation. Under Mr. Alexander's beaming gaze, first we sang "Joy to the World" and "Adeste Fideles," before settling to the rhythms of the worship service, which scarcely varied.

After a blessedly brief sermon and the Apostles' Creed, we lined out two psalms together and concluded with the Doxology. "Praise Father, Son, and Holy Ghost, Ah-men," we chanted. Mr. Alexander read the one hundred and tenth psalm to us, and we bowed our heads for his asking of God's blessing on our behalf.

At last we all rose and filed out, one pew at a time, Almyra glowing in her new rose muffler as she held Mrs. Alexander's arm, then Caroline and Matthew, a spark of Christmas hope in their eyes and a nod to confirm they'd come after their noon dinner, which in turn would allow time for the three o'clock visit I'd promised to make to Almyra. Slowly, the threads of this tangled moment smoothed themselves. I made sure to accompany my mother closely, so she'd know I appreciated her efforts, and our menfolk trailed behind us.

To my surprise, Mrs. Alexander and Almyra stood with Mr. Alexander at the exit from the church. This was a new custom to witness! Smiles all around and exchanges of Christmas greetings cheered us, despite the solemnity of a community in mourning. How would Old Mo Cook manage without the tavern? Did others yet realize the inn itself and its family were vanishing from our village? I shivered a moment. Perhaps in a way it was all my fault: If I hadn't called out "Papa! Do something!" we might not have stopped for the horse being beaten, and reported the owner, and offered it a home—which led to the horse barn across the road being set afire. And it wasn't even our own barn that paid the consequences, and not my father but Caroline's, dead in the flames!

I stopped walking and took a deep breath. This was neither rational nor Godly. Once more, I allowed Miss Farrow's long-ago reassurance about blame and fault and God to repeat in memory: "When it strips us of the people we love, we blame ourselves, and we blame our God," she'd told me. Then I must convey that to Caroline this afternoon: Her father's death did not mean she must retire from life herself. Was that right?

My mother, who had paused with me, saw something clearing in my expression. "That's the way," she urged. She began a hymn our congregation had learned earlier in the year, even though it wasn't meant for Christmas: "All things bright and beautiful," she caroled, and I joined in, "All creatures great and small, All things wise and wonderful, The Lord God made them all."

As we reached the end of the last verse, we trekked briskly up our track, to reach the kitchen before the men: "How great is God Almighty, Who has made all things well."

Someday, I mused as we poked the woodstove into action and shifted pans, perhaps I'll write a song. A hymn. About the importance of feeding our friends. About sheep, and setting the table, and not being afraid. I laughed aloud, aware I'd just outlined King David's own twenty-third psalm.

At that moment the men arrived, minus my father, of course, who was taking "just a quick look" inside the barn. William and Helen pulled up in their sleigh, and we made an affectionate fuss over their arrival. A merry feast ensued, of roast mutton and baked potatoes and rich golden squash and carrots, almost sweeter than when they'd been harvested, all swimming in butter and gravy. A Christmas pudding stretched us all near bursting, even as Matthew and Caroline arrived and were persuaded to help polish it off.

Soon after the meal, my brothers, including William, insisted they needed to sit in the parlor to read the past week's newspapers and smoke some tobacco that William contributed to the day's pleasures. Helen assisted my mother in clearing the dishes and packing away any remaining edibles. And I took Caroline aside and conveyed to her: *Almyra needs a visit. Let's take her gift to her.*

We found some paper and tied it in place around the album we'd stitched, and my mother added a festive length of ribbon. The snow still fell, though modestly and in a warm air that made it half melt on the way, so in turn we set the package inside a small sack and made our way through the village to the parsonage. A candle in each window gave an air of sweetness to the ordinary house, and I noticed a swag of evergreens, tied with a bow, next to the kitchen door.

We found Almyra and Mrs. Alexander at the kitchen table, marking fabric for embroidery and picking out a sampler design as well. This suited us all for conversation, and, over the course of an hour, I was pleased to see Mrs. Alexander trying out some hand gestures with Caroline, and Almyra becoming downright adept with the letters of the alphabet. We laughed often, while outside the snow vanished and a pale but welcome December sun lit the last few minutes of the afternoon. As it set, I nudged Caroline; we should head back, before darkness fell.

First, though, with care to include Mrs. Alexander in the conversation, I proposed that we all make a visit on Monday, weather permiting, to Miss Farrow in St. Johnsbury. Almyra wondered who this was, and why we should visit someone so far distant; her aunt, however, more experienced in such interactions, said only, "I think it would be a very good visit for you girls to make. I'll have some yarn ready for you to take along. Let's watch the snow and hope for the best."

I did not need to restate this for Caroline, as she'd followed both the words and the friendly expression—she reached forward and placed a kiss on Mrs. Alexander's cheek and embraced Almyra.

And then, at last, it was just Caroline and me, back to our usual closeness, walking arm in arm in the dusk toward my mother and the proposition I desperately hoped my parents would choose to offer—and Caroline, to accept.

CHAPTER 33

The last calm hour of the day settled in softly glowing Christmas beauty, as Caroline and I pulled close to the kitchen table to listen to my mother. The men were all in the barn, she said; she passed us tea and lit the candles and sat between us, half turned, so that as Caroline watched Mama's lips and expression, she could also see my hands filling in details as needed.

To my surprise, the proposal did not begin with Caroline's situation, but with a story of the "old days" in the village that my mother told. She'd been newly married to my father and still unable to cook much more than eggs and griddle cakes. Far from her family, who lived in Maine, she struggled to be the perfect wife and every day fell short, she said. She used to go walking each afternoon to weep a little and try to grasp the winding back roads. The fields, she told us, were still half woods, and wagons of newly cut logs passed often.

A new sort of wagon arrived in the village one day. The drivers, stern faced and unyielding (my mother made a ferocious expression!), had brought their daughter to marry a cousin who wanted to open an inn. (We gasped as we guessed.) Yes, the young Mrs. Clark had come to North Upton. Her parents unloaded her and her one bag of clothing, with two rolls of fabric and a set of English china for a dowry, and pressed a coin into the hand of the local minister to solemnize the marriage—and promptly left, to tackle the two-day journey back to where they'd started.

My mother, barely sixteen at the time, presumed she'd seen the arrival of someone who'd be far more desperate and unskilled than she herself. And it gave her hope that she might at least be a comforter, instead of someone always needing comfort. Instead, she found that Hannah Grace, newly Mrs. Clark, could laugh and make merry about almost anything, from burned bread to lumpy potatoes to darned socks that no longer had room for all the toes of the owner's foot.

Caroline marveled as the story unspooled: *My mother?* she questioned again and again. It seemed impossible. "Your mother," came the confirmation.

Then followed the tale of the second child born, the one who proved unable to coo back to her mother because she hadn't heard the sounds to begin with. The one who was Caroline. And the arrival of the fierce, unyielding grandmother from far away, who blamed the young mother and insisted the child be sent away. "She cried for months," my mother confirmed. Caroline wept in sympathy.

So, Caroline gestured, *I should go with her now and be the daughter she wanted to keep?*

"If you do," my mother challenged, "will you be the merry woman who went her own way and loved life? Or the one who yielded to her mother's grim sense of what belonged and what didn't?"

Caroline rose from the table and stood looking out the window, to avoid both our faces for a long few minutes. I felt like I held my breath until she turned back to us.

If I go with my mother, will she be happy again? she asked.

My mother's sad expression told the truth: Mrs. Clark no longer wished to be happy in that way. She held her losses like a wound with a bandage she could tear off, again and again, watching the cut place bleed more each time. Caroline could choose to go with her mother anyway, and be present, and absorb some of the deep anger. But happy again? Not likely.

Now my mother drew out Sarah's letter, still folded, and set it on the table as a marker. She asked Caroline: "What does it feel like to teach the children who do not hear?"

Baffled at the turn of topic, Caroline stared. My mother repeated the question and had me translate it with my hands. But I knew Caroline understood. Slowly, she began to describe two of the children in the last class she'd taught: a boy so withdrawn into himself, beaten and more, that they'd had to bring a kitten into the room and place it in his hands in order to earn a response from him. And an older girl who'd lost her hearing after a case of mumps, and who still believed she'd regain it and so refused to take part in any lesson or connection. Caroline had taken her shopping, time and again, pulling her into dressmaking and lace and more, spending months to bring truth back into the girl's world, and to cast out shame.

As she conveyed these stories to us, I saw a woman I hadn't seen often: confident, joyous, even triumphant. One who knew her value and prized her skills and loved the students in her care. One who could do anything she chose to accomplish.

Yes, my mother began to sign back. *Yes, that's right. Yes, that's how it feels. That's freedom, the kind given by heaven to make the world a better place. To light up one child's life. To bring two children back to friendship and love. That's teaching.*

Tears streamed down both of their faces and began to leak from my own eyes. Sarah's own declaration sat mute on the table, a silvery moon to the golden glow of strength and generosity I could see before me.

All at once, I couldn't hold silent any longer. *I want to teach something important, the way you have,* I gestured. *I want to learn that, in Illinois. Are we going there together?*

Of course we are, Caroline replied. *Meet me at the inn an hour from now. You can help carry my bags.*

I'll bring my mother, too, I told her.

Good, Caroline declared. *Now I need to go to say goodbye.* At the door she stopped and turned back to us, an expression of sudden fear on her face. *But Matthew,* she gestured.

My mother rose and said slowly, "Matthew made up his mind earlier. He is staying at the inn, to rebuild it. We will help him. He is in the barn with Mr. Sanborn, working. Men love to work together," she added, smiling.

Caroline's glow returned. *I'll be ready in an hour.*

And she was gone. I ran to fetch a lantern, and I slipped outside as soon as I could get my cloak and boots into place. But the moon had risen, and Caroline had already followed its gleam, to the main road and the inn's front door. I retreated to our kitchen and watched the parlor clock until it was time.

My mother and I pulled a small wooden sledge behind us, as we carried our storm lantern down the track to the road, then crossed it. I tapped at the door. It opened. Peter again. He called out, "Ma! They're here!"

A moment later, Mrs. Clark hurled a sack of clothing toward us, followed by a pillow and blanket, then shoved Caroline out the door. "You always take my children, you Sanborns, don't you? Fine! Take this one and keep her. She was never good enough to begin with. And don't ever speak to me again, or write to me. I'm finished with this place and you. You've cost me too much. I hate you all!"

She slammed the door shut, and I heard the latches fall into place. I wrapped an arm around Caroline, whose swollen cheek and bleeding lip spoke of a vicious blow. My mother scooped up a bit of snow to hold to the bruise.

Caroline signaled, *I made my choice, for what I love. My mother did that once, too, yes?*

"Yes," my mother agreed. "Let's go find Matthew and make supper."

On Monday morning three of us sat with Miss Farrow at her kitchen table, in the back of the impressive brick mansion in St. Johnsbury where another judge resided. Miss Farrow, the judge's housekeeper and live-in cook, re-filled the teapot at the end of the three reports: Sarah's by letter, Almyra's amid giggles and side comments about cream soup, and, last of all, Caroline's, in a shared chorus of her gestures and my quiet clarifications when the need arose, and Almyra's gasps.

"Ah, ladies," Miss Farrow sighed, "I'd add my own tale to yours if we had another day to spend together. But with Mrs. Sanborn expecting to carry you along back to North Upton at three, I fear we'd best move ahead to making some plans."

Caroline looked a question at all of us, and Almyra said, "Why?"

Miss Farrow, her dark, curling hair pinned up snugly into her cap, her tan skin freckled with increasing age, her eyes dark with both anger and determination, turned to me and said, "Tell them, Alice."

I stumbled at first. It was necessary to speak aloud to Almyra especially, while catching as much detail as I could in my hands. Other than in the strange intimate language Caroline and I shared, I didn't have practice in speaking two languages at once. Or so it felt, as the grandfather clock in the distant parlor began to chime the hour, and time itself ran short and urgent.

"People are dying each day under the Slave Power's brutal force," I started. "Families are torn apart. Sarah's is only one. There are more than three million Africans enslaved in America now."

Caroline asked for the number to be repeated. Almyra marveled: "Millions?"

"Three million," I confirmed. "And we who treasure freedom need to reach out and end the slaveholding, the torture, the killing. Together."

"How?" my friends demanded as one.

"Together," I repeated. The American Anti-Slavery Society; the legislators fighting to right the laws and Constitution; the surging ocean of persons drawn to action by Mr. Thaddeus Stevens, Mr. William Seward, Miss Lucretia Mott, the sisters Grimké. Miss Farrow brought a tintype of Frederick Douglass to show them, and two of his books. I turned the conversation back to the moral roots we all knew were right: no more slaveholding.

How? asked Caroline again, with her face enforcing the message of her hands. *How does a teacher take part? Two teachers heading west? How does a girl?* She placed a hand on Almyra's, gripped it as if to protect her.

Almyra said, "A minister to be. Perhaps I will even read law. Tell her, Alice."

I did, as quickly as my fingers could. Caroline cast a glance of fresh respect and affection at Almryra, who returned the hand clasp and leaned forward for a quick short embrace.

Miss Farrow rapped gently on the table for attention. "Caroline, Alice, I believe your journey will take you through Albany. We have things to send to the ladies there, and to Mr. Douglass. I'll start stitching them inside comforters and such, so you can carry them without risk. Almyra, we need you most of all now."

Almyra nodded eagerly. "When do I start?"

"Today," said Miss Farrow. "Mr. Eli Thayer is about to stir up a revolution of his own, if I'm seeing the future clearly. And I believe I must be. You'll begin to make the lists of people willing to head to the Territories and fight with the ballot to contain and defeat the Slave Power. The time is coming rapidly, and we must prepare and be strong."

I romanticized it for a moment. "An ardent flame of freedom will seize this land, won't it?"

Miss Farrow said bluntly, "It has already started to burn. And we, my friends, are carrying the matches forward."

Almyra beamed. "I've always wanted to make things right," she said plainly. "Go west, Alice, Caroline. I'm here. And I'm staying, to take hold."

Miss Farrow leaned forward and grasped all our hands in hers. "To take hold," she repeated. "To make things right. To follow the call of justice, wherever it will lead."

"Amen," I murmured, spelling it with my fingers as I spoke. "Amen."

EPILOGUE

Albany lay behind us, with Mr. Frederick Douglass and Mrs.
Lucretia Mott and so many remarkable people. I half wished we
could have lingered there.

But Buffalo lay ahead of us, and then the miles of rails
through the New York and Pennsylvania lands beside the Great
Lakes and into Ohio. I counted the states again in my mind:
then Indiana, and then at last Illinois, where Uncle Martin
expected us.

At my side, Caroline took a stocking out of her reticule for
mending. Unlike most of the ladies around us in the elegant
passenger car, she declined to knit. She'd explained to me:
Grasping the needles in two hands at once silenced her
completely. But with a stocking curled under one arm and the
much smaller darning needle, her fingers could flutter free readily, to comment or draw my attention.

From my own reticule I drew a book: *Roughing It in the Bush*,
by Susanna Moodie, which Mrs. Mott's friends assured me
would make Illinois seem very civilized and comfortable by
comparison. I propped it open on my knees so that Caroline, if
she chose, could read along with me.

I must describe this to Almyra, I thought for the tenth time
at least in that bright morning: the telltale reek of tobacco smoke
on the men's clothing each time they came from the other
railroad car to ensure that we were comfortable, or to beg
another sandwich from our sack. How Mrs. Susan B. Anthony

described the Syracuse convention for women's rights. About an entire rail car belonging to the postal service, where clerks sorted letters as the train rumbled along. The view to the west, so open, always calling us.

I wondered also—Almyra, Miss Farrow, North Upton: what news from home?

THE HISTORY BEHIND
THIS ARDENT FLAME

Readers of the preceding volume in the Winds of Freedom series, *The Long Shadow*, already know that North Upton is based on the real Vermont village of North Danville. The inn building and the farm remain; so do the generous hearts of the people. The actual churches and parsonage do not have the geographic relationship I've built here, but I hope I've made up for that with detailed research on timing of hymn use.

I have generally named characters for members of my own family, which has ties to many North Danville family lines. Historic figures like Clarina Howard Nichols, Eli Thayer, and Thaddeus Stevens are real, although their personalities are imagined, with affection. The tie between Thaddeus Stevens and Vermont is authentic, as is his connection to the Underground Railroad—which, as historian Jane Rokeby reminds us, was an "Aboveground Railroad" in Vermont in the years before the Civil War, since Black Americans in the Green Mountain State were generally "free and safe." For the history of Black American communities in Vermont, see the work of Elise Guyette.

Children in Vermont who lost their hearing or were born without it were indeed often sent, if their families were willing, to residential schools that might be outside the state. The one in Hartford, Connecticut, was the earliest in America, and I noticed it first because a child from my town of Waterford, Vermont, resided there in the 1800s. Jean Linderman, historian for the school, provided background, and this important note on its name:

"During the time period of your story, the school's formal name was 'The American Asylum, at Hartford, for the Education and Instruction of the Deaf and Dumb.' But everyone referred to it as 'The American Asylum.' This is the term that would be appropriate for your story. All of our records from that time use 'American Asylum,' or just 'Asylum.' The Deaf Community rallied to have the words 'Asylum' and 'Dumb' removed from the name, but that didn't happen until 1895. Only after 1895 was the school named 'The American School, at Hartford, for the Deaf.' That remains its proper name, but people refer to it as 'The American School for the Deaf' (or, ASD)."

Language changes; today the term "asylum" would be considered both offensive and prejudicial in this context, so I've avoided it in the story.

Harriet Beecher Stowe and her sister Catherine Beecher did have connections to that school, as Jean Linderman confirmed. But I am not a Stowe scholar, and I have allowed myself room to imagine Stowe's first meeting with Caroline on the train.

Finally, I hope you are reading this note, as intended, after reading the novel. Because here's a hint for Book 3 of Winds of Freedom: Keep your eye on Almyra, and, if you have time, rediscover the efforts of Eli Thayer. Adventures ahead!

ACKNOWLEDGMENTS

A writer often labors alone. I am grateful for the amazing research, support, question-answering, and reassurance that accompanied me in writing *This Ardent Flame*.

My read-along team, whose expectant presence keeps me moving into each new chapter, is Cheryl Minden, Lois Allen, Joan Weston, Jean Linderman, and Gerry LaMothe, Jr., for this book.

Research on "North Upton" and the 1850s depended on Gerry LaMothe, Jr., Liz Sargent, railroad pro Gary Aubin, Tom Ledoux, Paul Chouinard, and the region's small local historical societies, as well as countless books, articles, and the actual newspapers of the time. Jean Linderman provided amazing material from the American School for the Deaf in Hartford, Connecticut. Laura Stevenson, Jessie Haas, Elizabeth Everts, and Barb Kristoff consulted on horses, dogs, sheep, and such. Steve Adler, thank you for the text of the Vermont laws of that time.

For newspaper runs and other stress relief and endless courage, my thanks to Alexis Savino and Caitlin Irwin.

And for research, images, attention, and most of all love (and tolerance for late suppers), I credit (always and forever, through life and beyond) my b'shert, Dave Kanell.

ABOUT THE AUTHOR

Beth Kanell lives in northeastern Vermont, with a river at her feet and a mountain at her back. Exploring American history led her into crafting the Winds of Freedom series, of which *This Ardent Flame* is Book 2; Book 1 is *The Long Shadow*. Outside the series are three earlier published books: *The Darkness Under the Water*, *The Secret Room* (which is a sort of 160-years-later sequel to *The Long Shadow*, also set in fictional North Upton), and *Cold Midnight*. Her books of adventure travel, her regional histories, and most of all her poems contribute to how and why she writes. Visit http://bethkanell.blogspot.com to get better acquainted and to find resource materials for all of her novels.

The employees of Five Star Publishing hope you have enjoyed this book.

Our Five Star novels explore little-known chapters from America's history, stories told from unique perspectives that will entertain a broad range of readers.

Other Five Star books are available at your local library, bookstore, all major book distributors, and directly from Five Star/Gale.

Connect with Five Star Publishing

Visit us on Facebook:
https://www.facebook.com/FiveStarCengage

Email:
FiveStar@cengage.com

For information about titles and placing orders:
(800) 223-1244
gale.orders@cengage.com

To share your comments, write to us:
Five Star Publishing
Attn: Publisher
10 Water St., Suite 310
Waterville, ME 04901